CRYSTAL DOORS

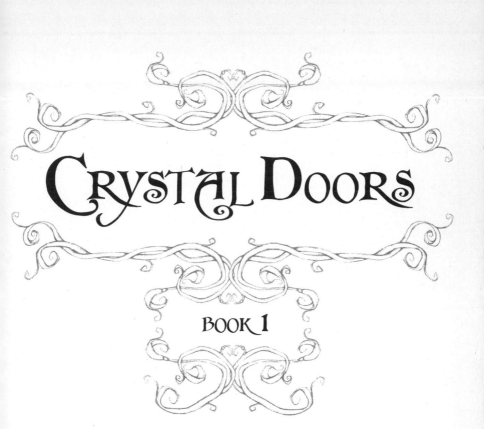

CRYSTAL DOORS

BOOK 1

REBECCA MOESTA

AND KEVIN J. ANDERSON

LITTLE, BROWN AND COMPANY
New York ❧ Boston ❧ London

Little, Brown and Company

Time Warner Book Group
1271 Avenue of the Americas, New York, NY 10020
Visit our Web site at www.lb-teens.com

First Edition: June 2006

Library of Congress Cataloging-in-Publication Data

Moesta, Rebecca.
    Crystal doors / Rebecca Moesta and Kevin J. Anderson.—1st ed.
        p. cm.
    Summary: Two fourteen-year-old cousins are accidentally transported to the island of Elantya,
site of ancient magic, vicious creatures, and fierce battles produced by a territorial feud with the
sea-dwelling merlons, conflict between the bright and dark sages, and the cousins' own mysterious
roots.
    ISBN 0-316-01055-3 (hardcover : alk. paper)
    [1. Islands — Fiction.   2. Cousins — Fiction.   3. Fantasy.]   I. Moesta, Rebecca.   II. Title.
PZ7.A5435Cry 2006
[Fic] — dc22

                                                                                    2005017048

10   9   8   7   6   5   4   3   2   1

Q–FF
Printed in the United States of America

This book is for
CATHERINE SIDOR

Acknowledgments

We'd like to express our special appreciation to

John Silbersack and Robert Gottlieb of the Trident Media Group for supporting this project from the beginning.

Jennifer Hunt and Phoebe Sorkin Spanier for their enthusiasm and insightful editing.

Diane E. Jones, Catherine Sidor, and Louis Moesta of WordFire Inc. for their long hours and invaluable comments; Megie Clarke, Paul and Lacy Pfeifer, Jonathan Cowan, and D. Louise Moesta of WordFire Inc. for keeping things running smoothly in the office.

Our families for putting up with our eccentric schedules and for introducing so many new people to our books.

Igor Kordey for his brilliant concept artwork and imaginative designs.

Sarah and Dan Hoyt and Rebecca and Alan Lickiss for local cheerleading.

Kristine Kathryn Rush, Dean Wesley Smith, Deb Ray, Lisa Chrisman, Mary Thomson, Cherie Buchheim, Brian &

Jan Herbert, Maryelizabeth Hart & Jeff Mariotte, Brad & Sue Sinor, Max & Erwin Bush, Letha Burchard, Janet Berliner & Bob Fleck, Leslie Lauderdale, Kathy Tyree, and Ann Neumann for their friendship, decades of long-distance encouragement, and keeping us sane in an insane world.

Dean and Gerda Koontz for years of invaluable advice.

1

A WARM SALTY BREEZE ruffled Gwendolyn Pierce's blond hair as she stared across the ocean. She let her mind sail all the way to the horizon. Anything seemed possible out there.

Gwen squinted against the golden flare of sunlight reflected from the waves. For centuries, the lure of the sea had cast a spell over mankind. The briny waters held beauty, danger, and mystery in equal portions. *Sea monsters. Explorers sailing off the edge of the world. Ghost ships. Undersea kingdoms.*

Intrepid sailors crossed the uncharted waters to find adventure in distant lands, exotic ports with new goods to trade. Fishermen hauled their catch from the bountiful waters. Artists, writers, and philosophers drew inspiration from the restless depths. The potential of the seven seas seemed limitless.

"You kids hungry yet? Or do you want to hit the rides right away?"

Gwen lowered the brochure-map of the Ocean Kingdoms Learning Center and Amusement Park. "I want to see some exhibits first, Uncle Cap."

Dr. Carlton Arthur Pierce — nicknamed Cap for his initials — regarded his niece with affection and good humor in his hazel eyes. "Don't forget to have fun, too, Gwen. You're so serious." The brilliant yet eccentric former archaeologist had given up a day of his strange experiments with crystals so they could all visit Ocean Kingdoms.

"Of course I'm serious." She drew her slender form up to its full height. "I'm going to be an oceanographer or marine biologist, maybe even study at The Scripps Research Institute." A love of the sea, and water in almost every form, was one of the many things Gwen's mother and father had passed on to her. In the two years since her parents' death, Gwen had become increasingly serious, but she couldn't help it. Only by immersing herself in study did she find refuge from her feelings of loss and grief. But today she was supposed to have fun. She forced energy into her voice. "In other words, it's never too early to start learning!"

A suntanned hand yanked the map from her grasp. "Sheesh, Gwen — take off the Spock ears for a while, okay?" Her cousin Vic grabbed her by the shoulders and turned her in a slow circle so she could see the roller coasters, flume rides, concession stands, and gift shops. The air smelled more of popcorn than salty ocean. "It's an amusement park, so let's try to be amused."

"Actually" — she pointed to the brochure — "it's a Learning Center, too."

"Come on, Doc. Play now, work later." Vic used the nickname he had given her when, at age six, she announced she was going to be "Dr. Pierce" someday, just like her dad. Now Vic looked longingly at the rides. "Here's a plan: we get all sticky with cotton candy, wash off with a drench on the Raging Riptide, and then stuff ourselves with corn dogs and giant pretzels. You know, have some *fun*! Then, if there's time, we can look at an exhibit or something."

"Goof off all day?" Gwen planted her sandals firmly on the turquoise-painted concrete. "I'm the oldest, and Uncle Cap said I get to choose first."

Her cousin made an exasperated sound. "Sheesh. Older by five hours. Big deal. That's a trivial percentage of fourteen years, you know, so don't try to pull rank on me. Besides, I'm bigger than you are." Years of competitive swimming had made the cousins equally lean and fit, but in a recent growth spurt Vic had grown a few inches taller than Gwen. He pointed to a flume ride that looked like a three-story-tall cement wave frozen in place. At its base lay a glittering sapphire pool. "Doesn't that look cool?"

"It looks *wet*." Gwen pulled herself free. "The exhibits will be more —"

Dr. Pierce broke in. "I'm the captain of this ship, and I propose a compromise. I say we grab some churros from this vendor here and eat them on our way over to the South Pacific Kingdom. Then we ride the Ripple Conveyor through the underwater tunnel in the aquarium."

Gwen retrieved the wrinkled map from her cousin. "If that's the aquarium with all the miniature volcanoes around it — I'm in!"

"Yup, you just might be. If you don't climb out of your rut, I'll make sure you see plenty of fish." Vic cracked a wicked smile as his father handed them each a fried doughnut stick. Vic waved his churro in front of Gwen, ignoring the sugar that showered onto his black Mad Scientists' Union polo shirt. "Mmm, the food of the gods. Cinnamon and fat and about a million empty carbs."

Gwen primly stepped around her cousin. Although Vic and his dad finished their treats in two minutes, she took small bites as they walked up the gentle slope toward the aquarium.

"Hey, I wonder if Ocean Kingdoms has a suggestion box," Vic jabbered. He often made oddball comments that came out of nowhere. "Wouldn't it be cool if they'd let us use skates, bikes, or skateboards in here? We'd move faster and hit twice as many rides."

"And exhibits," Gwen added.

Uncle Cap tapped a finger on his lower lip as he considered. "Think it through, Vic. There'd be more accidents, and that would increase the park's insurance rates and lead to higher entrance fees. It could cause traffic-control issues, injuries, unfairness to the elderly or handicapped who might not be able to ride bicycles or skate. And if the park owned the equipment, there'd be problems like sizing skates and bicycles, equipment breakdowns, maintenance, providing safety gear and changing areas for the skaters. There are a lot of second- and third-order consequences."

Gwen smiled; this was typical of her uncle. Once given a problem, Dr. Pierce would work at it until he found a solution, often by instinct or by the seat of his pants. Vic and his father were similar in that. On the other hand, Gwen's approach to problem solving was painstaking and methodical, though not always more successful. Since the mysterious car accident that had killed her parents, Gwen's strategy of organization and structure had become a way for her to impose order on the world, to make sense out of life.

Because she had no other relatives, Cap — her father's identical twin — had moved Gwen from Berkeley, California, to live with him and Vic in Hawks Hills near San Diego. Adding to the strange circumstances surrounding the deaths of her parents, Vic's mom — Cap's wife — had vanished a week later. No one seemed to know where she had gone.

Bound together by the unexpected tragedies, Dr. Carlton Pierce, Vic, and Gwen had formed a new family. For two years now, the "twin cousins" — born only hours apart on the same night — had been raised almost as brother and sister. They attended Stephen Hawking High School together and shared many of the same classes and friends.

"Maybe," Vic said, unconvinced, "but we'd still get around a lot faster."

Gwen turned her violet eyes to the sky, begging the heavens for patience. "What's your hurry? Maybe walking is the best way to see the park." Making a mental list, she ticked off the reasons on her fingers as she spoke, pointing to each digit in turn with her half-eaten churro. "One, most people here could use the exercise — think of all the calories in this food!" She gave the churro a twirl before tapping it to her second finger. "Number two, the designers of Ocean

Kingdoms spent millions of dollars developing its ocean theme, creating the whole illusion."

"You mean like painting concrete blue, so that it looks, um, 'just like' water?" Vic gave a snort.

Gwen ignored his interruption. "If you rushed by, you wouldn't get the overall effect. For example, as we move toward the South Pacific Kingdom, they gradually add more and more of the area's distinctive culture."

"Ooh-ooh! Volcanoes!" Vic pointed to a miniature cone-shaped mountain at the side of the path. It erupted every few seconds with "lava" that was really just water with a red light beneath it.

"See? If you took skates or a scooter, you'd miss a lot of the ambience," Gwen said. "Like volcanoes."

"And the shops." Her uncle indicated the ubiquitous thatched huts with names like Easter Island Trader or Polynesian Playthings. "Merchants don't want visitors going by too quickly."

"Plus, there's the island music." Gwen waved her churro like a baton, pretending to direct the ukulele tune that drifted from the speakers hidden in the palm trees. Then she touched the churro to her third finger. "Number —"

"Seven?" Vic tried to derail her train of thought, a game he often played.

She shot him a warning glare. "*Three,* these people are on vacation. They come with families or friends to get away from it all. Walking from kingdom to kingdom gives them a chance to take their lives at a more relaxed pace." When Vic mocked her serious tone by playing an air violin accompaniment, Gwen rushed on to her next point. "Number —"

"Googol?" It was the biggest number Vic could cite, a one followed by a hundred zeroes.

"Number four." She tried to wither him with the power of her eyes. "Amusement parks don't have the capacity for all the visitors to be on rides or in exhibits at the same time. So walking disperses the crowds from point to point. Rushing faster only creates bigger bottlenecks and backups."

Uncle Cap nodded. "Good point, Gwen. It also gives visitors a chance to gorge on food that they shouldn't eat, and buy souvenirs that they don't need."

She smiled. "That too. And also —"

"Fourteen B?" Vic intoned.

She punched her cousin's shoulder in mock exasperation. He often acted a lot more than five hours younger than she was. "Number five, you dork —"

She never got to make her point. They had reached the section of the park called the South Pacific Kingdom. "Pick a seashell and stand on it." Uncle Cap hurried them onto the conveyor. "Quick."

"Please watch your step," a robotic voice droned from a speaker in an oversized replica of a spiny rock lobster.

The conveyor carried them down a tunnel. The clear arched roof offered a spectacular view of the aquarium around them. Gwen quickly forgot her list, and Vic dropped his impatient complaints as the darting sea creatures caught their attention.

The exhibit's coral reefs were populated with sea urchins, frilled anemones, and slimy curtains of algae. Gwen studied the various species, identifying them from labels and drawings mounted on the glass: shrimp, seahorses, bright feathery crinoids, seastars, cruising sharks, sea fans, striped lionfish showing off their venomous spiny fins, moray eels, triggerfish war-painted in blue, brown, white, and yellow. Orange-and-white clownfish and zebra-striped angelfish swam among blobby sponges.

The underwater scenes mesmerized them all and, for a time, transported them to another world — exactly as Gwen had wanted.

2

THOUGH TIRED FROM WALKING, drenched from the rides, and queasy from eating so much junk food, Gwen was truly enjoying herself at Ocean Kingdoms (and not just the educational parts). It seemed like such a long time since she had lost her parents, but bittersweet memories still came back at unpredictable moments. She wished they could be there.

Uncle Cap instituted what he termed an Anthropologically Sound Method of maintaining harmony between the cousins: Before they left the aquarium, Gwen and Vic each chose the activities they most wanted to do, then Dr. Pierce arranged them in geographical order to avoid unnecessary backtracking. Any complaints about the other's pick resulted in a lost turn in the rotation.

The three of them saw a giant water clock, visited kelp-bed experiments, blasted at targets with water cannons, and went on splash rides that soaked Gwen's hot-pink tee and white shorts. Vic's thick brown hair got drenched and dried a mess, though he didn't seem to notice.

After a long day, Cap suggested that they attend the main theater's four o'clock Marine Spectacular, which had performing dolphins, sea lions, and a killer whale. Vic and Gwen both agreed, though for different reasons. When they got into the amphitheater, Gwen hurried toward the front to get a good spot. Vic couldn't help teasing her. "Guess you want to be close enough to smell the fish, huh?"

"I want to be close enough so *you* can get splashed."

"Too late." He plucked at his wet tee shirt. "Already soaked."

They found seats in the second row, near the ramp where the trainers and aquatic actors would stage their performances. As the open-air auditorium filled with young couples, senior citizens, laughing teenagers, and parents herding children or maneuvering rented strollers, Gwen scanned the rows of benches, the crystal blue water of the exhibition pool, the fabric banners depicting Shoru the trained killer whale. She looked at her watch — another ten minutes.

At the moment Gwen felt more relaxed than she had in the past two years. At times, Uncle Cap reminded Gwen so strongly of her father that she could almost believe he had never died . . . and she found that troubling. Was she betraying her own parents by accepting Uncle Cap and Vic as her replacement family? Such thoughts were sobering and disturbing, but how could she help seeing the uncanny similarities between her father and his twin brother?

Uncle Cap and Reginald Ivan Pierce — "Rip" to his

friends — had studied the same subjects and gotten the same university degrees in anthropology and ancient history. The brothers had made a brief bid for independence from each other, Uncle Cap in the Air Force and Rip in the Marines, but after serving their required stints they applied to graduate school at Berkeley, became roommates, and earned PhDs in historical archaeology.

On a dig in the dense jungles of Mexico's Yucatan Peninsula, a pair of exotic and beautiful sisters had stepped out of nowhere and into the brothers' lives — Kyara and Fyera, who would become Vic's mom and Gwen's mom. Both women were now gone. Gwen missed her parents and knew Vic must feel just as bad for his lost mother, though she, at least, might still be alive. . . .

When the Marine Spectacular finally started, it was a welcome distraction from Gwen's uncomfortable thoughts. Recorded music blared through the speakers. The host, a tanned man with curly dark hair and a bright smile, stood on a high podium above the water. Underwater gates opened, and six gray bullet-shaped dolphins streaked out in a choreographed water ballet. Female handlers in tight wetsuits swam along with the dolphins, holding on to their fins. Sea lions clowned, bouncing beach balls back and forth; an enormous walrus provided more comic relief.

Vic laughed at the host's corny jokes, while Gwen tried to observe the creatures as a marine biologist would, studying the traits that made them so well adapted to living in the water. She was impressed with their intelligence and training.

After all other performers had cleared the tank, a black-and-white creature swam out to great fanfare and many cheers. As soon as Shoru the killer whale appeared, curled into the air, and dove under the water again, Gwen could see why he was the star of the show. Shoru amazed the crowd with his tricks and showed an incredible ability to understand and follow commands. If Vic could follow instructions that well, Gwen thought, he'd probably do better in school!

The curly-haired announcer called for a volunteer from the audience. Glancing around to see who would be chosen, Gwen was astonished when Vic grabbed her arm and waved it in the air. "Here! My cousin wants to do it."

Gwen tried to yank her wrist free. "No, I —"

"*Over here!*" Vic shouted, then elbowed his cousin. "Come on, Doc. You want to be a marine biologist. Here's your big chance to get up close and personal."

Gwen wasn't exactly averse to the idea; she just didn't like being forced into something she hadn't planned. Before she could think of a rational reason for resisting, the announcer pointed at her. "I don't know which one of those two is more enthusiastic, but we have our volunteer. Young lady, please join us!"

The audience applauded. Some of the children who had raised their hands reacted with obvious disappointment. Uncle Cap gave Gwen an encouraging smile, and she got uncertainly to her feet.

"Hurry now!" the announcer prodded. "Shoru's hungry. Don't make him wait for his snack."

As if in a dream, Gwen found herself moving toward the aisle. When she and Vic were younger, their mothers had taught them *zy'oah*, a form of self-defense that combined unconventional techniques of balance, observation, evasion, and improvisation. Although the instruction had demanded poise and alertness, at the moment Gwen felt anything but self-assured and graceful.

A trainer led her to a ramp at the edge of the main pool, where a big bucket of fish waited. Gwen thought the trainer was cute, with a lifeguard's build, a nice tan, strawberry-blond hair, and blue eyes that were entirely on her. *Everyone's* eyes were on her, for that matter, and she felt distinctly awkward. The trainer hopped up onto the platform and reached out. Taking his hand, Gwen stepped up beside him, noting that she was almost as tall as he was. After the trainer asked her name, he tapped a microphone on his collar and said, "Everyone give a big hand to Gwendolyn Pierce, who's going to help me do something . . . fishy."

A ripple of laughter passed through the audience. For a moment she was thrilled to hear her name come across the loudspeakers. She glanced over her shoulder and saw Vic grinning and Uncle Cap with a wistful smile. A sad smile? Was he missing his lost wife? Gwen felt another pang for her own parents.

The story of how Cap and Rip Pierce had met the two beautiful women out in the middle of an isolated Yucatan jungle still seemed so romantic. "It was as if Kyara and Fyera were forest spirits who just magically appeared," her father had told her once.

The sisters were anything but twins. Kyara, Vic's good-humored mom, was full-figured and stood nearly as tall as the brothers. She had flowing dark hair and eyes as warm and sweet as pools of melted chocolate. On the other hand, Gwen's slender and serious mother, Fyera, was shorter, with baby-fine flaxen hair cut to chin length. Her gray-green eyes, the color of a stormy ocean, were in keeping with her reserved and thoughtful nature. Neither of them looked at all like the locals. They spoke perfect English and understood the esoteric work that Cap and Rip Pierce were doing out at the digs.

According to the stories, the moment their eyes met, Cap and Kyara were smitten with each other, and Rip and Fyera could not be parted. Both sisters loved the sea, especially the nearby blue Caribbean, and a few weeks later the two couples were married in a private ceremony on the beach near the ancient Mayan ruins of Tulum.

The mysterious sisters assisted Rip and Cap with their archaeology project, where their uncanny knowledge of languages proved helpful, not only with the local villagers, but in interpreting the markings on unusual artifacts. After three months at the dig, the Pierce brothers returned to the United States with their new brides, who were already pregnant. On May fifth of that year, Fyera gave birth to Gwendolyn Uma Pierce; five hours later, in a remarkable coincidence, Kyara had a baby boy, Victor Ivan Pierce.

Neither Gwen nor Vic knew much about their mothers' families. Though they raised their children with unmistakable love, Kyara and Fyera were reticent to talk about their pasts. Gwen had always suspected that her father and uncle knew a lot more than they revealed — and now it was too late. Gwen found it enigmatic, like a fairy tale, and clung to the strange aspects. . . .

"All right, Shoru!" The announcer's voice boomed through the loudspeakers. "Time to eat." Alone inside the big tank, Shoru plunged from one end of the pool to the other like a hungry puppy excited for his dinner.

Startling Gwen out of her memories, the handler reached into the plastic bucket, pulled out a dead fish, and extended it toward Gwen. She wasn't squeamish about fish or slime — no potential marine biologist could afford to be. Gwen took the fish from the trainer, who flashed her a smile. She held on to the tail, the caudal fin, and studied the fish, trying to identify the species.

When she glanced again toward Uncle Cap and Vic, Gwen noticed a strange man sitting two rows behind them. He had unusual eyes that looked wrong, somehow, and thick eyebrows furrowed in an expression of intense anticipation. A chill ran down her spine. Why did that man give her the creeps? Everyone else in the audience was cheering and whistling, but the man just stared.

The cute trainer cleared his throat. "Gwendolyn — if I were you, I'd concentrate on the giant set of teeth that are heading this way." His stage-whispered words boomed across the loudspeakers. Everyone laughed.

Gwen flushed with embarrassment, then turned back to the killer whale, mentally kicking herself. She'd never been so close to a large marine mammal before. This was a dream come true!

Swimming from one end of the tank to the other, Shoru kicked up quite a froth with his passage. The killer whale seemed agitated, and she could sense a bit of uneasiness from the handler, too. He tried to cover it, but Gwen could read the concern on his face as he went on with the show.

"Hold the fish out, like this." He took Gwen to the edge of the platform and she extended the dripping snack so that it dangled over the water.

She had seen this trick before and knew what was supposed to happen. The killer whale would rise out of the water and, as gently as a kiss, take the fish out of her hand, and probably splash her to the amusement of everyone in the stands.

But Shoru surged forward like a black-and-white torpedo. He launched from the water, mouth yawning open to reveal a set of sharp white teeth. Fishy breath came up at her, smelling like a clogged drain in a seafood restaurant.

Shoru was rising too fast, coming too close. It looked like he was going to attack her! This wasn't supposed to happen! She let the fish drop, but the killer whale ignored it, lunging toward her instead.

The trainer acted swiftly. "Look out!" He dove to the side and tried to pull Gwen with him from the platform but missed because she was already moving. Her body instinctively re-membered the *zy'oah* tricks her mother had taught her. She sprang backward to the edge of the platform, grabbed the rail, and swung to safety as the killer whale struck the end of the ramp where she'd been standing only an instant before. Shud-dering, Gwen watched Shoru crash back into the pool. As he swam away, the killer whale seemed confused, like a sleep-walker who had just awakened and didn't know where he was.

The trainer scrambled to his feet. "Are you all right?"

"Was that really part of the show?" she said, panting. The audience cried out in alarm; a few chuckled nervously, convinced the "accident" had been staged to add thrills to the performance. Uncle Cap and Vic scrambled toward her from the amphitheater seats.

In a wavering voice, the announcer tried to cover the mistake. "It looks like Shoru was hungrier than we thought." He forced a weak laugh.

Nodding that she was okay, Gwen looked back toward the agitated people in the stands. Oddly, she noticed the strange, dark-browed man sitting cool and emotionless while everyone else reacted with great concern. If anything, he seemed disappointed. . . .

Uncle Cap and Vic rushed to her, full of alarmed questions. When she looked up again, the stranger had silently slipped out of the amphitheater.

3

WHILE THE AUDIENCE CLEARED from the amphitheater, a florid-faced man wearing a tie and an Ocean Kingdoms uniform hurried toward them. "Miss, I am so sorry for any inconvenience Shoru's poor performance may have caused you. I assure you Shoru has never misbehaved in any way before. Thank goodness it was such a minor incident." His dark eyes tried too hard to be sincere, while he downplayed the danger Gwen had just faced.

Minor incident? Inconvenience? The man made it sound as if the killer whale had done little more than splash a bit of water on her. Gwen's weak knees seemed only now to be comprehending how close she'd come to being chomped.

"You should have seen it from where we were sitting!" Vic broke in, sounding more excited than afraid. "Sheesh, those jaws only missed you by an inch or two!"

"I apologize for your distress," the administrator said. "Please accept our hospitality while you calm down. I'll show you to the VIP area, where we serve our finest refreshments." Gwen's stomach was already queasy from all the junk food they had eaten. Another round of refreshments didn't sound very appealing.

Uncle Cap seemed a bit jumpy. "That really won't be necessary," he told the administrator. His voice sounded strange and distant. "It wasn't Shoru's fault." He kept glancing around, studying the last few people leaving the stands, as if expecting some new threat to leap out at them. She wondered if he had seen the creepy man, too.

"I'd rather just go home," Gwen admitted.

"Of course, of course!" said the administrator. "But let us offer you some small tokens of our regard. Nobody should leave Ocean Kingdoms without a pleasant memory of their time here. I can authorize a free annual pass to the park, and any souvenir you would like from the shop near the park entrance."

He bustled them out of the amphitheater to the nearby Aquatic Emporium. "Now you just look around in here, Miss. And you, too, young man. Find yourself a souvenir — as if this day wasn't memorable enough!" He gave an unconvincing chuckle. "I'll just run to my office to get you some releases to sign. No hurry. Take your time."

Gwen knew the man was trying to make sure she didn't file a lawsuit against Ocean Kingdoms. Her uncle certainly realized what the administrator was doing, but he seemed more preoccupied and unsettled than she had ever seen him. Gwen bit her lower lip. "It *was* an accident, wasn't it, Uncle Cap?"

A one-of-a-kind accident . . . just like the mysterious car wreck that had killed her mother and father. *Accident.* Even the police had been baffled. Her parents' car had fallen through a high bridge on a rugged section of the Pacific coast. They hadn't driven off the highway, but dropped *through* it. Several girders and support plates had been missing — not fallen away, broken off, or cut apart. Just . . . missing.

Clearly troubled, her uncle shook his head.

"I thought — I thought I sensed something," Gwen said. "I saw a strange man in a row not far behind you, and his eyes looked wrong somehow. He was watching me as if he *knew* something was going to happen."

A shadow crossed Cap's face. "We have to go home, kids. It would be best if we got away from here as soon as possible. There's no telling . . ." His voice trailed off.

Vic was pawing through the sweatshirts, stuffed dolphins, plastic Shoru toys, T-shirts, and puzzles. "Just a minute, Dad. That man said we could have anything we want in here. I'll make it quick."

"All right, hurry up." Uncle Cap still seemed distant, and for some reason, his gaze lingered on the five-sided medallion Gwen always wore on a leather cord around her neck. Her mother had given it to Gwen at her birth. Vic's mother had given him one exactly like it, which he kept as a fob on his keychain.

The pendants were five-sided, paper-thin disks of irides-cent metal the size of a penny, etched with a strange design of loops and angles. Fyera and Kyara had never explained the significance of the medallions, but the unusual symbols had always intrigued Gwen.

After the Lost Spring — Uncle Cap's name for the three months following the death of Gwen's parents and Kyara's disappearance — her uncle had become obsessed with the exotic symbols. Giving up his tenured professorship, Dr. Pierce took a job as a curator for a local museum and spent much of his spare time researching the medallions. He scanned the symbols into his computer and ran worldwide searches for similarities, for any clue that could lead him to his missing wife. He found nothing. . . .

Vic chose his souvenir in less than three minutes, a muscle tee tie-dyed in shades of green and blue that said:

SEA CREATURE.
SEE CREATURE SWIM.
SWIM, CREATURE, SWIM.

Still flustered by what she had been through, Gwen agonized over the selections for a full fifteen minutes, while Vic shifted from foot to foot. "Come *on*, Doc. I could have built a working submarine out of an oil drum and a couple of table fans by now." He took out his frustration by scratching a mosquito bite on his arm until it bled; he asked the woman behind the counter for a bandage.

Finally, the Ocean Kingdoms administrator came back, still all smiles, with season passes, a bag of "VIP Goodies," and — almost as an afterthought — release forms for them to sign.

Gwen was astonished at how quickly Uncle Cap signed them. "Don't worry about it." He seemed to be brushing the man aside. "Come on, kids. We really need to get out of here." He looked around again, very wary.

"I still need to pick something." Gwen narrowed her choices to a baby pink camisole tee with OCEAN PRINCESS spelled out in glittery silver bubbles and a lilac hooded sweatshirt with the same design.

Vic whispered, "The sweatshirt's more expensive. Get that."

Hovering nearby, the Ocean Kingdoms man overheard. "Please, take them both. I insist. In fact —" He picked up a pair of zippered jackets in dark green fleece with embroidered logos and gave them to Vic and his father. "Take these, too, with our best wishes."

After curtly thanking the man, Uncle Cap hurried them past the jostling crowds to the parking area. Vic was already making plans about the next time they could use their season passes. "I wouldn't worry about that," his father said. "I don't know when we'll be back." He looked quickly over his shoulder, as if someone might be following them. "I've decided we should lay low for a while, keep out of sight. In fact, we may . . ." His voice caught. From his stricken expression, Gwen wondered if he was suddenly reminded of how his wife had vanished.

"Uncle Cap, what's wrong? What are you talking about?"

Vic's eyes were also wide. "Hey, does this have anything to do with those big crates that arrived yesterday?"

Gwen knew her uncle had been excited about the shipment — assorted chunks of exotic and expensive crystal. It didn't seem likely he would want to pack up and drive off so soon. She wondered if the creepy man in the audience was involved somehow. A rival researcher, maybe?

"Yes, a big breakthrough . . . I hope. I'll be getting you both up at three-thirty in the morning — no complaints, now. This could be the key to . . . well, let's just wait and see if it works."

"If what works?" Vic asked.

Uncle Cap's voice was agitated. "I need you two where I can protect you. Pack an overnight bag — a change of clothes, a toothbrush, a book — I'll take care of the rest. We'll leave early, but I've got a lot of work to do before then." Cap unlocked the car doors for them. "After what happened today, it's more important than ever that I get everything right."

4

HER ALARM WENT OFF at 3:30 the next morning, though "morning" might have been too optimistic a word for the hour. Exhausted from their busy day at Ocean Kingdoms, not to mention almost being eaten by a killer whale, Gwen had gone to bed early. She was still agitated after what had happened, and even more so because of Uncle Cap's very obvious concern. He wouldn't explain anything.

Knowing she'd be getting up before dawn, she kissed her uncle goodnight and went upstairs while he continued to bustle around with great determination, hauling crates of crystals into the solarium, a large glassed-in area just off of the living room. Unsettled, she packed a few things in her yellow duffel, put on fresh underwear, set the alarm clock, flopped onto her bed, and immediately dropped off to sleep.

Even though her uncle had promised to wake them, Gwen

set her own alarm. Her parents had always taught her to be self-reliant. She could still hear her mother saying, "If something is important to you, don't rely on anyone else. Do it yourself."

Bleary-eyed, she rolled out of bed, wearing her pendant and underclothes. She pulled on a pair of cropped white jeans and the new pink cami, wondering where Uncle Cap would be driving them. The tension in the air told her this wasn't going to be a surprise "vacation," though school wouldn't start for another month yet. She threw on the lilac Ocean Kingdoms hoody just as a tousle-headed Vic appeared in her doorway wearing his Sea Creature shirt, old jeans, the green fleece jacket unzipped, black Vans skater shoes, and a small backpack slung over one shoulder. "Did I sleep through Dad trying to wake me up?"

"He hasn't come up for us yet." Gwen slid her feet into a pair of white sandals. "I wonder if he even went to bed last night."

"Did you see all those crates he was unpacking? They looked like a geologist's treasure chests," Vic said. He and Gwen both shared their mothers' love for crystals and geodes of all sorts. "Sheesh, when Dad gets involved in some project, he could work right through an earthquake and a solar eclipse at the same time."

Gwen picked up her duffel. "Then he may not realize what time it is. Let's go put our stuff in the car. Any idea where we're going?" They kept their voices low and walked quietly in the pre-dawn hush.

"It's a surprise — an adventure." Vic was always better at rolling with the changes than she was.

"Do you think he's outside already?" Gwen asked. "I didn't hear him."

"Don't worry. I've got my key," Vic whispered, tucking the medallion key ring into the front pocket of his jeans along with the tiny LED flashlight Gwen had given him this year on their fourteenth birthday. "Just in case Dad locked himself out."

"That would be a switch." Twice in the past month the cousins had decided to go for a midnight swim in a neighbor's outdoor pool and had accidentally locked themselves out of the house. The first time, they had rescued themselves with the spare key under the terra cotta planter by the door, but Vic forgot to put it back, once again earning his nickname of "Doctor Distracto." The second time, they'd been forced to wake Uncle Cap to let them in. Tonight, though, they were prepared.

They were creeping down the stairs toward the garage when they heard a low, throbbing hum from the glassed-in solarium. Exchanging surprised glances, they headed toward the sound instead of going outside.

As they approached, Gwen saw her uncle adjusting and repositioning massive clusters of exceptionally clear quartz crystals around the room. Dr. Pierce was spending a lot of time arranging them with absolute precision.

"What's Dad still doing that for?" In the darkness, Vic squinted at the lighted dial of his watch. "Weren't we supposed to be going somewhere? There isn't time for another experiment."

She dumped her yellow duffel on the floor. "I have a feeling he's not ready to go yet." Vic set his backpack next to her duffel, and they went to the solarium doorway.

Through the glass ceiling, stars twinkled in the pre-dawn sky. Dr. Pierce had arranged mirrors, prisms, and lenses all around the floor and mounted them to the glass walls. He fidgeted with the mirror and prism angles, adjusting and readjusting them just so. "A key." He kept referring to a parchment diagram in his hand. "I still need a key!"

Gwen knew how much her uncle hated to be interrupted when he was concentrating. Vic, though, had no such compunctions. "Hey, I've got keys." Fishing for his keychain in the pocket of his jeans, he walked into the room.

Gwen hurried after him. "Uncle Cap, didn't you want to —"

As they stepped into the network of crystals arranged all around the solarium, their night-adjusted eyes were suddenly dazzled by a bright light that was refracted and echoed by the prisms and mirrors. The air around Gwen and Vic sparkled like a million glowing shards of glass.

The smells of salt and ozone filled her nostrils. Gwen could see only her uncle's outline silhouetted against a blaze of light. Vic grabbed her arm.

Dr. Pierce cried in triumph. "It worked!" A brief flash lit his face, and she saw his dismayed expression as he tried to reach out to them. "Wait! Vic, Gwen, we have to go together! My Kyara —"

She could still feel her cousin's hand on her arm as dazzling facets spun around her, blurring everything: the room, the crystals, her uncle's outline, even Vic. In slow motion, Gwen felt herself falling, swept along as if the universe itself were rushing down a drain. Like the worst part of the flume ride at Ocean Kingdoms —

Vic yelled something she couldn't understand. His voice cut off abruptly with a thwacking sound. A moment later Gwen's head hit something cold and flat and hard, and the only stars she saw were inside her head. They quickly faded to black.

5

BY THE TIME VIC cleared the cobwebs from his throbbing head, the room had stopped spinning. Incomprehensible shouts filled the air around him, men's voices in a strange language. Someone was ringing a bell . . . or maybe it was just his head ringing.

"Ow." He kept his voice low, since yelling would have hurt too much. Vic found himself lying on something cool and hard — the Spanish-tiled floor of the solarium, he supposed, though he was reluctant to open his eyes. The hard floor felt comfortable and reassuringly solid after the nauseating fall he had experienced.

A strange though not entirely unpleasant odor tickled his nose. He tried to draw a deep breath and coughed. Fire? The smoke from something sweet burning? Had his father's array of crystals exploded in the solarium? Vic ordered his eyes to open, but an unaccountable drowsiness held them shut.

What if the house was on fire? Could the shouts be coming from firefighters? What if Gwen and his dad were both unconscious? What if his own drowsiness was a sign of smoke inhalation and asphyxiation? He needed to move. No time to think.

Vic pushed himself to his hands and knees, remembering the warnings from his best friend, Jordan, who volunteered at the local fire station two days a week after school. "Never stand up in a smoke-filled room. Try to stay low."

Vic finally opened his eyes to scan for Gwen and his father, then blinked several times. The air was indeed filled with smoke, but it was canary yellow, fuchsia, turquoise, tangerine, and emerald. Bright daylight streamed into the room from overhead. Daylight? Could he really have been unconscious for hours?

Coughing again, Vic blinked and crawled forward low to the floor while the shouting continued to hammer at his ears. Just as he spotted Gwen's sandaled foot, strong hands grabbed him and propelled him away from the smoke. A moment later, Gwen appeared beside him, half carried by a tall, clean-shaven young man with dark brown hair, heavy eyebrows, and deeply tanned skin.

The man holding Vic up had flowing white hair, pink cheeks, and a beard, like a classical painting of Moses — or maybe Santa Claus in a velvet toga. He wore midnight-colored robes flecked with silver. The younger man, dressed in a knee-length tunic, reminded Vic of a bronzed Roman soldier from a gladiator movie.

Vic and Gwen both leaned against the cool marble wall for support. *Marble?* The men held up their hands and said something in a strange language, yet their meaning was clear: Stay here.

The younger man picked up a folded blanket from a basket on the floor and began flailing at the smoke, while the white-bearded man unfurled a parchment-colored scroll and began reading in a stentorian voice.

Gwen called past the two strange men who had apparently rescued them. "Uncle Cap, where are you?" There was no reply. "Taz, what's going on?" she asked Vic, using his nickname borrowed from the wild cartoon character.

"I don't know, but I'll bet I can figure it out." Suddenly the answer came to him. He chuckled aloud, which set him coughing again from the smoke. "Relax, it's just a dream. We'll wake up soon."

She gave him a withering look. "*You* might dream yourself in a place like this, but I certainly wouldn't."

Vic imitated her withering look. "Classic fantasy paradox, nano-brain. I could just be dreaming you."

"Well, how do they figure it out — in books and movies, I mean? Pinch each other?" Vic responded by punching her in the shoulder. "Hey!" Gwen rubbed her upper arm. "That's gonna be a bruise. Twit."

"See? That hurt, but it doesn't really prove anything. Here's a better test," Vic continued almost as if he hadn't heard her. "Tell me something I don't know and would never have thought of."

Gwen nibbled at her lower lip while Moses/Santa droned

on in his strange language. "How about this? 'Whan that aprill with his shoures soote, The droghte of march hath perced to the roote, And bathed every veyne in swich licour, Of which vertu engendred is the flour . . .' "

Vic shook his head. "Whoa! Now you're speaking strange languages too?"

"It's the first few lines from the prologue of *The Canterbury Tales* by Chaucer."

"You're right, I wouldn't have thought of that. What's it mean in English?"

"That *was* English, just an older form. Now you tell me something I would never guess."

"Oh, easy. Jordan has a crush on you."

Gwen's mouth opened and shut. A rosy pink flushed her cheeks. "You . . . you made that up."

He gave her an eyebrow shrug. "*You* didn't think of it, did you?"

Just then, the old man's voice fell silent, and the clouds of multicolored smoke dissipated, giving them a clear view at last. Vic's jaw dropped as he saw the amazing chamber in which they stood. Definitely not the solarium anymore.

"I couldn't have dreamed this better myself." Then he suddenly realized what was missing. "But where's Dad?"

6

WITH THE EVIDENCE RIGHT before her eyes, Gwen could not deny that their situation, whatever it was, was real. Impossible, illogical, ridiculous even — but definitely real.

The two strange men stood chattering next to a cluster of charred-looking crystals, very much like the arrangement Dr. Pierce had been building in the solarium before the wild flash of light. On the floor and walls were curved mirrors, angled prisms, and wide distorting lenses like funhouse reflectors.

The room had a vaguely Greek or Roman feel to it, with marble walls, arched doorways, open windows, and support columns flanking an entryway. At one end of the oval room a spiral staircase corkscrewed up toward the ceiling. *Where are we?* A year ago, Uncle Cap had taken Gwen and Vic on a private tour of the Getty Museum in Malibu, which was laid out like a Roman villa. But she couldn't recall any rooms quite like this.

Scanning the broad oval chamber, Gwen saw shelves full of stoppered vials, racks crammed with thick scrolls, and a long table on trestles that was cluttered with parchments, glowing crystals, more mirrors and lenses, chunks of scrap metal, a variety of unrecognizable implements, and blown-glass beakers filled with colorful fluids. Enormous aquariums built into the curved wall contained colorful fish, peculiar shell creatures, and glowing eels.

"Looks like some sort of secret clubhouse for mad scientists," Vic said.

"Or a medieval alchemist's laboratory. How did we get here?" She rubbed her temple where she had struck her head on the hard floor. Where could she have fallen *from*? She and Vic had been walking across the solarium floor. "Do we have amnesia?"

Running a hand through his messy brown hair, he gave her one of those don't-be-ridiculous looks. "Huh. I don't remember getting amnesia."

"Very funny." Gwen thought this over for a moment. "But we got up in the middle of the night. Now it's broad daylight. We've obviously missed something in between. How can we be sure that it's only been a few hours, instead of days?"

"First of all, if it was that long since I ate, my stomach would be rumbling like a 6.9 earthquake by now. And remember at Ocean Kingdoms when you were taking forever to pick out your sweatshirt? I kept scratching at a mosquito bite, and they gave me a bandage."

"Right," she said, "a kiddy bandage with a little octopus on it."

Vic pointed to his arm. "Same spot, same bandage." He peeled the strip away, and the mosquito bite beneath it was still large and raw. "See? It's barely started to heal."

"Okay, then, what's your theory, Einstein?" Gwen was irritated at his logic but more bothered that she hadn't figured it out for herself.

Their two strange benefactors stood before them again. The bearded man touched a finger to his temple, to the center of his chest, then held out his flat-palmed hand and waited expectantly. The dark-haired young man made the same gesture, holding his hand palm-side down and parallel to the floor between himself and Vic. The strangers said something in unison that Gwen assumed must be a greeting.

"What do you think we should do?" she asked Vic.

"Maybe it's a secret handshake."

Gwen glanced at the older man's hand, which did look as if it were outstretched for a handshake. "Sure, why not?" With a bright smile to demonstrate her friendliness, she clasped the bearded man's hand and shook it briefly. "Nice to meet you."

Likewise, Vic grabbed the younger man's hand and pumped it twice before letting go. "And we have no idea what language you're speaking. You can't understand a word we're saying, can you?"

Moses/Santa frowned, then whispered to the younger man, who left the room. Motioning for the cousins to stay with him, the older man spoke in a ridiculously slow voice, as if that would make him more comprehensible.

Gwen sensed the man's growing frustration. "I'm Gwen and this is my cousin Vic. We're from America."

"We may need a translator. Habla usted Español?"

The white-bearded man looked back at Vic with apparent interest but no understanding.

"Um, parlez-vous français?" Gwen added.

"Er, uh — Sprechen Sie Deutsch?" Still no response.

"Right. Definitely going to need a translator." Gwen looked about the room, hoping for some inspiration.

Just then the handsome dark-haired man returned with a petite, elfin young woman who looked about Vic and Gwen's age. The girl wore a creamy long gown that draped over one shoulder and flowed down her petite body in elegant folds and ripples like a toga. Curly copper hair fell past her waist. The girl touched a finger to her own temple, to the center of her chest, and held her hand out just as the two men had. Next, the elfin girl touched the fingers of her left hand to the center of Gwen's forehead. Her name was Lyssandra.

Gwen jerked backward, losing contact. "Hey! You speak English!"

Vic looked at his cousin strangely. "Why do you think that?"

Gwen was exasperated. "Duh? Just now she told us her name is Lyssandra."

Vic looked even more confused. "But she didn't say a word." He glanced at the copper-haired girl. "Is Gwen right? Is your name Lyssandra?"

The girl nodded and pointed to herself. "Lyssandra."

Vic's aquamarine eyes lit with understanding. "Did you *hear* her say something when she was touching your head?"

Gwen thought about it. "Well, no. Not words, exactly, but —"

"Cool! She's telepathic." Vic grabbed Lyssandra's hand and placed it against his own forehead. A delighted smile spread across his face, and he laughed out loud.

Gwen stared. Was the girl really telepathic? That was impossible. Maybe she should reconsider the theory that this was all a dream — albeit the most vivid one she'd ever had.

Still, her cousin's delighted expression did not go away. Lyssandra's hand dropped from Vic's forehead, and he grabbed Gwen's arm, speaking excitedly. Now she couldn't understand what *he* was saying until Lyssandra touched her forehead again, and suddenly Vic's words made sense.

"— an interpreter and a telepath. If you'll just stop squirming, Lyssandra can prep your mind so that you can understand the language! Sheesh, and you call *me* Mr. Attention Deficit Disorder!"

Amazed, Gwen felt a shifting and repositioning of thoughts in her brain. Lyssandra spoke aloud. "I am preparing your mind to understand Elantyan, our common language. Because this island is the connecting point for many worlds, our ancestors created a language with simple rules to make it easier for people from all cultures to learn."

Gwen grasped each word clearly now, but the sentence still made no sense. Something about an island? Many worlds?

Finished, Lyssandra let her hand drop to her side, and she stepped away from Gwen. "Can you understand me now?"

"Sure. Does that mean that I'm —"

"Speaking Elantyan? Of course you are. I gave the translation center in your brain the basic rules and vocabulary of our speech. It will automatically translate our language into terms you can understand. While you remain here on our island of Elantya, your mind will convert your speech to our words — though the concepts may still be foreign. I myself speak eleven tongues fluently, and Elantyan is by far the simplest. It is also the easiest to communicate to another mind. It would take weeks or months to teach you another language in the same fashion."

"Cool," Vic said.

Lyssandra smiled. "In our world, your names would be Viccus and Gwenya. May I call you that?"

"Where exactly are we?" Gwen asked. Something just wasn't making sense. "What is this place?"

"Such discussions can wait," the bearded man broke in. "I am Sage Rubicas, and this is my apprentice Orpheon." He gestured to the swarthy-skinned young man. "Hmm, now that you can communicate, please tell us how you came to be here. It is most intriguing."

"Uh, we were kind of hoping you could tell us that." Vic scratched his nose. "We don't have a clue."

Orpheon crossed his arms, and his heavy eyebrows drew together. "Did someone unlock the crystal door for you, or did you find the door open?"

Gwen glanced at the graceful arched doorways. "Uncle Cap was doing something with crystals and mirrors, then there was a flash of light."

"And that is how you came through a crystal door to us?"

Vic muttered, "Yep, a transporter accident. Didn't see that one coming."

"But where was the Key?" Orpheon prodded. "You couldn't open a crystal door by yourselves."

Vic dug in his pocket and pulled out his keychain medallion. "A key? You mean this?"

Rubicas reached for it in astonishment. "Hmm. Where did you get this?"

Vic handed it to him. "On my thirteenth birthday Dad said I was old enough to have a key to the house. Or do you mean the little flashlight?"

Orpheon pointed to the small five-sided medallion. "*This*."

"It belonged to my mom. Gwen has one just like it."

She pulled the pendant on its leather cord out from under her sweatshirt.

"It is made from xyridium, a valuable metal — that much is certain. And I have seen the symbol before," Rubicas admitted. "Hmm. I must think further on this. Lyssandra, would you be so kind as to show our guests the city and answer their questions? It will give me time to consult my scrolls and confer with Orpheon." He gave the key chain back to Vic, who put it in his pocket again.

As if she were asked to do this sort of thing all the time, the girl blinked her cobalt-blue eyes. "I would be honored, Sage Rubicas."

Lyssandra led Gwen and Vic to the spiral stone staircase at the far end of the oval room. Climbing up, leaving the smell of colored smoke behind, the copper-haired girl explained, "Elantya is a gathering place for scholars from far-flung worlds. Sages and students come here to learn mathematics, alchemy, magic, agriculture, metallurgy, philosophy, astronomy."

The three of them emerged onto an observation deck at the top of a sunwashed white tower. A fresh salty tang filled the air. The elfin girl spread her hands to indicate the island realm all around them. "This is my favorite view. Is it not beautiful?"

Below lay the most spectacular and *foreign* cityscape Gwen had ever seen. Terraced gardens, vineyards, and orchards climbed the steep and rocky hills. Streets zigzagged up the slopes, which were crowded with whitewashed buildings. A perfect turquoise sea deepened to sapphire as it stretched to the edge of the world, and the cerulean sky held a few cottony clouds. Colorful ships plied the island's harbor, sailing from the sheltered water to the open ocean. Gwen turned a full three hundred sixty degrees to take in the panorama.

Beside her, Vic said, "Hey Dorothy, I don't think we're in Kansas anymore."

"That's for sure." She gave a shaky laugh. "I'm not sure this place even has a Kansas."

7

WHILE THEY ABSORBED THE view of Elantya, Vic wondered if Gwen was trying to concoct some rational explanation. Vic wasn't usually so overloaded with amazement, but his own mind was whirling so fast the thoughts didn't have time to form words, much less sentences.

This island was the coolest place he'd ever seen. He only wished his father could be there with them. Vic was fairly certain Dr. Pierce was all right — after all, *the two cousins* had been the ones sucked into a strange new world! — but by now his dad must be awfully worried.

His thoughts ricocheted to another question. Had his father *expected* this to happen? He was always talking about his important experiments, and he'd set up a crystal array very similar to the one here in Rubicas's lab. Just before the solarium flooded with retina-searing light, his dad had called out,

"Kyara." Had he been *trying* to do something with the crystals, an experiment that had sent Vic and Gwen here?

Though concentrating in school was difficult for him, Vic had a sharp mind and could synthesize bits and pieces of what he had learned — snippets from speeches, phrases from textbooks, remembered experiences — to create plausible explanations. A self-proclaimed "gadgetologist," Vic used his uncanny intuition to figure out how things worked. He flew by the seat of his pants and often saw connections before anyone else did. When a subject truly interested him, he could teach himself things, too. He had even learned to play the guitar without taking lessons.

Of course, his unorthodox approach landed him in trouble when he leapt before he looked, trusting his instincts. Many teachers despaired of helping him, or even getting him to sit still. In math class he often lost points because he couldn't show in writing the exact steps by which he reached the correct answer. He just "knew" it.

Gwen teased him about the way his mind bounced from one thing to another, but Vic did not see his supposed "attention deficit disorder" as a weakness. He had read a college-level psychology textbook in which the author theorized that hyperfocus and distractibility were survival traits for hunters in the wild. And both Cap and Rip Pierce had assured Vic that he was endowed with "untamed genius," much like Albert Einstein, who had himself flunked math. Not a bad comparison, he supposed.

If he and Gwen had somehow managed to land themselves next door to Oz, then Vic would have to gather as much information as he could. Maybe his mind could fit the puzzle pieces together and find a way home . . . or bring his father here to Elantya.

When they descended the spiral staircase and returned to the chamber, bearded Rubicas and his apprentice were crouched beside a blackened crystal, studying it, rearranging the fragments. The once-glittering gems now looked like lumps of charcoal.

Vic gestured with his chin to the two men. "So, uh, are these guys mad scientists, or what?"

"They are certainly not mad," Lyssandra said. "Master Rubicas is one of the wisest sages in all of Elantya."

Overhearing them, Orpheon flashed the elfin girl a wolfish grin. "And how would you describe me?"

Lyssandra blushed, turning away from him. "Orpheon, apprentice to Sage Rubicas, is beginning his fourth level apprenticeship at the Citadel."

Sage Rubicas bobbed his head absently. "Mmm. He is one of the most brilliant sages in training that we have. Orpheon achieved the highest level of apprenticeship in less than two years, and I may soon promote him to journeysage. I do not know what I would do without him."

The younger man gave the sage a nod of thanks, and Vic could tell by Orpheon's smug expression that he had no doubt as to his status in the fourth level . . . whatever that was.

"What's the Citadel?" Gwen asked. "Some sort of training program?"

Rubicas answered, "It is a place of learning, a center of knowledge and enlightenment."

Vic grimaced. "Oh. You mean a school?"

Lyssandra brushed her fingertips along his forearm, tasting his knowledge and memories. She laughed. "Oh, no! Schools like those are for little children. The Citadel is entirely voluntary, a place of growth and enrichment."

"More like a university, then?" Gwen asked.

Lyssandra touched her fingertips to Gwen's hand and read the thought in her mind. "Closer . . . but not precisely. Those who study at the Citadel stay as long as they choose in order to reach their desired level of knowledge. A novice may work to attain the rank of apprentice, journeysage, neosage, sage, or master sage. I am a second-level apprentice in Translation and Diplomacy. Perhaps you do not have a similar concept for —"

"Surely that can wait," Rubicas interrupted, still fixated on the problem they posed. "We wish to clarify the method by which Gwenya and Viccus came to be here at all. How did the crystal door open? We cannot be certain what allowed you to pass through."

"Um, what door?" Vic looked around.

"The crystal door that Orpheon and I were hoping to create. We were using the rarest and most potent type of aja crystal, brought here from Afirik in hopes of establishing a new crystal door in the center of Elantya. If all had gone as planned, we would have brought a Key sage directly from Chian. Regrettably, the crystals all caught fire at once and poured out multicolored smoke, so we were unable to open a door after all. But you two appeared. Hmm, so something did go right, did it not?"

"And something went wrong, too." Orpheon pointed to the scorch marks on the marble floor. "Those were very valuable crystals."

"Yes," Rubicas mused. "Still, there must be a Key. What was it that allowed these children to pass through? Hmm. Something on the other side?"

Vic was about to point out that at fourteen they weren't exactly *children,* when Gwen said, "Maybe my uncle's crystals and mirrors tapped into your complex array here and leap-frogged us into the middle of your experiment."

Orpheon gave Gwen a slow smile. "Or perhaps it was your xyridium medallions?"

Rubicas nodded. "It may also be related to the star aja crystals, which we had never tried for this purpose before."

"In other words, it could have been a thousand things," Vic said.

Gwen's shoulders slumped. "You *can* send us back home, can't you?"

"Perhaps," Rubicas said. "*If* we could recreate the conditions. Hmm."

Orpheon shook his head. "These were the only star crystals we had, and now they are ruined. Few other sages around the city have star aja, but we have been anticipating a new shipment for some time. The trading vessel has not yet arrived. It was due to bring both the star aja and a new instructor from Afirik four days ago."

"Can't we use some other kind of crystal?" Gwen persisted.

Rubicas blinked his inscrutable gray eyes. "If the door opened only because of the star aja . . ."

"Then we must wait until our shipment arrives," Orpheon finished.

"If, however, the power surge came from the crystals arranged by your own sage —"

"My father," Vic corrected.

Rubicas continued as if he hadn't heard him. "If he linked with the crystals in this world to open a new and unexpected door, then we must re-create the experiment. Do you think he will try again on his side?"

"He won't give up on us," Vic said stubbornly.

8

IN AN OBVIOUS EFFORT to get the unexpected visitors out of the way while the sage and his apprentice contemplated the problem, Lyssandra glided to the door. "Let me show you more of our island."

Trying not to let anxiety and uncertainty get the best of her, Gwen met Vic's gaze, violet sparring with aquamarine. Unconsciously, at least, both of them had realized at a young age what a powerful effect their unusual stares could produce, and people often remarked on what extraordinary eyes the "twin cousins" had. She knew without asking that Vic was ready to jump into any adventure, but she hesitated. Someone had to keep a level head here.

Gwen glanced around the damaged laboratory, not really wanting to leave. Unpredictable situations made her worry. "What if the crystal door unexpectedly opens up again when we aren't here? What if we miss our only chance to get back home?"

Vic was enjoying the moment without worrying about future problems — as usual. "Come on, Doc! You know you'll regret it forever if you don't see everything that's here. That would be like going to the Grand Canyon on vacation and staying in the car."

It irritated Gwen that her cousin didn't seem concerned. So much was still unexplained. On the one hand, she wanted to analyze the evidence in the chamber — mirrors, burned crystals, and so on — to see if she could logically deduce what had happened. On the other, she probably ought to learn about this strange world in order to better take stock of their situation.

"All right, let's see. Number one, we're stuck here anyway for the moment." Gwen ticked off the list on her fingers. "Two, our medallions are made of xyridium, a metal that seems well known here, but we never found anything quite like it on Earth . . . so maybe our moms have some connection to Elantya. Maybe there's a clue here somewhere. Three, we have no idea what might help us get back home, so we'd better learn all we can. Four —"

"Four, this place is cool," Vic interrupted, taking her by the arm and propelling her into the corridor toward Lyssandra. "Explore now, make lists later."

Although she saw no imminent danger in looking around, Gwen didn't like knowing that she couldn't return to her familiar Earth whenever she wished. What if she and Vic were stranded here for the rest of their lives? Maybe she worried too much. At least Lyssandra, Rubicas, and Orpheon seemed friendly enough.

Outside, the air was fresh, scoured by pleasant breezes. The sky was the perfect color of a robin's egg, and the temperature was warm but not oppressive. A soft wind stole away droplets of sweat as soon as they formed.

Lyssandra led them along flagstoned streets, some wide and some narrow, down the hill on which Sage Rubicas's tower laboratory stood. Gwen quickly forgot her immediate concerns and stared in fascination. At first, she tried to keep the delight from her face because she preferred to present a calm, sensible image. But with the wonders of Elantya all around her, it was hard to be aloof.

At primary intersections, a profusion of colorful flowers attracted butterflies and sluggish bees. Aqueducts flowed with swift silvery water alongside the avenues. Tiny canals criss-crossed the streets, flowing downhill or uphill with the aid of pumps. Floating containers bobbed along the narrow channels, carrying scrolls, crystals, and occasional flowers or food.

"Those remind me of sushi boats," Vic said.

"Or messages in a bottle," Gwen said. "Is this like a pneumatic-tube messaging system?"

The petite young woman waved a hand toward the floating containers. "Those packages are enchanted to go to a certain person, and they float through the network of channels until they arrive at the correct destination. We have other communication systems, of course, but this one is very efficient."

"Great way to send the mail," Vic said with a grin.

"We normally use skrits for mail and spell scrolls," Lyssandra said, "but since skrits can only carry three times their own weight, we use the water channels for other deliveries."

Gwen was about to ask what "skrits" were, when they came to an area where tall, tapered silver towers stood like giant toy pinwheels. The thin curved blades flashed as they rotated. The pinwheel petals alternated between quicksilver mirrors and angled prisms, spinning a flurry of rainbows and dazzling reflections into the air like water droplets from a whirling sprinkler.

Gwen stared, then consciously closed her mouth so she wouldn't gape like a fish out of water. Lyssandra looked at the towers. "Those are mirrormills, coated with a reflective film of aja crystal. They catch and split the magic energy inherent in sunlight, then store it in luminous jars, so that Elantyans can use the power wherever it is needed."

"Like solar energy cells?" Gwen said.

Lyssandra touched her arm, took the concept from Gwen's mind, then pursed her lips. "An inaccurate comparison, but useful enough. You must adapt to the fact that everything in Elantya functions differently from the way to which you are accustomed."

"I may not know how it works," Vic said, "but I bet I could figure it out."

Gwen noticed that all of the buildings were made of stone or whitewashed bricks, with many crystals and metal supports. "I don't see much wood."

"We are a small island at the center of all crystal-door trade routes. Although we have access to stone, sand, and some metal ores, as well as crystals that we can either mine or grow from natural elements, wood is scarce here. Our ships and docks come from other worlds where wood is plentiful. Because so much of what Elantya needs must be imported through the crystal doors, we take great care to put everything to its wisest use."

"I guess that would have an effect on architectural styles."

Men, women, and children from many races walked past them, dressed in colorful costumes that originated from diverse cultures. Different worlds? Different universes? Gwen couldn't deny the strangeness all around her.

Some people rode in low wheeled carts with colorful sails flapping out in front of them. Catching the breezes, the sail carts glided along the smooth streets, picking up speed down the slopes and then rolling uphill. Overhead, kite gliders carried one or two passengers, who pedaled to turn the broad scoop-shaped propellers.

From what Gwen could see, some of the "magic" was based on physics rather than sorcery, but some things were undeniably magical. She wondered if this was what her own world might have looked like if the Renaissance had occurred at a time when arcane spells could work alongside science.

Ornate water clocks spun paddle wheels that dumped dippers of water into cylinders calibrated with the hours of the day. The excess current spilled down chutes to turn gears that propelled mechanical figures of outlandish animals and dancing imps.

"It's like something from the mind of Leonardo da Vinci on too much coffee," she murmured.

"I was thinking more of Dr. Seuss," Vic said. "I sure wish I had my digital camera. I left it in my backpack by the solarium door." He groaned with frustration. "Nobody's going to believe any of this back home."

They turned the corner of a domed building whose windows were shaded by flapping orange and purple awnings. Gwen heard a hissing noise and the clank of metal footsteps.

A gleaming contraption with pulleys and cables plodded toward them on a pair of thick short legs, like a robot built from a child's construction set. The artificial walking body was studded at every joint with what appeared to be rubies, emeralds, and sapphires, each jewel shimmering with a hidden fire. Bubbles circulated through veinlike tubes. Set atop rectangular shoulders, a compact aquarium tank formed the machine's "head." The water-filled dome contained an exotic living creature — a rippled mass that might have been a cross between a sea anemone and a jellyfish. A frilly ridge surrounded the brainlike lump, studded with a ring of eye protrusions.

"Whoa, what's that?" Vic said.

Lyssandra motioned her two new friends forward. Moving with a cautious, ponderous grace, the walking device stopped in front of them. A bubbly voice came from a pair of horn-shaped speakers embedded in the armored chest, reminding Gwen of the sounds Vic used to make when he talked through a drinking straw in a glass of soda. "Greetings, Mistress Lyssandra."

"A good day to you as well, Sage Polup," she said with a quick bow. "These two strangers came through a crystal door during one of Sage Rubicas's experiments. I am showing them Elantya for the first time."

~52~

The anemone creature floated closer to the faceplate to get a better view with its ring of eyes. "I hope you find Elantya to be as rewarding, and as safe, as I have." With a hiss of building power, the walker lifted one heavy leg and then the other. "I must be off to a meeting of the Pentumvirate."

Lyssandra said her farewells, echoed by Gwen and Vic, though the two were mystified. "And what was that? An alien?"

"Sage Polup is an anemonite from beneath the sea. In the ocean, his people are mobile, but they are unable to live or move on land, so our sages created that special survival tank for him. With spells and science, he can walk among us and go about his business through the streets of Elantya."

"Why did he want to leave the ocean?" Gwen's brow furrowed. "Does he work here?"

"Maybe he's a foreign-exchange student," Vic said.

"He is one of our teachers, and Elantyan students learn much from him. Anemonites are famed repositories of ideas and knowledge, forming a great brain trust when they cluster on the sea floor. This makes them both valuable and vulnerable. Sage Polup's fellow anemonites are now oppressed, held in thrall by our enemies, the merlons."

"Mer-what?" Vic asked.

"Merlons. An aquatic race that lives in cities beneath the waves. After Elantya was created here to guard the crystal doors, the merlons came to resent our tiny patch of solid ground on their world. They wish to drive us away, but Elantya's master sages and our own reservoir of knowledge protect us. Still, the merlons have not given up."

"And what do the merlons use anemonites for?" Gwen asked.

"To fight us. Though the anemonites declared their neutrality in the conflict, the merlons enslaved them, forcing these great thinkers of the deep to devise spells and tactics against us."

"In other words, they're like hostage weapons scientists," Gwen said.

"Sorta sounds that way," Vic agreed. "I watched a TV special about how the Nazis forced scientists to make weapons for Hitler during World War II, even though they didn't want to."

Lyssandra watched the artificial walker turn the corner and disappear down the street. "Sage Polup escaped from the guarded anemonite beds and came to us. One of our divers found him in the harbor a year ago, pleading for asylum. Polup warned us of a growing threat to Elantya. The merlons mean to remove this island from their oceans. From time to time they have destroyed our docks, shredded our fishing nets, and damaged our ships. They intend to move against us again . . . and soon."

"Let me get this straight," Vic said. "You're being threatened . . . by mermaids?"

"Mer*lons.*" The young woman touched his arm, and paused a moment to read his thoughts. "I can see in your mind a picture of what you are thinking, and you could not be more wrong. The merlons are far more horrific than anything you can imagine."

"Closer to the Creature from the Black Lagoon, then?" Vic said.

Lyssandra wore a troubled expression. "Ah, I see now. Yes, that is closer to reality. Sage Polup advises the Pentumvirate, our governing council of five leaders, but he spends most of his time teaching."

"In other words, a visiting professor," Gwen said.

"A jellyfish professor driving a robot!" Vic chuckled. "Am I the only one who finds that funny?"

The telepathic girl's eyes were solemn. "Would you truly judge him by his appearance rather than by his mind? That is not our way, Viccus. Elantya is an egalitarian city, and the Citadel welcomes students and instructors of any race or species from all the worlds linked by crystal doors — medical specialists and weather readers from Chian, shamans and tribal musicians from Afirik, philosophers and mathematicians from Grogypt. Students come to learn the complexities of intelligent life in all its forms. You will see this for yourself. While you are in Elantya, it would be simplest to let you stay in student rooms at the Citadel. Perhaps you two will learn from us and add to our reservoir of knowledge by telling us of your world, where things are different?"

"Oh, it's different there, all right," Gwen said.

"Then you will fit in well. We each carry special knowledge. Scholars and scientists, mystics and philosophers, come from different civilizations to practice their arts, to share their learning, and to see other points of view."

Vic pointed to the sky. "Ooh — look!"

Looking up, Gwen spotted a rectangle of purple cloth fringed with gold tassels sailing among the scoop-powered gliders. A young man in billowy pantaloons, a white silk shirt, and short vest rode cross-legged atop the carpet, guiding it along.

"You've got to be kidding me." Vic whooped with delight. He nudged his cousin. "Five bucks says we're about to meet Aladdin."

"A flying carpet?" Gwen put her hands on her hips. "That's impossible."

"Why is it more impossible than any other design of glider or aircraft?" Lyssandra said. She waved to the young man on the flying carpet, and he came around to land in front of them.

"Because . . . because it just is," Gwen insisted.

"You must learn to dispense with your preconceptions, Gwenya."

9

AFTER THE EMBROIDERED RUG settled on the flagstones with a flurry of gold tassels, the boy stood up and brushed off his fancy clothes. He ran a critical eye over the interpreter. "You are looking very tired today, Lyssandra. Bad dreams again?"

Lyssandra studied the ground at her feet. "Shipwrecks . . . all night. It seemed so real, so familiar. I'd rather not discuss it."

He shrugged and looked instead at Gwen and Vic. "A new pair of novs?"

"These are not novs," Lyssandra said.

"They certainly look like novs. They are dressed very strangely."

While Gwen self-consciously smoothed her rumpled sweat-shirt, Vic rolled his eyes. "Let me get this straight: A guy in poof-pants on a purple flying carpet thinks *we're* dressed strangely? Maybe we should try introductions now, fashion advice later."

Gwen suspected they had just been insulted by the apparently wealthy young man, and she wasn't ready to let it slide — even if he *was* way cuter than Shoru's handler from Ocean Kingdoms. "What're novs?"

With a quirk of his full lips, the young man said, "Usually ignorant, in my opinion. Unfortunately, I, too, am a nov."

Lyssandra added, "The term 'nov' is short for novice. New students at the Citadel."

"In other words, freshmen," Gwen said.

Vic heaved an exaggerated sigh at Gwen. "So even after being transported to an amazing fantasy land, we still can't escape school?"

The long-haired girl politely presented the newcomers. "Gwenya and Viccus arrived through a new crystal door during one of Sage Rubicas's experiments."

Without introducing himself, the boy with the flying carpet raised his dark eyebrows. "It is not possible to create new doorways since the Great Closure."

"Rubicas has been trying," Lyssandra answered with a distant smile. "Never underestimate a master sage."

With a flourish of his right hand, the young man bowed to them. "I am Ali el Sharif." He deftly rolled his carpet and tucked the thin cylinder under his arm. "I will walk with you for the time being," he said as if he were doing them a favor. "After enjoying the breezes and looking down on everyone, perhaps I should stretch my legs a bit." From the care he showed for the rug, Gwen could tell it was a treasured possession.

Sharif had a strong cleft chin, olive-green eyes, and wavy dark hair that covered his ears. His shoulders were square, his back straight, and he moved with a poise that suggested extreme confidence and a cultured upbringing. He seemed well aware of both his handsome features and his surroundings.

"Sharifas comes from the flying city of Irrakesh," Lyssandra explained. "He has been with us for six months, taking classes at the Citadel."

"A flying city?" Vic said. "Cool!"

Gwen was more skeptical, as always. "What exactly do you mean by a flying city?"

"It is a city that flies," Sharif said, his tone suggesting that the answer should have been obvious. "That is why we call it a flying city."

Gwen did not let him rile her. "A city can't just sprout wings, so how does it fly?" Of course, a few moments ago she wouldn't have believed in a flying carpet, much less a flying city.

Sharif's voice was even, almost bored, as if he had told the story many times before. "Irrakesh is a place of great marvels, with paved streets and tall buildings, minarets and domes. Long ago, to protect its people, powerful magic was used to uproot the city. Irrakesh drifts across the open skies, riding the desert winds. We glide far above the arid, trackless dunes and harvest our water directly from the clouds." As he painted pictures with his words, Gwen could see that Sharif enjoyed telling stories, even bragging a little about his world. "If you wish, I might consider arranging a visit for you. Someday."

"If we stay that long." Gwen looked at her cousin. "We're

still trying to figure out how we got *here,* and how we can get back. Your dad's got to be really worried by now, Taz —"

Sharif laughed in disbelief. "You do not know how to open the crystal door to your home again?" Then his olive eyes narrowed knowingly. "Ah, you must be one of the fortunate accidents for which Sage Rubicas is so well known?"

Lyssandra nodded. "Yes, another one."

"Not so fortunate for us, if we're stuck in Elantya," Gwen muttered.

"Sheesh, Doc, we just got here," Vic said. "Enjoy the moment. My dad's probably in the solarium right now trying to figure out what happened. This couldn't have been a complete accident, you know — he must have realized what he was doing. Have a little confidence."

After everything she had seen in the past hour, Gwen realized she didn't want to go home just yet, though she would have felt much better to know they *could* go back. She fingered the pendant at her neck. Why had Sage Rubicas been so interested in these medallions their mothers gave them? She really did want to find some answers. . . .

Lyssandra led her companions down the steep street and stone steps, past multicolored sculptures of blown glass and wind chimes made of flat-cut gems that created a beautiful high-pitched music. As they walked, Sharif reached into a mesh pouch around his neck and withdrew an object the size of a grapefruit wrapped in scarlet cloth. He removed the cloth to reveal a lovely crystal sphere, which began to glow. Inside the ball, Gwen could see the silhouette of a tiny female form.

"There, now you can shine, Piri," Sharif said. "I hope you had a nice nap."

The female figure stretched her tiny arms. Sharif tossed the crystal sphere into the air, and it drifted back down into his hand as gently as a soap bubble. He extended the clear globe toward the two newcomers. The miniature girl leaned closer to the glass, glowing aqua, and looking just as curious about the cousins as they were about her. The young man rolled the shimmering ball back and forth in front of a delighted Vic and Gwen, showing off.

"Looks like somebody put Tinkerbell inside a snow globe," Vic said. "Beam me up, Scotty, my brain is about to explode."

"And I thought Ocean Kingdoms had too much stuff to absorb in one day." Gwen peered into the crystal ball. "That's beautiful, Sharif. What is it?"

"A nymph djinni. Piri cannot yet survive outside of her protective eggsphere, so I carry her everywhere with me in a pouch."

Vic's eyebrows arched. "That doesn't look like an egg. It's not egg-shaped."

"You mean just because it's round?" Gwen asked. "Fish eggs are round. So are frog eggs and —"

"Okay, I get it. Anyway, that's the coolest pet I've ever seen."

"Piri is much more than a pet." Sharif's voice held a reproachful tone. "I am her master and protector. Very few people have a djinni, you know." He carefully polished the curved surface with the scarlet cloth, then rolled the sphere from the tips of his fingers up his arm to the shoulder and back again. "Piri is my companion and confidant. In my position, it is refreshing to have someone I can trust who wants nothing from me but security and affection."

The globe twinkled in variegated shades of pink, and the djinni danced inside, giggling silently while Sharif juggled her sphere. "Piri is quite helpful in the dark. Look how bright and rich her light is." He spun the ball on his fingertips, then let it roll down his arm again to his elbow.

Gwen could tell Sharif was just as proud of Piri as he was of his fancy flying carpet. "How do you make it change colors? The ball was turquoise at first, but now it's pink."

Sharif regarded her with annoyance. "Not 'it.' *She*. Piri's color changes with her mood. For example, pink is evidence of happiness, red represents anger, and so on. In a year she will become capable of small feats of magic — nothing extravagant at first, but eventually she will be powerful. Won't you, Piri?" Holding the ball close to his eyes, Sharif rubbed his nose against the glass. The sphere responded with a warm yellow glow, brighter than before.

Lyssandra took them to Elantya's main harbor. The docks stretched out into the sheltered water like tongues of slatted wood. Exotic ships with colorful sails came in and out of the port, dancing like butterflies on the waves.

Harbor workers unloaded crates from trireme ships tied up to the sun-washed docks. Lyssandra explained, "Each vessel arrives through a specific crystal door far out in the ocean, sailing from their world to this central hub."

"In other words, Elantya is like Grand Central Station," Gwen mused. "People come from far away and everybody meets here."

"Each crystal door requires a Key," Lyssandra said.

"Huh. My dad said he needed a key when he was arranging the crystals." Vic held up his keychain. "I tried to offer him this one, but —"

"A Key is a *person*," Sharif interrupted, as if they should already have known that.

Lyssandra said calmly, "A Key is tuned to a particular crystal door. Every ship carries at least one Key, so the captains can go back and forth on their regular route." She pointed out many people who wore garments, ribbons, or armbands bearing a symbol to indicate they were Keys.

Piri's crystal sphere flashed in the sunlight. Sharif inspected it for smudges before balancing it on the backs of his fingers and deftly rolling it back and forth. "I have been tested, and I have the potential to become a Key myself."

Gwen didn't ask the million questions that sprang to mind. Her brain was already so full of new sights and ideas that she was afraid she wouldn't have room to absorb one more fact.

Fortunately, Lyssandra took the opportunity to ask Vic and Gwen about themselves. When she learned that Vic and Gwen were "twin" cousins, the telepathic girl caught her breath. "A few nights ago, I had a dream about one of the ancient prophecies. It tells of champions who will rise up to defeat the dark tyrants and free the sealed worlds. It is strange how you almost fit the old legends." She sang a haunting tune:

"Born beneath the selfsame moon,
Only they may bind the rune,
And create the Ring of Might,
Right the wrongs, reverse the rite.

Sharing blood, yet not the womb,
Two shall seal the tyrant's doom.
Darkest Sage, in darkest day,
With his blood the price shall pay."

"That's, uh, strange all right," Vic admitted, ". . . whatever it means."

Gwen shaded her eyes and spotted another ship approaching Elantya's main harbor. All the sails were stretched tight, as if to squeeze out every last bit of push from the wind. It came in more swiftly than the breezes could possibly be pushing it, as if some magic had given it a burst of speed. Red banners flapped from the masts, and a bright flag flew from the tallest point. She wished she had some binoculars. "That ship certainly is in a hurry."

A flash of light and a plume of bright purple smoke shot into the air from the main deck of the racing ship, followed a few seconds later by the distance-muffled *thump* of an explosion. Everyone on the docks began to scramble to mount a response.

Sharif said, "Ships fly those banners only in the direst emergency."

Lyssandra motioned for them to follow her as she broke into a run. "The captain is sounding an alarm!"

10

ELANTYAN WAR GALLEYS SPROUTED oars as soldiers dipped long wooden blades into the water. A bell rang from a high tower, and dock workers hurried to prepare a slip where the captain could tie up at the main dock. Other ships dropped their sails and raised anchor, ready to respond to the news, whatever it might be.

Gwen and Vic crowded with Lyssandra and Sharif on the edge of the dock, listening to the dip of oars in the water, the rhythmic chanting of the soldiers as they drove their war galley across the harbor. Even in a frantic rush, though, sailing ships moved at a sedate pace compared to racing ambulances and police cars. They watched the intricate slow-motion drama as the galleys approached the larger vessel, tied up alongside it, and added the power of their oars to escort the ship to the Elantyan docks. Sages in colorful robes climbed aboard the sailing ship and stood at the bow, reading from spell scrolls to add momentum. The red alarm pennants fluttered in the breeze. More purple smoke rose up.

The whole process took almost an hour, during which time Gwen felt the sense of urgency grow. Vic, on the other hand, was bored and knelt on the dock boards to watch fish flit around the weed-grown posts beneath the pier. He trailed his fingers in the clear water. Laughing, he waved his cousin over. "Hey, Doc, look at this — a sea monkey the size of a Barbie doll!"

She saw a doll-sized figure that looked like a man with a fish tail, swimming and waving his little hands, desperate to get somebody's attention.

Lyssandra caught her breath when she saw the creature. "An aquit! They are the messengers of the sea." When the telepathic girl reached into the water, the aquit eagerly swam to her, allowing itself to be cupped in her palms. She drew it up, dripping, and set it on the warm boards of the wharf.

"Elantya!" it squeaked. "A message for Elantya."

"Did you just come from that ship out there?" Sharif demanded. "The one with the emergency?"

"No. I swam here all the way from the reefs."

"We can accept your message," Lyssandra said in a quiet, encouraging tone. "Go ahead."

The amphibious creature straightened, shimmered, and suddenly took the form of a small human. Gone was the mermaidlike fish tail. Gwen couldn't tell if this was an illusion or actual shape-shifting. The aquit now looked like a man dressed in captain's robes, wearing the mark of an assigned Key for one of the crystal doors.

Lyssandra blanched. Noticing, Sharif said, "What is wrong?"

"That captain. I recognize him — from my dream."

The tiny man's face was distraught, his voice hoarse. "This is Captain Argo, en route from Afirik. We are under attack! Merlons have stranded us on the reefs of Ophir. They cut the anchor chain and drove my ship onto the rocks. The merlons are surrounding us, closing in!

"I am heavily loaded with a hold full of star aja crystals. I have twelve able-bodied sailors aboard, as well as a sage from Afirik and his apprentice, both on their way to Elantya. I am arming everyone, but I doubt we will survive this night." The figure of the captain bent over and spoke toward the floor. "Go now! Take this message to someone from Elantya. Swim as fast as you can!"

"Cool," Vic said. "The aquit must be kinda like a living recording device — a chameleon that can absorb the words and image of whoever is talking."

Finished with its message, the creature shifted back to its normal form, balanced on his merman tail. Lyssandra splashed it with water from beneath the dock to refresh it. "Would you like to go back into the sea? Or would you prefer a tank where we will feed you?"

"Tank, please," the aquit said in a piping voice. "Too dangerous out there. Sharks, merlons, sea serpents. . . . I was chased by predators all the way."

Without explaining his actions, Sharif hurried to one of the ships tied to the dock, spoke to a concerned-looking first mate, and soon returned with a borrowed ceramic basin, which he filled with sea water. Once placed in the basin, the aquit happily swam in circles like a tiny person in a miniature swimming pool.

Finally, the inbound ship arrived at the docks. The guardian galleys rowed away, leaving the sages and sailors to guide the ship in. Working together, harbor crewmen rushed forward to catch ropes and tie them to big rings on the pilings.

Sailors on the ship's deck bellowed orders, and sweating men and women turned a winch that raised a sturdy fishnet into the air and swung it on a block and tackle over to an unloading platform on the wharf. "This is all we found floating out in the open water," one of the seamen called down.

When the net was emptied of its contents, Gwen could see splintered wood planking from the hull of a large ship. Attached to one piece of scrolled deck rail was a xyridium plaque inscribed with identification symbols. Lyssandra recognized the markings. "That was Captain Argo's ship."

"There seems to be very little left of it," Sharif said.

Seamen spoke in superstitious whispers. Embedded in one of the planks was a burnished reptilian scale the size of Gwen's hand. The scale shimmered with rainbow ridges, and she tried to calculate the size of the creature that had shed it.

As the dock workers spread out the debris retrieved by the newly arrived ship, Vic touched his cousin's arm and pointed in uneasy disbelief at the long deep grooves that had been gouged into the hull planks of the destroyed ship. She immediately recognized what they were.

Claw marks.

11

VIC'S IMAGINATION CONJURED UP plenty of frightening images from the wreckage of Captain Argo's ship. Sea monsters? Scales from something the size of a dragon? Claw marks? He swallowed hard.

Rumors swiftly circulated around Elantya's harbor. Lyssandra set the aquit's basin in the middle of the crowded dock and had the chameleon messenger repeat its story in the form of Captain Argo. Watching the image, Vic realized that the desperate man was almost certainly dead now. Hearing the terrible news, many of the captains, sailors, merchants, and robed Keys grew anxious. Restless, Vic paced up and down the waterfront, eavesdropping wherever he could.

"And you are sure you spotted no survivors? No sign of Captain Argo?" one of the sages asked the captain of the newly arrived ship. "How much wreckage did you find?"

"A lot of flotsam and jetsam, and most of it looked *chewed*." Many workers muttered uneasily. "Even without the threat of the merlons, the currents around the Ophir reefs are treacherous, swift, and erratic. I was not going to let my ship be pulled onto the razor coral. I ordered my crew to get away from there fast."

"We saw thick planks and masts that had been snapped in two," said his first mate. "What if the merlons are using sea serpents again? We did not dare search for long."

"And then a line of dark clouds came from the horizon," said a third sailor. "So we decided to make for Elantya as fast as possible."

"Couldn't there still be somebody in a lifeboat? Or clinging to wreckage?" Vic asked.

Lyssandra closed her blue eyes briefly, then opened them wide. "Yes. In my dream, there *was* someone. . . ."

The captain looked at Vic without recognition. "Considering what we saw and all the time that has passed, it is not likely. The currents out there are harsh. Even without sharks or merlons, the reefs could grind you into sausage meat."

"But you don't know for sure unless you look." Vic grabbed Sharif's white silk sleeve. "I've got an idea! You and I could go search for anyone floating with the wreckage. Your flying carpet can carry a couple of extra people, can't it?"

"Indeed it can." He gave Vic a skeptical look. "Though I seldom accept passengers. Flying carpets are very rare. Right now, mine is the only one in all of Elantya, a gift —"

"Whoa, flyboy. Search now, brag later, okay? We need to hurry. What if someone's floating out there hoping to be rescued? With my good eyesight, I can help you look. I promise not to spill anything on your expensive upholstery."

Considering the matter as if he were a wise judge, the boy from Irrakesh unrolled his carpet on the dock. "Yes, this I can do." He knelt on the woven surface, neatly spreading and arranging the tassels. "And this would be a good time to see how fast it can go — provided Viccus does not fall off."

Lyssandra looked uncertain. "Should we not consult the Pentumvirate? We have no authority to make such a decision."

Vic groaned. "I don't know how it works here in Elantya, but where we come from there's an important first rule of emergency protocol: Act now, discuss later. Better to apologize afterward — if you *have* to — than to waste time waiting for permission." He stared at the mangled wreckage, imagining what some poor victim might be facing right now.

Biting her lower lip, Gwen surprised him with her support. "Normally I'd say Taz — Vic — is too impulsive, but this time I have to agree. Lives may be at stake. Though I think a bit of Vic's motivation may come from wanting to ride on the magic carpet."

Vic shrugged an eyebrow. "Does it matter if I have a little fun while I'm doing the right thing?"

"No, I suppose not. Good luck. I wish I could go, too."

"At most I can take one person to help me search," Sharif said quickly.

"Right. We need to save room for any survivors."

Lyssandra had no choice but to accept the decision. "I will inform the Pentumvirate."

Sharif sat at the front of the carpet and looked over his shoulder as Vic situated himself at the rear.

"I don't suppose this rug has safety belts?"

"Sit cross-legged, and you will keep your balance better."

Gwen turned to Sharif. "If you fly too fast, can the wind blow you off the carpet?"

"No. On my carpet the wind never feels stronger that a light breeze." He glanced back at Vic. "If you fall from the carpet, I will try to catch you. But it would be more beneficial if you did not fall."

"Got it," Vic said. "I think I can handle that."

Gwen still looked worried. "You *sure* you want to do this, Taz?"

Crossing his legs, Vic smiled reassuringly. "*Someone* has to do it."

"Just be careful!"

"Tell that to *him*." He tapped Sharif on the shoulder. "He's the pilot."

Sharif put Piri's crystal sphere into its open-weave pouch and hung it around his neck, so the glowing djinni could see better. He traced his fingers along the complex patterns of interwoven gold thread. With flares and sparks, the carpet's embroidery began to shine in different illuminated patterns, like a shifting neon sign. Vic thought the rug's design looked like the circuit paths of a personal computer's motherboard. There were far too many interwoven designs for him to study them all without getting dizzy.

Gently, as if they were sitting on the palm of a giant hand, the rug lifted into the air, its gold tassels dangling down. As they gained altitude, Vic suddenly thought of the fact that only a thin rectangle of fabric separated him from a long drop. His stomach lurched.

Several sailors waved at them, but most continued their tasks without glancing up, as if seeing a flying carpet were nothing surprising. For them, maybe it wasn't.

The carpet rotated to orient itself on a new course, then sped forward, gliding silently across the air currents. Vic laughed as breezes blew through his thick hair. "Does your djinni use fairy dust to make us fly? Should I be thinking happy thoughts?"

"As you wish," Sharif said. "Our flight is driven by the spells embroidered into the rug with threads of sun aja."

"Ah, that makes sense."

The carpet soared out of the harbor toward the open ocean in the direction from which the new ship had come. Vic could barely sit still as he peered over the side at the long plunge. If he did fall off, Sharif would have some time to swoop down and intercept him — but he didn't want to test his new friend's reactions or flying skills.

Elantya's inner harbor was filled with fishing boats, cargo vessels that had sailed through crystal doors, sailboats, sharp-prowed guardian galleys, even training vessels filled with students. Bright orange sails with yellow and red markings made them look like tropical fish from the aquariums at Ocean Kingdoms.

The upthrust island was covered with white buildings, stacked like barnacles one upon the other. A spectacular lighthouse tower on an extended spit of land shimmered with dazzling green flames to guide vessels to a safe haven. While Sharif piloted the carpet, Vic got a good view of the windward side of the island where big waves crashed against wet black cliffs. Trickling white rivulets ran down into tide pools. Weeds and flowers grew from crevices, and seabirds swooped to snatch insects from the air.

As the carpet increased speed, the breeze remained steady and refreshing. *Kind of like riding in a convertible on a warm day,* Vic thought. The carpet's gold tassels fluttered. Vic felt more exhilarated than frightened.

Sharif bent low as they raced over the ocean, far faster than most ships could sail, and the djinni globe swung forward in its mesh pouch. Glowing blue with earnest concentration, Piri pressed herself against the curved side of her eggsphere and stared down at the water where seabirds skimmed the waves in search of fish.

Soon, the island dropped far behind them, dwindling to a tiny smudge on the horizon. Then even that was gone.

"Sharif!" Vic raised his voice to be heard above the constant breeze. "Do we have a map or a compass? How will we find our way back?"

"The embroidery in the flying carpet carries all the maps and charts we could need. It is very sophisticated. I have already traced in our destination for the Ophir reefs. I could easily fly back to Elantya with my eyes closed."

"Well don't close them yet, or we might miss any survivors."

Sharif chuckled. The heavy globe pendant around his neck shimmered white, and the tiny djinni moved her hands, signaling. "Ah, Piri reminds me that she could also lead us back, if need be. She has a good sense of direction."

The open seas stretched out blue-green as far as he could see, and Vic began to realize how isolated the island of Elantya was. Was it the only speck of land on this whole planet? Yet it was at the center of all the crystal-door gateways.

After about an hour of fast flight, Vic found himself shifting restlessly on the cushion of fabric and air. Ahead he spotted a white foamy patch where waves churned around black rocky reefs that were mostly submerged.

They descended, circling low over the rocks. As they had expected and feared, Vic and Sharif saw broken driftwood and a long floating mast with a tangled blue sail. From his high vantage point, Vic could see tiny chunks of wreckage drifting in all directions, as if the ship had exploded and sprayed debris out into the ocean currents.

"The reefs stir up the water," Sharif said. "Any survivors may have been driven far out on the open sea."

"Good thing your carpet can cover a lot of distance," Vic said. "Spiral outward, and maybe we'll see something. With both of us watching —"

"And Piri," Sharif said.

"— how can we miss anything?"

As they cruised over the reefs, Vic could hear the churning sounds. Anyone trying to swim in that maelstrom would have been caught and smashed. Farther from the dangerous rocks, Vic and Sharif discovered another part of a mast drifting slowly by. Large, predatory shapes swam about beneath the water. Giant sharks, perhaps? Or prehistoric sea monsters?

They probably would have devoured any helpless person floating in those waters. How could there be any survivors?

But Vic didn't say that out loud. He was an optimist, after all.

Sharif circled farther from the Ophir reefs. By the end of two hours, they saw no more debris, but they continued to spiral outward, making sure. When they were on the verge of giving up, the boy from Irrakesh saw something on the water's surface.

"It's another piece of debris." Vic shaded his eyes and squinted into the bright sunlight. "No, wait! There's a *person* on it!"

Sharif urged his flying carpet to greater speed, skimming just above the choppy waves. Piri's sphere glowed an urgent orange.

As they came closer, the two young men made out a floating yardarm from the ruined ship. Sodden ropes dangled in the water, and a single dark-skinned woman clung to the wood with one arm while struggling and thrashing against an underwater enemy.

"Looks like she's fighting something," Vic said.

"She is fighting for her life. Hang on."

Spray splashed into the air, and the flying carpet closed the distance.

The female survivor gripped a long polished wooden staff. One end was pointed like a spear, while the other end was crowned with a polished stone as large as a billiard ball, adjacent to a curved hook. The girl jabbed her spear into the water, lifted it out dripping a mixture of sea water and red fluid. Blood? A gray torpedolike snout rose out of the water and opened a huge maw of sharp teeth. The girl twirled the staff and brought it down with a hard smack.

"We've got to save her. Those look like sharks!" Vic said. "We, uh, didn't happen to bring any weapons, did we?"

Sharif cast him a haughty glance. "We have speed. That will have to do for now."

The bedraggled survivor did not panic as she fought. Vic didn't think she had seen her rescuers coming yet. Sharif glided to a spot above the girl whose arm still hugged the floating yardarm. Their appearance scattered the prowling sharks. The waterlogged survivor looked up at them, her large eyes drooping with utter weariness. Vic could see sharp fins cutting the water as the startled sharks immediately began circling back in.

Sharif brought the magic carpet low, and Vic leaned over the edge, reaching out to take the girl's outstretched hand. "I hope this thing doesn't tip over. Come on!"

With lithe grace, the survivor pulled herself out of the water as the sharks approached. She kicked off against the slippery floating yardarm for leverage, pushed with the wooden staff in her other hand, and sprawled across Sharif's embroidered carpet.

Three angry sharks raced in with open jaws, but Sharif had already touched the golden threads, and the carpet ascended out of reach of the snapping teeth.

As if it were a perfectly normal occurrence to be picked up by a piece of flying cloth, the bedraggled dark-skinned girl pulled her lean legs onto the carpet, arranged herself at the center so as not to overbalance them, and laid the wooden staff across her lap. Panting and dripping and weary beyond words, she looked at her two rescuers. "Thank you," the girl said in a hoarse, parched voice.

"We, uh, thought you might like a lift," Vic said.

"I will repay your kindness. And your names will be added to the Great Epic."

12

THE SOLE SURVIVOR'S NAME was Tiaret. A rangy girl from a place called "Afirik," she was no more than a year older than Gwen and Vic. Her eyes were an amazing amber color, like those of a lioness, and she wore short animal pelts that hugged her muscular body like a second skin. When Vic and Sharif returned with her, Gwen thought the two young men looked insufferably pleased with themselves, though she had to admit to a bit of admiration for the rescue.

Everyone gathered in Elantya's main water-clock square to hear the weary girl's story. Tiaret clutched her battered-looking staff, as if ready to keep fighting. Her eyes swept around the square; she seemed as intrigued by the crowd and the city as they were with the exotic newcomer.

Already alerted to the emergency, the five members of the Pentumvirate hurried from their council chambers. Gwen watched the colorfully robed representatives march together down the sloping streets, escorted by functionaries and advisors.

"Pentumvirate members are called virs," Lyssandra whispered quickly as they took seats on curved stone benches near the trickling water clock. "Each wears a bright color — yellow, blue, red, green, or white — that corresponds to one of the five elements."

"*Five* elements? There are over a hundred on the periodic table. My chemistry teacher made us memorize them."

"No, only five: earth, air, fire, water, and spirit," Lyssandra said.

"Then what about nitrogen, helium, iron, sodium — all those?"

The elfin girl's expression turned thoughtful. "In studying a thing too closely, one may see more details but gain little understanding."

Obviously the translator did not consider that society on Earth might be more sophisticated and advanced than in Elantya. "In other words, concentrate on the big picture?" Gwen smiled at this cultural simplification and admitted, "Chemistry sure would have been easier with only five elements. . . ."

After the Pentumvirate members had taken their places on the stone benches, Elantyan workers erected poles across which they stretched dyed fabrics to form an awning that shaded the virs from the sun. The crowd that had gathered was anxious to hear Tiaret's story, and the survivor seemed eager to tell it, but the Pentumvirate would not be hurried.

Tiaret gratefully accepted the fresh water and soft blanket brought to her, but when the virs offered her a spot in the shade, she chose to sit in the open. She folded her long legs and held her staff in both hands, propped like a scepter between upthrust knees. Its round, polished stone head glinted like a bloodshot dragon's eye in the bright light. "I have been cold and wet for far too long. I prefer to be out here on the smooth stones, soaking up the warm sun. I feel my bones may never be dry again."

Tiaret had long hair twisted into ropy strands, bound and decorated with beads and tiny pendants of copper and polished stone. Prominent cheekbones above a delicate chin gave her face the appearance of being heart-shaped. Her lips were generous, her nose strong, her teeth white and straight.

"I must tell you, and I must tell you all of it," the girl began. "Among my people, storytelling is an important skill not to be rushed. Every person plays a part in the Great Epic and, whether we see it or not, the Epic is a part of us, as well." Her voice was rich and resonant, made to carry beneath open skies, across whispering grasses. "Kundu was one of our greatest warriors and talespinners. In spite of my youth, I fought by his side in the Grassland Wars, and he taught me everything he knew. He is gone now. His storyline in the Great Epic has ended." Her breath hitched. "And so this duty falls to me."

Tiaret turned her gaze to the five council members under their awning, then to her rescuers Sharif and Vic. When Gwen's cousin grinned, obviously proud of what he and Sharif had accomplished, Gwen resisted the strong urge to elbow him in the ribs.

"My Master Kundu was coming to Elantya to teach self-defense techniques, veldt magic, and storytelling. I was his best student. In my village out on the savannahs, he had already instructed everyone in his skills. Since the Grassland Wars were over, he felt that Elantya — and all the worlds through the crystal doors — needed his knowledge. He brought me along to become a student at the Citadel." She maintained her composure with a visible effort.

Gwen hoped Vic wouldn't get distracted and start whispering to Sharif before Tiaret had finished. Gwen wanted to hear every word of the story.

"One bright, warm dawn, Master Kundu and I caught a pair of horned zemus — stallions who wanted to see the world beyond the wanderings of the herd. After Kundu convinced the zemus of our need, the stallions allowed us to climb onto their striped backs. We rode for three days across the hot grasslands to the coast, where caravans brought regular shipments of star aja from mines in the mountains. Trading ships came to the coast. Master Kundu was sure one of the ships would give us passage through the crystal door to Elantya.

"When we reached the seaport village, the horned zemus began to snort, unsettled at being too close to so many humans. So we dismounted and turned them loose, then walked barefoot the rest of the way to the town. Master Kundu was old, but very strong. He could walk for days if he needed to.

"In the village we met Captain Argo, who agreed to take us aboard, provided that we helped him load his ship with aja crystals. So we labored for two days, carrying cartloads of rock." She grinned. "Kundu and I shamed the captain's own workers out of their laziness, and the vessel was loaded in half the normal time. We set sail, carried away from the coast by a freshening breeze as the tide went out. We left our beloved Afirik behind and sailed into waters that were unknown to me.

"I had never seen the ocean before — so much water! Once we lost sight of the shore, I felt as if I were drowning in the vastness. Master Kundu had sailed twice before to Elantya, and he reassured me. Captain Argo showed me his astrolabes and star charts, explaining how he could navigate without landmarks. I was unfamiliar with this skill. Even out in the broadest brown savannahs, there are trees and distant hills for landmarks, but the ocean was green-blue and smooth, extending forever and ever. I found it very humbling."

Tiaret gave a wan smile and looked at her listeners, then took another drink of water before she continued.

"Captain Argo was the Key, master of his own ship. He was born in Afirik and could open the crystal door directly to Elantya once he arrived at the proper coordinates. Our ship sailed through the night and half of the next morning before we reached an otherwise unremarkable spot in the middle of the ocean. Master Kundu and I came forward to watch the opening of the crystal door.

"Argo stood at the bow of the ship, looked out at the waves, and read the words of the spell tattooed with aja ink on the skin of his forearm. When he finished his chant, the air and water in front of us changed. It was as if the sky itself had been painted on glass, and Argo's spell shattered the pane. In front of us the water and air broke, cracked open, and on the other side of an invisible door lay a different sea, different waves, different clouds.

"His crew worked the sails, and the ship cruised forward. They had made the passage so many times they just went about their jobs, but I was fascinated. The vessel passed through the open door, gliding into the waters of this world. Behind us, the gateway closed again, a thin mosaic reassembling itself in the air, restoring the wall between universes. And we sailed on toward Elantya."

Tiaret closed her amber-gold eyes for a moment, as if hesitant to move to the next part of the story. She shifted her grip on the polished teaching staff. Gwen leaned forward to hear better.

"Our ship rode low in the water, its hold heavy with the rare star aja Elantya had ordered. We expected no problems." She drew a heavy breath. "No problems . . .

"On the second day out, the lookout spotted two sea serpents with gold and blue scales, and serrated fins like the edge of a broken sword. They rose out of the water on our starboard side, spitting sea foam from their fanged mouths. They approached our ship, and I could see their large slitted eyes. Master Kundu stood on the deck holding his teaching staff." She lifted the polished weapon in her hand; Gwen realized that it must have belonged to the girl's teacher.

"The giant serpents circled us. Their sharp fangs were as long and curved as the tusks of an elephoar. Most frightening to Captain Argo, though, were the unmistakable designs *branded* on the sides of their sinuous necks — geometric symbols, like tribal markings etched into the serpent scales and painted with enamel. The creatures wore spiked metal collars, golden harnesses, and silver linked chains." Tiaret paused to let the implication sink in. "Someone domesticated these sea serpents, kept them in thrall."

"Merlons," whispered one of the Pentumvirate members.

"The sea serpents swam beside the hull, then departed, slipping under the waves and swimming away. Once, in my childhood, I had seen enormous pythanas hanging from trees in the rain forest, but these were beyond my ken.

"The crew was uneasy, and Captain Argo put everyone on watch. Master Kundu and I trained on the deck, practicing our fighting skills together, but he kept his eyes on the water. We saw lines of black storm clouds gathering on the horizon. From afar, I observed a silvery waterspout, a fearsome weapon of weather. The clouds and the waterspout seemed to stalk our ship. Captain Argo told me the merlons have powerful sages who can affect the weather.

"On the third night since departing from Afirik, our ship drifted into treacherous waters. We were still far from Elantya, and we could see whitecaps curling over the submerged coral. The captain's charts showed a safe path through the Ophir reefs, but it would be a challenging course, and Argo did not want to negotiate the maze until daylight. At the edge of the reefs, two crewmen threw our anchor overboard. The chain dropped barely ten feet before it snagged on the rugged coral, and our ship was uneasily tethered in place.

"All the crew was on edge. The air smelled of lightning, but we saw no rain. The stars were out like a million silvery eyes watching us from the thickets of night. I spread my blanket on deck and tried to rest. The captain had offered us a small cabin, but Master Kundu and I preferred sleeping in the open. Closed spaces make me uncomfortable. The breezes from the ocean had been peaceful on our journey. But not this night.

"As the high moon spread its cold light across the deck and rigging, I felt a sudden lurch, and the ship began to drift. The anchor chain slapped against the hull with an empty clank. The crew shouted an alarm. Our anchor had been severed from below!

"I heard a splashing sound close to the hull. All around us, breakers foamed on the reefs. As I looked over the deck rail I could see moving figures, manlike but flashing and slippery. When they broke the surface, their bodies glittered with water and slime in the moonlight. Their skin was covered with scales, their faces wide and sleek, as if someone had crossed a dragon with a human. Master Kundu told me what they were." Tiaret looked at the Pentumvirate. "Merlons, of course."

The city leaders nodded.

"Cut loose from the anchor, the ship drifted in the currents, drawn toward the reefs. Captain Argo shouted orders. Men scurried up the masts to unfurl the sails. We were adrift and out of control. But the men could not climb fast enough, and the winds died of their own accord as soon as the first cloths were stretched tight.

"We ran aground on the grinding rocks. Loaded with its heavy cargo, our ship scraped against the rough black rock until its belly split. I heard wood splintering below, and the vessel lurched to a halt, throwing three men overboard. Others were flung to the deck. The ship tilted. Water rushed in, and crystal ore spilled out.

"The captain understood who our attackers were. He went to the tank in his cabin and withdrew both of his pet aquits. He dictated a message and turned them loose overboard. We all knew the aquits would never reach Elantya in time to bring us help, but we hoped at least they would inform you of what had happened, if we all died that night."

"One of the aquits did arrive," said the white-robed vir from her bench. "That was how we knew to look for you."

Tiaret was engrossed in her memories of that terrible night. "With our ship stranded on the reefs, the merlons moved in. They knew we could not escape. I saw the creatures outlined in the pale glow as they converged like hunting leopards around a weakened ibex. They swarmed out of the water, climbing up the severed anchor chain. Others clung to the hull planks, digging in their claws.

"I have seen harvester termites move across the savannah. They march together, overwhelming grasses, bushes, even trees with their sheer numbers. Nothing can stand in their way. And these merlons were even more dangerous, for they had weapons and a willful hatred toward us.

"A sudden storm whipped up, and cold rain pelted us, making the tilted deck slick. Our mast tipped as the hull continued to grind and splinter against the reef. The captain, his eyes glazed with despair, took out his sword and called us all forward." Tiaret's mouth was set in a grim line. "Master Kundu stood beside him with this teaching staff. I took a weapon of my own. Together we fought the hordes of merlons.

"They stink like rotting fish, and their inky, bottomless-pit eyes have a glazed look, like the eyes of a drowned man. They have flapping gills along their necks, but merlons can live in the air much longer than fish can.

"The attackers fought using their long claws and spears tipped with sharpened shells. Their scimitars had scalloped edges and flow holes cut through the blades. Three merlon warriors wielded spiked clubs topped with poisonous sea urchins." Tiaret stared at the water clock as clear streams continued to pour from one cylinder to another, filling basin after basin, raising the markers to keep track of the hours. The tinkling flow seemed soothing and hypnotic, but the storyteller did not relax.

"Even in our most extreme battles, I have never seen Master Kundu fight like such a whirlwind. I vanquished at least twelve merlons, and Kundu killed many more." She turned the staff's sharp point upward, showing dark stains, and ran her fingers along the curved hook at the handle. "The spear end, the hook, and the dragon's-eye stone were equally effective against them." Even from her sitting position, Tiaret twirled the heavy weapon a few times over her head, producing a distinctive whistling sound.

"Argo's ship had twelve crewmen, the captain, Kundu, and myself. Many sailors fought with their bare hands and fists, throwing themselves upon their scaly enemies." Her mouth turned down at the corners. "Two cowards jumped overboard, though I do not know how they intended to escape.

The sea was full of merlons and other sea creatures, and soon the water ran red. The cowards screamed and thrashed, begging for help, but we could barely help ourselves.

"I fought in a daze. After a time, my attention became focused only on survival, on swinging a weapon, cracking skulls, and stabbing scaly chests.

"Then the two sea serpents we had seen before joined the battle, but now they wore heavy armor. Their heads sported metal studs, solid lumps that turned them into living battering rams. They swam in from the open water, picking up speed, and crashed into the side of our ship. A single impact was enough to split the already damaged hull. One of the masts toppled, bringing down two sailors who had climbed to safety.

"The storm around us grew stronger. Waves hammered against the hull, and the sea serpents came back for a second attack. The ship was now cracked and began falling apart.

"I looked up, covered in green merlon blood. My own weapon was slippery with fishy slime, and when the enemy came at me again, I struck, but lost my grip. I found myself unarmed, with merlons closing in. Master Kundu saw it, too. He called my name, and —" She fell silent, wrestling with her terrible memory. "And he threw me his teaching staff. I did not ask for it, but he threw it to me and then flung himself at the merlons nearest him, punching and kicking. I caught the teaching staff and swung it, smashing the merlons close to me. I fought as hard as I could, trying to reach Master Kundu, so I could defend him. But I did not get there in time. Four merlons dragged him overboard into the water. I could not save him."

Tiaret closed her eyes as tears welled up. But she would not leave her story unfinished. "I realized then that only Captain Argo and I were left alive. I was on the other end of the deck, and I ran to help him, so we could stand back to back for our last battle. But seven merlons surrounded him. Though the captain slashed with his notched sword, the merlons overwhelmed him. I could not even see him go down in the flurry of scaly bodies.

"The sea serpents rammed again, and a broken yardarm fell past me, knocking one of the merlons aside. Desperately, I grabbed onto the yardarm and, as a heavy swell swept me overboard, somehow I kept my grip on the teaching staff. I plunged into the frothing water. Fortunately the yardarm was large, with good buoyancy." She gave a wry smile. "Out on the savannahs of Afirik, one has little need to learn how to swim."

"Nor on flying cities," Sharif admitted in a whisper to Vic. "I never learned to swim, either, until I came to Elantya."

"Perhaps that is one of the things we can teach you here, Tiaret," said another Pentumvirate member, a bit too cheerily.

The girl was nearly finished with her story. "The storm carried me away. I drifted for a long time, and soon the sharp reefs were out of sight. I do not think the merlons knew I was alive. Obviously they expected no survivors.

"I clung to the floating yardarm for more than a day, trying to imagine how I might reach safety, how I could survive. I am accustomed to solving my own problems, but I had nothing to work with, no way to guide my course. I did not know how to navigate, so I could not guess where Elantya might be. I had no water and nothing to eat other than a few small fish that I caught with my hands.

"On the second day the sharks found me. I climbed onto the yardarm as best I could and used the teaching staff to defend myself. The sharks circled and came closer.

"I have fought lions before. They are honorable predators with minds and grace, and it is a great challenge to defeat one. But a shark is simply a machine with jaws. It swims, and it attacks. I discovered that the snout is their sensitive area, and many of the sharks that came close soon retreated with sore noses. I thrust with the spear and stabbed one in its dark, soulless eye. I managed to draw blood, and the other sharks fell upon their comrade, treating him as food easier to obtain than myself.

"I saw symbols branded on their gray bodies — symbols similar to those I had observed on the sea serpents. Merlon symbols. I knew my hours were numbered. Once the sharks reported my position, the merlons would come. I vowed to defend myself and survive as long as possible. Wet and aching, miserable and hungry, I recalled the color of the warm veldt, the smell of sunlight on dry grass, the sound of the blades rustling together in a lullaby, and wished I had never left Afirik."

She looked pensive, then glanced at Sharif and Vic. "These two, Sharifas and Viccus, found me just as the sharks returned. No doubt the merlons were on their way. I owe my rescuers a debt that I do not take lightly." Tiaret hauled herself to her feet and leaned on the battered teaching staff. When she squared her shoulders, her expression was bold and determined. "And now that I am here, if you give me food, fresh clothes, and a chance to rest, I am prepared to begin my studies."

Her tawny gaze swept the audience. "If the merlons are indeed gearing up to attack this island, then every citizen of Elantya must learn how to fight."

13

THE GIRL FROM AFIRIK insisted on walking unassisted from the square. Elantyan sages hurried her off to the Hall of Healers, where they could patch her wounds and watch over her while she recovered. Although Tiaret was obviously weary, her amber eyes flashed with a clear resolve to recuperate as quickly as possible in order to be ready for another fight.

While the five virs held intensive meetings to discuss the news and make vital defensive plans, citizens spread the news of the merlon attack. "By the end of the day," Gwen said, "everybody on this island will know Tiaret's story."

"Yup, and they'll probably embellish it to make it even more fantastic." Vic grinned, still proud of himself. "Maybe they'll even exaggerate my heroic acts."

"Our heroic acts," Sharif said with a sniff. "Tiaret's story is so fantastic, I doubt they will need to embellish much."

Lyssandra stretched her thin arms. "It has been a long day, especially for you two, Gwenya and Viccus. Follow me to the student quarters at the Citadel. There should be rooms available for you two."

"Just temporary quarters, remember," Gwen said. "We're planning to go home as soon as we can."

"Rest now, plan later. It'll be like going away to college and living in a dorm." Vic wished his cousin weren't always so pessimistic, even though they'd both been through some substantial tragedies for anyone their age. Of course, it was different for Vic. He still had his father and could always hope his mother might return someday, while Gwen knew both of her parents were dead. The mystery and all the unanswered questions were the hardest parts to handle. Uprooting her whole life and moving in with her uncle and cousin must have been traumatic enough — but it was nothing compared to being yanked through a magical door to Fantasy Island!

Sharif unrolled his embroidered flying carpet. "I shall fly ahead and make arrangements. Since I know Vir Questas personally, I can secure exceptional quarters for our new friends." He flew off before anyone could argue. Vic wished he could have gone on the flying carpet, too.

"Won't the Pentumvirate members be too busy right now to bother with finding housing for us?" Gwen said.

"There are always plenty of rooms," Lyssandra assured them.

The Citadel buildings crowned one of the island's rolling hills. The structures included a large forum, open classrooms, and experimental laboratories, as well as living quarters, a common area, and a dining hall. Vic thought it looked like a prep school and university rolled into one.

Sharif circled over their heads, then landed in a courtyard in front of them. With well-practiced ease he jumped off of his rug and rolled it up, careful to align the edges. "They are preparing areas for you now. The evening meal is just being served. If we dine now, your quarters should be ready by the end of the meal."

Lyssandra raised her hand in farewell. "I will leave you with Sharifas."

"Where are you going?" Vic said, crestfallen. He had hoped to sit next to the copper-haired girl while they ate.

"I have a family and a home here in Elantya. My parents and my little brother, Xandas, expect me to join them."

Sharif said, "You two will eat with me and the other novs, apprentices, journeysages, and neosages. You will not lack for company."

In the crowded dining hall, long tables alternated with open spaces, and tall stone columns supported a roof made of sectioned colored crystal. Slatted panels could be opened to let air circulate, or closed to keep out rain. Sharif sat near the head of a table, taking the place as if it were his right, and indicated two open seats for Vic and Gwen.

Vic's stomach was growling. Though everything was strange, he reveled in it, and he looked forward to tasting Elantyan food. His dad had made a habit of regularly exposing them to dishes from different cultures. They often ate Moroccan, Brazilian, Greek, Mexican, Russian, Japanese, and Ethiopian cuisine.

When servers brought out platters of food, Vic wasn't surprised to see a lot of seafood, but these recipes were far different from anything on a menu at Red Lobster. Bowls of spiced mussels, clams, and larger shellfish were passed around. Fried tentacled things looked ready to fight back against anyone who tried to eat them. Several kinds of whole fish had been wrapped in grape leaves and roasted. The salads were made of pickled seaweed and edible cliff flowers.

Gamely, he scooped some clams onto his plate and then added a few of the floppy but intriguing tentacles. He saw that Gwen was eating parts of the meal with her eyes closed, but Vic happily tried everything. Though some of the textures were unusual (he particularly didn't like the rubbery suckers on the tentacles), the flavors were wonderful, with plenty of olive oil and garlic.

"Elantyan meals are quite different from those on Irrakesh," Sharif said. "I long for the food of home." He introduced Vic and Gwen to the nearest novs and apprentices, who came from a variety of cultures on different worlds connected by crystal doors.

Vic nudged his cousin with his elbow. "This isn't so bad, is it?"

"In other words, not quite what I expected? It certainly is different," she admitted. "I'd feel better, though, if Uncle Cap knew we were okay."

"Me too. But come on, Doc, look at all this brainpower around you — and these are just the students! Once you add Rubicas and all the other sages, somebody's got to find a way to open that crystal door again, or at least throw a message in a bottle through it so we can tell my dad where we are."

Gwen nodded reluctantly. "Maybe Sage Rubicas can talk to the Pentumvirate tomorrow and ask if they could help us."

"Good idea. See? There's no reason why we shouldn't get a good night's rest. Sleep now, tackle the problem fresh in the morning."

WHILE THE HIGHER-LEVEL students had private rooms either in the dormitories or near their mentor sages, each of the Citadel's nov dormitories featured a large communal area surrounded by dozens of narrow chambers along the outer walls. The chambers had no solid ceilings, other than the high roof of the main room that housed them.

"It's kinda like those cubicles they have in big office buildings," Vic observed.

The main rooms were lit by bright crystals. Vic remembered what Lyssandra had said about there being little wood, so of course they wouldn't burn fires or torches.

Gwen blinked, swept her eyes around the dormitory, then looked back at him. "Where are the doors to the rooms? For that matter, where are the bathrooms? Aren't there separate areas for girls? Something . . . nicer, maybe?"

"Do not worry, Gwenya. I made certain you received one of the nicer rooms." Sharif showed Gwen and Vic to the two cubicles on either side of his.

Each of the small chambers consisted of a thick pad and a

blanket on a carved stone riser, a main back wall and a pair of shared half-walls that were two meters high. The "ceilings" and entrances to the quarters were draped with opaque curtains to provide privacy and to darken the rooms for sleeping.

The island had hot and cold running water from underground springs, and backup supplies from rain-filled cisterns in the hills. Each of their rooms was equipped with a small trickling fountain that served as a sink set into the back wall and, opposite the stone bed riser, a flagstone lifted to reveal a discreet hole in the floor, through which they could hear the distant sound of flowing water.

Gwen's mouth opened, closed, opened again. "That's not what I think it is — is it?"

Sharif enjoyed her obvious surprise. "Yes. Did I guess correctly that you would not choose to share the group facilities *outside* the building?"

"Good call, Sharif. Right, Doc?" Vic couldn't wait to see how Gwen would cope with life in such a rustic environment. He didn't mind at all.

"Perhaps you will be comforted to know that only novice quarters are so . . . basic," Sharif said.

Gwen looked in chagrin from her new bed to the side walls, to the pit toilet, and back to Vic. But he grinned at her. "You know what Mom always used to say. 'Life is what we make it . . .' "

" '. . . and life makes us what we are,' " Gwen finished with a sigh. "Thank you, Sharif."

"Yup, thanks," Vic said. "I sure wish I'd brought my toothbrush, though." The young man from Irrakesh showed them how to use the frayed end of an aromatic twig to scrub their teeth. The wood tasted of cinnamon and ginger, and Vic's mouth felt refreshed and clean when he was finished.

As he was settling down for the night, having drawn the curtains across the ceiling and door of his cubicle, Vic heard a commotion in the communal area. He climbed off his bed, pulled aside his door curtain, and was delighted to see a lost-looking Tiaret at the center of the dormitory. "Sheesh, I thought they took you to the Hall of Healers to spend a few days recuperating!"

The dark-skinned girl still wore her spotted pelts, but they were clean and dry now. Bandages covered wounds on her arms, legs, and cheek. Though she tried to be strong, she had obviously not recovered yet from the dehydration and exposure from her ordeal.

"I do not require further assistance from the healers," she said. "Master Kundu wanted me to study at the Citadel. I will not disappoint him. I intend to begin immediately."

"Wow — and I was impressed when you were just kicking shark butt. You're welcome to join us," Vic said. "There's plenty of empty rooms." Gwen and Sharif had poked their heads out of their cubicles now.

Tiaret started toward them, leaning on the heavy teaching staff. "There is little time to rest if the merlons intend to attack. Tomorrow I meet with the Pentumvirate in an emergency session." She took another step, then hesitated, swaying dizzily. "I must —"

"Whoa." Vic caught Tiaret before she could collapse. "Okay, I think you might be overdoing it just a bit."

"Don't push yourself, Tiaret," Gwen said. "Nobody will think less of you if you give yourself some time to recover."

Sharif gestured to a vacant chamber, and the two cousins helped Tiaret onto the empty bed. The injured girl grudgingly lay back. "This is most embarrassing."

"But not surprising. Think of everything you've been through," Vic said.

Sharif brought Tiaret a cup of water. "My people have a saying: Self-pride is the enemy of wisdom."

"Perhaps you are right. I should sleep. It would serve no good purpose if I were to collapse in the midst of battle."

Vic laid the teaching staff next to the bed's stone riser. "It's right here if you need it. I'm counting on you to keep us safe if any monsters attack in the night."

"I will protect you, Viccus."

When the crystals dimmed and all the students settled down to sleep, Vic heaved a long sigh and lay back, exhausted. They were in a strange, new environment, and so many unbelievable things had happened to them that he hoped Gwen would not lie awake and restless all night.

"I sure hope nobody snores," Vic muttered. Before he knew it, he fell asleep.

14

GWEN KNEW SHE NEEDED to rest and clear her mind so that she could begin solving their problems in a logical and organized fashion. Finding a way home, communicating with Uncle Cap . . . after that, maybe she could relax and enjoy all the remarkable sights of Elantya.

At dawn, when the novs got out of bed and went through their morning routines, she and Vic fumbled through the unfamiliar activities. Vic hovered close to the girl from Afirik, making sure she was recovered. Tiaret seemed much stronger, however, and Vic seemed disappointed that she didn't need his help. Tiaret was already talking about improving the island's defenses. Gwen felt sorry for any merlons the dark-skinned girl might encounter from now on.

With the rolled carpet tucked under his arm like a treasure map and the glowing sphere of Piri hanging at his chest,

Sharif joined them. He smiled at Tiaret. "I trust you need no further rescuing this morning?"

"I am quite safe at present," she said.

Vic volunteered to go with Tiaret to meet with the Pentumvirate, but Gwen reminded him that they were supposed to go see Sage Rubicas again. "We've got our own mystery, Taz. Let's figure out how we got transported through that crystal door. Lyssandra is probably already at the tower waiting for us."

Vic frowned, as if the decision was difficult. Obviously, he wouldn't have minded spending time with either Tiaret or Lyssandra.

Sharif broke in, "I will escort Tiaret to the Pentumvirate."

"That is not necessary. I have a very good sense of direction." The lean girl grasped her teaching staff and headed off toward the government buildings. Sharif hurried after Tiaret anyway, pretending to show her the way.

While the students went to lessons in the Citadel buildings, Gwen and Vic made their way to the sage's laboratory watchtower, which stood on one of the highest points in the city. Lyssandra met them outside. Vic beamed when he saw her.

"Sage Rubicas and Orpheon are preparing to meet with the Pentumvirate," the telepathic girl said.

The twin cousins explained their hope that Rubicas would ask the Pentumvirate to assist them.

"Do you think they'll agree to help us?" Gwen asked.

"The Master Sage will certainly present your unusual case to the five virs." Lyssandra frowned. "But I must caution you that they may be more concerned about the merlon threat."

"Sure, who needs to worry about two misplaced teenagers?" Gwen said.

While the three teens talked, the bearded sage and his assistant bustled out. Overhearing their conversation, Rubicas waved a finger at Gwen. "Hmm, now do not worry. I will ask the virs to help you. Do not underestimate the significance of your arrival. Mysterious strangers should not be able to come from a world whose crystal door was sealed in the Great Closure. The magical and scientific issues are most intriguing."

"We will see what the Pentumvirate has to say," Orpheon added, pushing past them.

"Wait here for us. You can . . . hmm, find something to occupy yourselves."

"And do not cause further damage," Orpheon warned; then the two men hurried down the steep street.

Entering the main chamber, the three looked at the disordered laboratory room. The sage's chambers were still in need of repair from the smoke damage, flash explosions, and crystal meltdowns. "Wow, did we do all this?" Vic asked.

Gwen said, "We should help clean up the mess. It was our fault . . . sort of."

"What if Rubicas has this junk organized in a special way?" Vic asked. "The, uh, randomizer technique of organization."

"Just like your room, Dr. Distracto."

"Hey, I know where everything is."

Gwen picked up one of the blackened shards of crystal. A faint whiff of exotic smoke still hung in the air. "I want to help. I feel like we should be doing something."

Lyssandra sorted through the singed scrolls strewn on the

floor and across the table. "I am certain Sage Rubicas would not mind."

Together, Gwen, Vic, and Lyssandra reassembled and polished the magical equipment, cleaned the windows and shelves, and scrubbed scorch marks from the marble walls and floors.

"So . . . what kind of troubles have you had with the merlons before?" Gwen asked. It seemed like something they needed to know.

Lyssandra looked at her. "Month by month, their acts of aggression grow more bold. Our fishermen's nets have been slashed, anchor lines cut, and docks undermined. In the last year we have had to bring in large shipments of lumber to rebuild three docks."

"What have they got against you?" Vic asked. "This place is practically a utopia."

"Save for Elantya, the rest of this world is ocean. The merlons resent our presence and would gladly leave the crystal doors unguarded and available to any conquering tyrant who can find a Key. Although for many generations the merlons tolerated and ignored us, they have recently resorted to overt violence, such as the attack on Captain Argo's ship."

"So what ticked them off?" Vic asked. "Did somebody dump toxic waste into the sea?"

"We do not know. We have had very little contact with the merlons. But something must have changed to incite them to this bloodshed."

The three friends had most of the clutter cleaned up by the

time Rubicas and Orpheon returned from the Pentumvirate meeting, talking intensely about defensive options, new spell ideas, and potential weapons.

Gwen and Vic met them with hopeful eyes. Rubicas seemed startled, as if he had forgotten all about the two newcomers. "Ah, hmm, when I told them about your amazing arrival, the five virs were mystified to hear of a new crystal door to a world we had thought cut off from us by the Great Closure!"

Orpheon was stern. "But Elantya is much more concerned with the new merlon crisis, as I had anticipated."

Rubicas nodded somberly. "Tiaret was there to answer questions, and several fishermen came forward. Admiral Bradsinoreus of the patrol galleys produced records to show how many ships have gone missing in the past year. The pattern is obvious: The merlons are already waging war against us." The bearded sage spread his hands in an apologetic gesture. "This could threaten all of us, and so the virs' priority is clear. I am sorry they cannot help you, at least not now. Our Protective Vir Helassa was quite adamant."

Gwen hung her head. "Sure. We understand."

Drawing his eyebrows together, Orpheon added, "Helassa's exact words were, 'We have greater considerations than the demands of two uninvited children. They will have to wait until the crisis is resolved.' Some virs were skeptical of your story and even suggested that you might be spies for the undersea realm. In fact, Vir Pecunyas suggested it was very convenient and suspicious that you arrived just when another ship was attacked."

"Sheesh, you've got to be kidding!" Vic said with a snort.

"Vir Pecunyas was definitely in the minority." Rubicas looked embarrassed. "However, many do not like the idea of our poking around in new worlds and trying to open sealed crystal doors. Helassa herself asked if we had learned nothing from the Great Closure."

Gwen was about to ask what he meant, but as the sage glanced around the room, he suddenly noticed that all the clutter had been picked up. His face lit with delight. "Hmm, excellent! Orpheon and I need to get to work right away. The Pentumvirate ordered us to prepare extreme measures against the merlons." He picked up several scrolls and sniffed them, as if to see whether the flames had damaged the sparkling ink. "Oh, yes, and they said you are welcome to remain in Elantya under my protection for as long as you need."

"And as long as you dwell among us in peace," Orpheon added. "In the meantime, Sage Rubicas and I cannot waste time or resources helping you find your way back home."

Rubicas tried to sound reassuring. "Someday when we are once again at peace with the merlons, we will have the leisure to assist you."

Gwen's heart sank as she recognized that any chance of getting back to Uncle Cap and Earth would be a long time coming.

15

SO THEY WERE ON their own. It wasn't what he'd expected, but at least Vic knew this was going to be interesting. He loved to jump into problems and puzzles, using anything he could find to piece together a workable solution. But first he needed more information. He cleared his throat to get the old sage's attention. "So what's the story with this merlon misunderstanding, conflict, war . . . whatever you want to call it? Tell us more about the merlons."

Rubicas started climbing a set of copper rungs set into the wall frame between his tall aquariums. He carried a small bowl of dried insects to feed the fish. "It is a long story, spanning many centuries. It began —"

The scimitar of Orpheon's voice sliced the air. "All merlons hate land-dwellers, and wish that Elantya would sink back beneath the waves. That is all you need to know." He reorganized the spell scrolls.

Vic could barely keep himself from laughing. "I was, uh, hoping for a little more detail than that."

Orpheon looked in frustration at the sage. "If you plan to engage in lengthy storytelling, Master Rubicas, perhaps I should search the storehouses for lesser aja crystals? We need to replace the star aja that was damaged when these two came through the crystal door."

"Hmm, a fine idea, Orpheon."

Without further encouragement, the assistant strode out of the laboratory room in a huff. The sage lifted an access hatch on top and began dropping bug bits into the bubbling aquarium water, humming to himself. Inside, four frisky aquits swam to and fro, chasing fish and making the glow eels shine even brighter. Rubicas mumbled, distracted. "I keep telling Orpheon this is his responsibility, but he ignores it. Frankly, I think he dislikes my aquits because they always swim away from him."

Vic found himself strangely drawn toward the aquariums. He pressed his face close to the glass. "How can anyone not like miniature mer-people?"

Gwen prodded, "You were going to tell us about this long-standing conflict with the merlons?"

Rubicas continued tossing bits of food into the tank. The aquits swam to the top and caught a few morsels in the air. Like an amusing trick, they briefly shifted their shapes to resemble the bearded master sage, then switched back to their fish-tailed bodies.

"Long ago the merlons did not care about land-dwellers or this island, but they are a changeable people, malleable in form and mind." The bearded sage paused and stroked his beard before continuing. "For many centuries, the merlons lived in these oceans, blissfully unaware of our comings and goings through the crystal doors. They had no idea of their world's unique place in the universe, at the center of all the connected worlds. Nor did they care."

He closed the lid on the aquarium. "Who created the crystal doors and for what purpose was a mystery, even to those endowed with the ability to open them. Then, about five thousand years ago, evil sailed through one of those doors on a ship known as *The Water Shadow*. It carried a family of dark sages — father, mother, daughter, son. Their knowledge of magic was great and their purposes were sinister. Ulkar, the father, was the most powerful and evil dark sage who had ever lived, and he meant to possess all of the worlds in the network of crystal doors. Or, barring that, to destroy them all."

"Quite an ambitious guy," Vic said.

"Through corrupt divinations, Ulkar's wife, Laetia, had abducted a talented Key. Ulkar, Laetia, and their two power-hungry children needed the Key's abilities to flee their world, which they had tried unsuccessfully to conquer. Taking along several hundred of their most loyal, most deluded, warriors, they forced the hostage Key to open a crystal door to this world. Then the family of dark sages worked a secret Blood Magic: For if a Key is sacrificed while a crystal door remains open, all those who pass through before it closes again will achieve perfect mastery over their bodies. Every cell, every muscle, every organ."

"In other words . . . what?" Gwen asked.

"Hmm. What, indeed? It means they can prevent themselves from aging, alter their appearance, render themselves immune to illnesses, and make their bodies heal quickly from all wounds save one."

Vic wanted to ask what that particular wound was — maybe a stake through the heart? — but he figured the sage would get around to telling it his own way.

"Those sound like pretty useful skills," Gwen said.

"Mmm. In a relatively short time, Ulkar's family and their deathless army conquered the world of Morzul and used it as their base. Azric, the son, and Aennia, the daughter, became great warlords. They expanded their armies, preparing to swarm through the crystal doors and seize other worlds. The first warriors who had accompanied them became powerful and virtually indestructible because of the Blood Magic. They became the new generals, ready to march from Morzul. Hundreds of worlds awaited them.

"Shiploads of dark sages and their evil armies sailed through the crystal door, again with captive Keys — whom they sacrificed, thus making their new expanded armies nearly immortal. The dark invasion seemed unstoppable. After the Blood Magic, the enemy armies could not be killed!

"Seven worlds were crushed and enslaved before a bright sage managed to sound the alarm from world to world. That sage, Qelsyn, was a Master Key — able to open every crystal door. He traveled through one after another in his kingdom's fastest ship, spreading the word. He managed to gather the strongest bright sages from a hundred different worlds; their ships arrived through crystal doors and all met here for a great convocation of sages so they could decide how to protect the worlds against Ulkar's evil family."

Rubicas climbed back down from the aquarium as his sea creatures snapped up the morsels he had fed them. "With such a large gathering on the surface of their waters, the merlons could not help but notice. Many swam up to investigate what was happening, and Qelsyn invited them to take part in the gathering. He explained that their ocean world had become a gateway for tyrants and murderers, but the merlons were uninterested in the affairs of land-dwellers. Seeing no reason for further participation, they returned to their kingdoms beneath the oceans."

Gwen nibbled at her lower lip. "I've seen people refuse to get involved even when an emergency is plain in front of their faces."

Rubicas took a seat on a metal stool. "Fortunately for us, the ambitions of the dark sage family proved to be a poison among them. Laetia, fearing the ever-growing power and violence that Ulkar demonstrated, schemed to have her son, Azric, assassinate him and take his place. Laetia lured her husband, made him let down his guard; then Azric, who knew the only weakness of their kind, struck Ulkar down."

"Ick," Gwen said.

"He must have been awfully strong to kill a supposedly immortal wizard," Vic pointed out.

"There is a way," the sage said. "A difficult and secret way."

"So, one down. What happened to the rest?" Gwen asked.

Rubicas scratched his white hair. "After Laetia vested all of

Ulkar's power in her son, Azric turned on her. He had neither love nor respect for his mother. 'You have already betrayed my father, your own husband. How long before you consider *me* too powerful — before you turn against me, as well?' So Azric killed his mother, too."

"Did I already mention *ick*?" Gwen said with a shudder.

"The daughter, Aennia, was not quite as corrupt as the rest of her family. When she saw the horrors and the bloodshed and realized how their armies were slaughtering the populations on world after world just to make them bow to her brother's rule, she broke with her own family. Aennia fled through the crystal doors and joined the bright sages.

"She met with Qelsyn and his fellows here on the oceans. At first they suspected this was a trap, that Aennia was a spy. But she had truly changed sides, and in fact she and Qelsyn fell in love. Eventually they wed and had several children, whose descendants are still among us."

"How romantic," Vic said.

"But that is not the important part of the story," Lyssandra said.

Rubicas took a deep breath and continued. "Over the course of weeks, the assembled sages shaped their plan. Because there is but one hub for all crystal doors, Azric's forces would have to pass through it to reach other vulnerable worlds. To prevent the immortal armies from sweeping from one conquest to another, Qelsyn, Aennia, and their allies resolved to bottle them up. The gathered bright sages used their most potent magic scrolls to lock the doors to the conquered worlds that had already fallen to Azric's mad ambitions.

"Only then did Qelsyn and Aennia, the two most powerful sages there, undertake a terrible and dangerous magic. In order to trigger the Great Closure and ensure that those tainted places would remain sealed, they unleashed the brightest of bright magic, which their newfound love for each other made all the stronger — and more demanding. The spell nearly got out of their control. It almost drained the very life from Qelsyn, but Aennia sacrificed her immortality to save her beloved. Both she and Qelsyn lived, and the crystal doors to Azric's conquered worlds were cut off forever — along with those to dozens of other vulnerable worlds. This was unintentional, isolating much of the network, but at least those worlds would be safe."

"Let me guess," Vic said. "Earth was one of them?"

"Most likely." Rubicas smiled. "So, you see, no one should have been able to come or go from your world — which is why I find your arrival so interesting."

Lyssandra picked up the story, which she had obviously heard many times before. "Just sealing some of the crystal doors was not enough. The place where the bright sages had gathered was the centerpoint. They knew that they could never again leave it unguarded."

The sage bobbed his head. "So we established a permanent presence. At the time, this world was entirely ocean — and we needed an island."

"An island?" Vic cried. "You mean you *made* this island? Cool!"

"It took thousands of bright sages five years to create Elantya, with its fresh water and rich soil, its harbors and fisheries, its Citadel for learning, its seat of government, and its common language. They drew this entire island up from beneath the oceans, creating a foundation of dry land at the center of the circle of crystal doors. The sages brought plants, birds, insects, establishing Elantya as their anchor at the hub of the crystal doors."

"You mean like a checkpoint?" Gwen asked. "A protective base at the crossroads?"

"Yes. But it has become much more than that," Lyssandra said.

Rubicas leaned his stool against the aquarium wall. From behind the glass, colorful fish tried to nibble on his wispy strands of white hair. "Certainly, the merlons were alarmed when this island started growing from the sea bottom. Bright sages tried to meet with them, to offer compensation to the undersea dwellers, but the merlons did not wish to trade with us. We offered every treasure or service we could think of, without success. We hoped we could give something of value to their people."

"Though we fished and sailed on their seas, for the most part humans and merlons did not compete for the same resources," Lyssandra said. "There was no need for conflict. We did not exactly live in friendship, but we left each other alone."

Rubicas took up the story again. "Hmm. But a century ago, merlons began making frequent trips to the surface and posted scouts to watch Elantya. Recently, reports of sabotage have become more frequent. We have sent emissaries to speak to them, to invite their leaders to meet with us, but to no avail. Either our emissaries find no merlons, or never return."

Lyssandra said, "Viccus and Gwenya have already met Sage Polup. They know how the merlons enslaved the anemonites, using the captives to build defenses and create weapons — weapons to be used against us."

"And there is another problem." Rubicas stroked his beard with one finger, deep in thought.

"Of course there is," Vic muttered with irony.

"When Aennia fled to join the convocation of bright sages, Azric was enraged that his own sister would abandon him. While his many immortal generals were expanding their forces on the seven conquered worlds, Azric slipped through a crystal door in search of Aennia. He meant either to kill her or take her with him. Thus, through bad luck, he was caught on this side when the Great Closure occurred. He is here in the free worlds, a seed of evil in our universe — while all of his armies are locked away."

"Lousy timing," Vic said.

"Of course it could have been worse," Gwen pointed out.

Lyssandra looked at the two cousins. "So, Azric has hidden for centuries, moving quietly among the worlds, searching for a way to undo the Great Closure, so that he can unleash his immortal armies and continue his conquest."

"And now the merlons are getting feisty, causing trouble," Gwen said. "Do you think there's a connection?"

Vic snorted. "There's always a connection."

"Therefore," the sage continued, "you see why I can offer little help to you in your troubles right now."

Vic raised an eyebrow. "You've, uh, got bigger fish to fry?" Gwen groaned.

Petite Lyssandra gave him a direct challenge. "In Elantya we encourage learning and discovery. The Citadel has much knowledge to draw from. You are welcome to study the problem yourselves and find your own solution."

"Then that's what we'll do," Vic said. "As Dad always says, 'No one cares about solving your problems as much as you do.'"

Discouraged, Gwen sighed. With long strides, she moved past the wall of massive aquariums without so much as a glance at the strange fish. "We're in a totally illogical world with mirrormills and spells and flying carpets and locked invisible doors. Right. We should have everything worked out in no time."

Vic looked at his cousin. "Come on, Doc. It might take a while, but we can find a way to get home — or at least send my dad a message to let him know we're okay. You can bet he's trying to solve this from his end, too. Trust me, I've watched those old MacGyver reruns on TV. We'll come up with an answer."

"Sure, but why stop there?" Gwen said with a touch of sarcasm. "Why don't we defeat the merlons and find Azric while we're at it?"

Rubicas smiled. "Hmm, you two certainly are ambitious! We would welcome such a victory."

Gwen flushed. "I was just kidding."

"Let's give it our best shot." Vic nudged her with an elbow, trying to cheer her up. "Try optimism first. There's always time to be a pessimist later."

16

BEFORE ORPHEON COULD RETURN from his errands, Sharif landed on the tower above the laboratory and ran down the spiral steps into the main chamber. Though he looked out-of-breath and windblown, he took special care to line up the edges of his carpet as he rolled it, making sure none of the tassels were crushed. Vic thought he took care of his embroidered rug the way some people polished and pampered their new cars.

Sharif lifted his chin. "During the Pentumvirate meeting, Tiaret suggested it would be a good idea to perform a security check, so I flew over the whole island. For the time being, Elantya is safe."

Gwen stopped her restless pacing and looked up at the young man from Irrakesh, smiling at him with a flicker of interest. Vic raised his eyebrows. Did his cousin have a soft spot for Aladdin Jr? That might provide some good opportunities for teasing. Of course, then Gwen would tease him about Lyssandra. Or Tiaret. Maybe he'd better just keep his comments to himself. . . .

Vic wasn't sure how he felt about being stuck on Elantya. Was he surprised that the Pentumvirate had not immediately offered every resource at their disposal to help the two go home? Not particularly. Was he worried that he didn't know when he might see his father again? Maybe. A bit. Was he intimidated by the prospect of attending a new school and risking spectacular failure even in this seemingly enchanted realm? More than a little.

Was he excited by the idea of having more time to explore this intriguing world? Absolutely! Was he bemused and enchanted by the petite interpreter with coppery curls, who seemed so bright and empathetic? Or was he more mesmerized by the lean, exotic, and beautiful girl from Afirik, whom he had helped rescue from terrible danger? He swallowed.

"Is your mind troubled, Viccus?" Lyssandra's hand on his arm startled him out of his reverie.

Vic flushed, hoping that she had not chosen that moment to look into his thoughts and imagination. "Oh, I'm fine. I was just . . ."

"That's Dr. Distracto for you," Gwen said. "Daydreams at the drop of a hat."

Lyssandra gave a puzzled frown. "I did not drop my hat."

Gwen rolled her eyes and smiled. If Vic wanted optimism, she'd give it to him. "Focus for a minute, Taz. Let's think through this. We got here somehow. There has to be a way to get back. It's only logical."

"They use spells all the time to open crystal doors. Why can't we just cast one of those to open our door again?" Vic asked. "Do we say 'Open, Sesame' or what?"

Sharif and Lyssandra looked at each other, both puzzled. "Is that a powerful spell in your world?"

"No, it's from a story," Gwen said.

"And a Disney animated movie. One of the good ones. Robin Williams is really funny."

Rubicas looked out the window, as if impatient for Orpheon to return with the necessary materials. "Spells do not work so simply. They must be carefully crafted, written in meticulous calligraphy on a specially prepared scroll. The magic works, but only if one knows how to shape it."

"Like writing down the right recipe," Gwen said.

"I don't use recipes when I cook," Vic pointed out. "I go by instinct, and it usually turns out great."

Gwen made an odd expression. "With a few spectacular exceptions. I seem to remember a tomato, mint, and pineapple soup. . . ."

"Well, *I* liked it."

Rubicas picked up one of the singed scrolls and opened it to display the intricate embroidery of letters and words. "When special sounds and phrases are written in aja crystal ink, the magic is locked into the scroll. It is released by whoever speaks the words. Spells are most powerful when written in the ancient tongue, with star aja ink. Fortunately, most people cannot read the complicated language."

Sharif crossed his arms. "It is the same in Irrakesh. Anyone can use small household spells written in the everyday language."

Rubicas squinted at the parchment in his hand. "*This* spell, though, is a work of art. Only a highly trained sage can work it."

"What does it do?"

"Hmm. I have had it for so long, I am not exactly sure. . . ."

"Here's the question," Gwen said. "If magic really works in Elantya, then why don't you just write a scroll that says 'Make an invisible shield to keep out enemies,' and be done with it?"

Rubicas explained patiently, "Magic is a great power, but of itself it has no knowledge. The words must shape the magic, tell it what to do. A short, simple spell in the vernacular language can work only small magic. But it takes intricate instructions in Ylijan, the powerful ancient tongue of the first sages, to perform more difficult functions."

"Hey, I get it. Like a computer program," Vic said. "The more you want it to do, the more complicated the program has to be. Some computer languages are simple, like Basic, and others are a lot tougher to learn but they can do more with fewer commands."

Preoccupied, Rubicas looked down at the scroll in his hand and began to read. Vic had never heard a language like it, rich and deep and almost musical; he could feel the power in the words. When the sage finished reading, he lowered the scroll, closed his eyes, and whispered, "S'ibah."

"See-*Baa*?" Vic said. "What does that mean?"

"It means," Lyssandra answered in a quiet voice, "'As it has been spoken, thus let it be done.'"

"All that in two syllables?"

The copper-haired girl shrugged. "As the master sage told you, the Ylijan language is filled with power. Much can be said with fewer words."

Vic and Gwen looked at each other, then glanced around the laboratory room. "But, uh, what did it just do?" Vic asked.

"It fizzled," Gwen said.

"Hmm, I doubt that. It is a very good spell, and I always intended to try it. Go take a look outside."

Sharif was the first to the tower window, with Vic close behind. With a crackling rustle, fingers of plants were crawling up the whitewashed wall. Vines stretched out of the rocky soil at the base of the tower, winding around the stones with woody brown stems and green clusters of leaves.

Rubicas peered over their shoulders. "Grapevines, I believe. I hope they do not grow too high — no one will want to pick the clusters if they are too far off the ground, and I would hate to see birds eat them all."

From the window, they saw Orpheon hurrying up the steep flagstoned path in the afternoon sunlight. He wore a frown on his handsome face as he looked at the vines, then shook his head in disapproval. Vic wondered why the assistant always seemed like such a killjoy.

Entering the tower, Orpheon set a heavy sack on the worktable. "I see you are playing with children, Sage Rubicas, and entertaining them with frivolous spells. Have you finished working on Elantya's defenses against a merlon attack?" His voice held a reproving tone.

Suitably chided, Rubicas moved away from the window,

which was now fringed with leaves. "Of course, of course. We had better get to work on that right away." The old sage looked at Vic and Gwen. "Sadly, my notes and the scroll I was using when you arrived were burned beyond use, so if you wish to learn more about the kind of magic you need, I suggest you visit the Cogitary."

"Sure," Vic said. "Uh, exactly what *is* a Cogitary?"

"A repository of scrolls, of spells and knowledge gathered from the worlds connected by the crystal doors."

"In other words, a library," Gwen said.

"A Cogitary. A place to think and learn."

Lyssandra said, "I can show you where it is."

"I will fly to the Hall of Healers. The sages wanted to inspect Tiaret's wounds again and urge her to rest," Sharif said. "I feel an obligation to see to these things, since I rescued her."

"Yup, *we* did." Despite a twinge of jealousy, Vic got the distinct impression that Sharif was trying to avoid spending hours digging through dusty scrolls in a library. Vic couldn't blame him. He would rather be flying on a carpet himself, but he *did* want to make sure he could see his father again.

Gwen had already gone from being a stick-in-the-mud to leading the charge. She was the first to the door. "As long as we're doing research, the Cogitary's as good a place as any to get started. The sooner we gather all the information we need, the sooner we can go home."

17

THE IMPOSING COGITARY WAS one of the largest build-ings in the Citadel complex. Built of polished white stone that shone with flecks of gold, the repository of scrolls consisted of five concentric pentagons which, from outermost to inner-most, grew progressively smaller in diameter but taller.

Lyssandra seemed very proud of the structure. "Each of the chambers encloses exactly the same amount of space."

With a soundless whistle, Vic tilted his head back to look at the high ceiling. Five-sided skylights alternated with sun crystals so the Cogitary would be well-lit at any time of day or night. "The number five must mean something special to Elantyans."

Beside him, Gwen gave a soft snort. "Brilliant deduction, Holmes. Our medallions have five sides, too, and I still can't help thinking that our mothers must have had some connec-tion with this place."

"If my dad was trying to open a crystal door, then I bet he thought coming here would help him find Mom." Vic blew out a long sigh. "There's so much they never told us — but I plan to ask him as soon as we get back."

Lyssandra spread her hands. "How would you like to begin your research?"

Gwen glanced around the huge angular library, then turned her violet eyes upward, as she often did when she was thinking. "First, I suppose we should find the crystal doors section and do some research."

"Always begin with the obvious." Vic put on a mock serious expression, pursed his lips, and nodded. "And then . . . ?"

"And second, we find out more about those aja crystals Rubicas used. He said they were rare. Your dad had crystals in the solarium, too. I wonder what kind they were."

"And twelfth?"

"*Third,* we gather the supplies we need based on what we learn. And fourth," she plowed on before Vic could interrupt her list, "we build an array like the one your dad and Rubicas were both using, then test it. If everything goes well . . . fifth, we go home. What could be easier?"

"Ah, five simple steps — that magic number again. And all so . . . conveniently vague." Vic stroked his chin with a thumb and forefinger now in a caricature of one of his father's curator friends from the museum. "Tell me again how we start doing number one — the research, was it?" He knew she hated it when he goaded her like this, but he just couldn't help himself. "I doubt there's any kind of Elantyan search engine or online card catalog." He looked at Lyssandra for help.

A tinge of pink crept into Gwen's cheeks. "Well, we ask someone, of course. There's got to be a librarian —"

She turned, ready to start looking — only to bump into a stocky older gentleman with a round, kindly face. His intelligent eyes were set above a doughy lump of a nose. "Actually, we call ourselves Cogitarians. How may I help you?"

Gwen's cheeks turned pink again. "I didn't know anyone was behind me."

The man folded his pudgy fingers in front of him. "I could not help but notice that you have been here for several minutes and have not selected a scroll."

"We've never been here before," Vic said. "We were just trying to get our bearings."

"Cogitarian Zotas will be glad to help you," Lyssandra said. "He has often helped me in the past."

The man's eyes sparkled. "One of the greatest pleasures of my work here is to introduce newcomers to our Cogitary. I am here solely to assist others in their searches. Please allow me to show you around. Once you understand our system, you will be able to find anything you need. Is this a project for the Citadel? Or a personal interest?"

Gwen cleared her throat. "Personal, but very important."

Lyssandra added, "My friends seek information about opening crystal doors."

Vic whispered to his cousin, "I think *that* was step one."

Zotas spent the next hour sharing the wonders of the scroll repository with Vic and Gwen. Each of the five-sided sections of the Cogitary was called a pentorium. With the exception of the arched doorways, the walls were lined floor to ceiling with shelves and cubbyholes, all stuffed with pre-served scrolls.

The lower shelves, the ones most easily reached, held the thickest scrolls, documenting a wide variety of topics from history to health, philosophy, magic theory, and science. The higher shelves held more delicate spell scrolls, all of them written with powerful aja ink.

As Zotas led them through an archway into the next pento-rium, something small and dark flitted through the air and darted down to hover in front of the plump Cogitarian. Vic thought it must be a giant flying beetle, but its movements were too precise and delicate. More like a hummingbird.

Gwen gasped. "Is that a fairy? A real one?"

Vic looked at the hovering creature and saw that it did in-deed appear to be vaguely human-shaped, but quite different from the ethereal Piri inside Sharif's glowing crystal sphere.

Zotas held out his palm, and the little winged thing lit on his hand. Vic saw that the flitting creature looked exactly like the Protective Vir Helassa, whom they had seen while Tiaret told her story. The figure wore a vaguely Grecian-looking scarlet gown that began on her left shoulder and swept in flowing folds across her bodice; it was clasped with a glitter-ing broach at her right hip, revealing a good deal of midriff and navel before flowing into a skirt that hung low on her hips and reached to her ankles in a fluttering crenellated hem.

"Wow," Vic said. "The amazing shrinking woman?"

Without looking up, the Cogitarian said with a chuckle, "Not Helassa herself, merely a skrit with a message from her." He spoke to the creature on his palm. "Message, please."

The skrit's imitation of Helassa fixed him with an imperious gaze. "I require three spell scrolls without delay: one for boiling large quantities of oil, one for a flame catapult, and one for healing burns. Do not keep me waiting. Sage Polup is assisting me with weapons. This is a matter of utmost urgency." The skrit put its arms down at its sides. "Repeat?"

"No, thank you," Zotas replied. "You may revert now."

The little figure shimmered and became a female figure five inches high, clad only in wings and a pair of tiny, transparent slippers. "Reply?"

Zotas raised a hand and made a circular motion twice in the air. "No need. Helassa does not want conversation from me. She just wants her scrolls." Two more skrits appeared and landed on his palm beside the first.

Lyssandra explained to the cousins, "Skrits are able to lift more than their own weight, but three scrolls are too heavy. They will each take one."

Zotas tapped the first skrit on the head. "A boiling oil spell to Helassa."

"A boiling oil spell to Helassa," she repeated, and zipped away with hummingbird speed.

Looking concerned, Gwen asked, "Helassa said it was urgent — are we under attack?"

Zotas pinched the bridge of his nose. "With Helassa, all matters are urgent."

As the other two skrits went to fulfill their assignments, Zotas continued the tour. In each of the pentoria, the marble floors were inlaid with mosaics depicting various subjects of the scrolls stored in that area — scenes of history, science, agriculture, magic. Polished stone benches ran down the center of each gallery.

The central pentorium was Vic's favorite. Like the other levels, the perimeter was lined with shelves of scrolls, but the upper third of the innermost chamber was made entirely of glass, rising into the air like a perfect five-sided crystal letting in sunlight. Carved reading benches and small trees encircled multitiered trickling fountains. Tiny crystals of sun aja dangled in the trees to provide light to readers after dark. Plump cushions strewn on the floor offered younger visitors a comfortable place to sit. A dozen novs, apprentices, and sages worked silently at tables, poring over scrolls and taking notes.

Gwen looked at all the other people in the chamber. "Do you have to be a wizard to use the spells on the scrolls?"

"You need only the ability to read." The Cogitarian smiled.

"We learned how to read before kindergarten," Vic said. "Both of us."

Gwen punched him lightly in the arm. "When did you learn how to read *Elantyan*? Just because Lyssandra helped us speak the language doesn't mean you can make out those symbols. They look like hieroglyphics to me, with a little Japanese and Arabic thrown in."

"Oh. Good point," said Vic, crestfallen. "We'll never be able to figure it out." Then he turned hopefully to the copper-haired girl. "Can you teach us to read Elantyan, like you taught us to speak it?"

Lyssandra shook her head. "Alas, Viccus, some things truly must be learned."

"Great," Vic said with a groan. "Looks like it's back to school again."

"The courses at our Citadel are enlightening, gratifying, and often entertaining." Lyssandra intentionally touched Vic's arm, though she didn't have to. "I would enjoy taking a discovery or a praktik with you, Viccus." She blushed and glanced at Gwen. "With both of you."

"Uh, maybe if this spell experiment doesn't work," Vic said, embarrassed by the attention. "All right?"

Meanwhile, the Cogitarian brought them an imposing rolled scroll. "This is in the ancient language, bound to the scroll with aja ink. As you see, it is much more complex than simple Elantyan."

"Now *that* looks like hieroglyphics," Vic said.

"Each time a scroll is used, some of its magic is released, and the ink becomes fainter. The power of the spell determines the number of uses before the scroll goes completely blank. Once a scroll is used up, it is returned here to be inscribed with a new spell." Zotas scanned the shelves, as if reorganizing them in his mind. "Common everyday spells — such as those for skrit summoning and heating stoves — are mass-produced from etched xyridium plates on a printing press overseen by sages in the Citadel, and they are written in simple Elantyan. A few are printed with phonetic icons, so that even children can access them."

The Cogitarian gave each of them a small, lightweight scroll, little more than a scrap of curled paper. "These are the easiest spells we have. They are for summoning skrits, and you can tell them which scrolls you would like from the shelves around here." He showed them how to interpret the easy icons, and then retrieved other simple spells from a shelf. "And these are translators. When you invoke the symbols, you will comprehend the concepts in the scrolls you are studying. You cannot access the magic itself, but you will understand what you are reading. Translator spells are designed for research."

"That's exactly what we need," Gwen said.

Pressing his fingertips together, Zotas said, "Please let me know if you have any questions." With a small bow, he left them.

After the cousins found an open table and seats, Lyssandra took her leave of them. "Now that you can be self-sufficient, I must see to my other duties. I have been neglecting my apprenticeship in Translation and Diplomacy." With that, she left the Cogitary.

Anxious to get started, Gwen unrolled her children's version of the skrit-summoning scroll and spoke the three sounds printed there, as the Cogitarian had explained. Nothing happened. She looked disappointed and was about to call Zotas back. "I know I read it just the way he told us, and I'm sure I got the sounds right."

"Sheesh, Doc! You try for two seconds and you're giving up already? Did you remember to say the magic word?"

"Oh, right! *S'ibah.*" Before she could draw another breath, a skrit hovered before her. "Aren't you cute! I need to see spell scrolls that have to do with opening crystal doors. Could you please get them for me?"

"Make as many trips as you need to," Vic added to the flitting creature.

Time and again, skrits delivered histories, essays, and treatises relating to crystal doors. Invoking the comprehension spells, the cousins scanned document after document, searching for ideas.

The door-opening spells had several variations, and thanks to the help of the skrits in the Cogitary, they "read" enough crystal door spells to understand the patterns and components a Key needed to use. Even Vic didn't get bogged down in all the studying. They both used up every bit of the skrit-summoning magic in their scrolls, but it was worth the effort.

While the skrits flew back and forth putting away scrolls they had used, Vic restlessly perused the lower shelves in the central pentorium. Suddenly, his heart skipped a beat. There, hand-drawn on the edge of a stone shelf that held a heavy scroll, was the symbol. *The* symbol. The one from the medallions their mothers had given them. He waved Gwen over and showed it to her.

She grew excited, too. "Maybe it's an omen? Let's read the scroll."

Reading the heavy parchment with the help of a comprehension spell, they discovered what none of the skrits had been able to find all day: a single pre-Closure theory for opening a new crystal door. It used water, prisms, and crystals in a complicated model. The angles for the array were exact, the separation distances perfectly specified and measured, the prisms tilted to magnify and reflect the crystal energies. Vic thought it was worth a try. It was their only lead.

Many hours later, when Vic's stomach was growling for an evening meal and darkness had begun to fall over the island, they found Zotas again and questioned him about the symbol on the shelf. With great surprise, he said he had never noticed it before and could offer them no explanation. Vic had suspected as much.

"May we take these with us to our rooms at the Citadel?" Gwen asked, holding up several scrolls.

The Cogitarian smiled. "Our skrits always remember who has a scroll. I'll let them know about this last one you found. When you are finished with a parchment, ask anyone to summon a skrit, and it will return the scroll to its proper shelf."

"Great," Vic said. "Now all we need is five star aja crystals to start our experiment. And while we're at it, maybe we should wish for a few million bucks and world peace."

Zotas cocked his head to one side. "Do you need the star aja temporarily or permanently? How long will your research take?"

"It'll be temporary — if this works," Gwen said. "A few days at most."

"In that case," Zotas said, "I know where you might borrow some."

18

THE NEXT DAY, ARMED with a diagram, some scrolls, and notes about several variations on the door-opening spell scrolls, Gwen and Vic spent hours going from sage to sage, classroom to laboratory in the complex of buildings and rooms that formed the Citadel learning center. They collected a basin, prisms, measuring devices, and the crystals. Zotas had pointed them in the right direction — as, Gwen suspected, Cogitarians were supposed to do.

Questas, the blue-robed Vir of Learning, used star aja crystals to increase memory retention and to compose remarkable, self-playing musical pieces. "I am afraid my crystals are quite small, and not nearly as powerful as the ones Sage Rubicas lost," the kindly Questas said, showing them the fist-sized clusters with an apologetic smile. "Star aja crystals are as rare and valuable as the learning experience. When he spoke to the

Pentumvirate, Rubicas told us that he believes you two are valuable, as well. You came from another world through a crystal door we did not even know existed. I am pleased to assist you in your attempts to reopen that portal, by lending you these crystals. Perhaps someday we can have an interchange of students and ideas between our worlds." With that, the Vir gravely handed over his treasure.

"Tell me — do you have music in your world?" the sage asked before they could go.

"All kinds," Gwen said. "I've got quite a collection of CDs and electronic files — that's how we play music. Vic likes harder stuff than I do."

"It gets better if you play it loud," her cousin said.

Though they were anxious to leave, Questas asked them about the kinds of music they liked. Since he had been generous enough to loan them the crystals they needed, Gwen felt obligated to tell him everything she knew, from classical pieces to hymns to Top 40 hits to loud heavy-metal songs. The cousins even sang or hummed to demonstrate the different styles.

"If you do manage to go back to your world and then return to us," the blue-robed Vir said, "I would love to hear some of this music."

"You bet," Vic said. "I can bring all of my 'desert island' music."

"Desert island music?" Questas arched his eyebrows. "What do you mean?"

"If I were stranded on an island, that's the music I would take to keep me company."

"We *are* stranded on an island, Taz," Gwen pointed out.

"Unless we can find a spell that works." She indicated the equipment they had collected. They thanked Questas again, then went back to Rubicas's laboratory.

THE RESEARCH BUILDING WAS as chaotic as ever. Rubicas was completely preoccupied with scraps and drafts of spells while Orpheon assisted him. With a wary look, the apprentice watched the two enter with their scrolls and crystals.

"Where did you get those star aja crystals?" Orpheon demanded. "Give them to me before you damage them."

"Vir Questas loaned them to us. We need them for our project."

"Well, there is no room in the laboratory for you to set up a whole new array." The assistant indicated the clutter of scrolls and glistening jars filled with aja crystal ink. "We are busy here on important work for the Pentumvirate."

Vic, ever the optimist, looked toward the spiral staircase. "We'll do all the work ourselves. How about the tower platform? There's plenty of room up there."

"Very well," Rubicas said. "It is good to see you so ambitious."

"We have a few questions first, though." Gwen rattled off a list, asking about how Rubicas's original array had been set up, why he and Orpheon had decided to use star aja, which versions of the door-opening spell they had tried, and what their chances of success were.

The bearded sage began to answer, but after a few minutes Orpheon interrupted. "Master Rubicas, you cannot allow these children to distract you from your urgent work."

Rubicas gave Gwen and Vic an apologetic look. "Do what you can. Perhaps I will find time to check in on your work later."

Orpheon's mouth was set in a disapproving frown. "At least they will be out of our way."

Gwen and Vic borrowed the last of the items they needed, and climbed the stairs to the tower. On the platform, they found a spot to spread their notes and the old magic scrolls.

"See, plenty of room to work," Vic said.

"Let me check. These distances and angles have to be very precise. According to the scroll, the prisms and lenses need to be exactly aligned." Gwen used a measuring rod to make sure there was enough free floor space to arrange the crystals according to the old diagram.

Hunkered on the platform, Vic shuffled through the scrolls they had borrowed. "Sure seems simple enough."

"Simple? We're trying to open a doorway between worlds. Don't expect it to be easy."

The Master Sage had explained that before the Great Closure, sages and Keys had occasionally opened new crystal doors, but the knowledge of that magic had been all but lost. Yet somehow, the combination of experiments by Dr. Pierce and Rubicas had apparently managed to do it again. Vic stared at the scrolls, moving from one to another and fidgeting. "Even though Rubicas's notes are gone, I bet I can figure this out. I'm going to get something to write on." He scrambled down the stairs to Rubicas's workroom.

With her distractible cousin gone, Gwen found it easier to concentrate. She paced, envisioning where the pieces would go. She set out the primary aja crystals and wiped them off with her Ocean Kingdoms sweatshirt to be sure they were clean.

Vic returned with a jug of water, a swatch of parchment, a bottle of sparkling ink, and a polished stylus. "Sheesh, I wasn't expecting a laptop or a word processor, but it sure is hard to find a pencil and scrap paper in Elantya!"

Gwen looked at him in surprise. "That's the special aja ink for writing spells! Are you sure Sage Rubicas said that was all right?"

"He wasn't using it. Besides, we're trying to write a spell, aren't we?"

Gwen wasn't sure about her cousin's logic, but she didn't argue with him. "As long as you didn't interrupt him."

"He didn't even see me." Vic squatted again, used a translation spell, and started to scribble something as he referred to the scrolls.

Gwen placed the empty basin at the center of the platform, then laid down the measuring rod and used a small piece of seashell chalk to mark her lines. She calculated the angles three times, being overly meticulous, and set a dot on the platform at the end of each starburst path where the star aja crystals would rest.

After she had marked the lines, she placed the fist-sized clusters of aja crystals at their endpoints and arranged a web-work of mirrors and lenses and prisms, radiating from the central basin like the streamers in Fourth of July fireworks.

"There, the spell's done." Vic held up the parchment on which he had written several lines. "Since I can't read or write the ancient language, I just used English. It follows the general pattern of all the other door-opening spells."

"English isn't going to work!" Gwen shook her head in disbelief.

"I never said it would. But Lyssandra can write it out in Elantyan and read it for us."

Gwen went back to measuring her angles again. Vic was impatient with her double-checking and triple-checking. "What's taking so long? I want to try it."

Gwen tossed her blond hair and glared up at him. "I'm not stopping you. There's no chance this spell will work anyway — especially if magic is dependent on good penmanship."

"Very funny." He filled the center basin with water from the jug, stepped back, cleared his throat, then read aloud:

"Honoring our good intention,
Take us to a new dimension.
Scroll and spell from ink and pen,
Let us see our home again.
Ground and fire and air and sea,
Make a door where it should be.
Spirit key unlock the door
That we've both been looking for.
Crystal door as clear as glass,
Open up and let us pass."

Seeing her reaction, Vic looked defensive. "What did you expect? More Chaucer?"

Despite her skepticism, Gwen held her breath. Vic waited. They looked at each other. Nothing happened.

Suddenly Gwen let out a laugh, remembering how Vic had chided her in the Cogitary. "So, Dr. Distracto, *now* who forgot to say the magic word?"

"Oh, right — S'ibah!"

The crystals in the array began to glow. Vic let out a cry of both surprise and triumph as he stepped back. The water in the basin bubbled and the air inside the complicated web of crystal lines rippled into a region of blur, like a steamy mirror after one of Vic's interminable showers. Then a patch at the very center turned as shiny and transparent as a window.

A window to Earth.

Gwen and Vic gasped.

"Uncle Cap!"

"Dad!"

There, at the centerpoint of the array, was an image of Dr. Carlton Pierce in the solarium of their house. He was reaching to adjust a lens in his arrangement when his head whipped around to focus on the new "window." He seemed to look directly *at* Gwen and Vic.

"I told you he wouldn't give up! Keep going, Dad — this has to work." Vic rushed toward the image of his father. "Gwen, come on! Who knows how long this door will last?"

But he passed right through the image of his father. At first he looked surprised, then crestfallen. "It's not a crystal door after all. Just a . . . a peephole back home."

His dad reached toward him. "Vic?"

"Can you hear us, Uncle Cap?" Gwen shouted.

The view sharpened even more, and Dr. Pierce seemed to be standing right in front of them, though he rippled like a heat-distorted image. His face lit with joy. "You're safe! Both of you made it to Elantya!"

Gwen couldn't believe what she was hearing. "You *knew* about this? About Elantya, and the crystal doors?"

"Yes, I was trying to get us all to safety. The three of us were supposed to escape that night — but only you two passed through. There was danger for you here on Earth. Azric already tried to kill Gwen."

Gwen suddenly felt cold inside, remembering the strange man who had watched so expectantly as the killer whale was driven to its unintentional attack. "*That* was Azric? The guy with the creepy eyes?"

"Azric?" Vic yelped. "He's the big bad guy, right? The dark sage who killed his parents, then went hunting for his sister? What does he want with us?"

"He was after your mothers, too. He engineered the accident that killed Gwen's parents, I'm sure of it. And now he's looking for you." Uncle Cap seemed frustrated to stay on the other side of the invisible barrier. "But at least you got away. You aren't safe here on Earth anymore. You'll have to stay in Elantya where the sages can protect you."

Gwen was having a very difficult time accepting what he was telling them. She had so many questions it was hard to know where to begin. Then the clarity and focus of the "window" started to fade. "Uncle Cap, what's going on? Please —"

He cut her off, sensing they were almost out of time. "Vic,

your mother is somewhere in one of the open worlds. When Kyara realized it was Azric who killed Rip and Fyera, she wanted to protect you children, and me, from him. She decided to confront him and escape back through the crystal door, hoping to lead Azric away from us. Her plan succeeded, at least for a while."

Dr. Pierce's image wavered, and some of his words were cut off. "— your powers. I'll keep trying to reach Elantya. Try to learn —" Again his words cut off, and he raised his voice to a shout now, though it sounded like a storm was howling around him. "Vic, find your mother! She may be hiding from Azric, but she —"

His words crackled, and they could barely see him now. The crystals were dimming. "Dad!" Vic shouted. Then the image faded away, leaving only a blur in the air. The basin was dry, and the star aja crystals no longer glowed.

Gwen and Vic stared at each other for a long moment, both speechless, their throats clogged with a thousand questions. Finally Vic said in a hoarse voice, "If we could do that with a spell written in English, imagine what'll happen when we use the *right* language!"

19

WHEN THE EXCITED COUSINS rushed back down from the tower into the workroom, even Rubicas reacted to their news with skepticism. "You two should not be able to work magic!" the sage said.

"Much less in a crude language that is not old enough to have developed true power." Orpheon took the scrap of parchment on which Vic had scrawled his spell. "And you used some of our precious aja ink? For your little . . . game? You had no training at all."

"Hey, it worked, didn't it?" Vic said.

"So you claim."

Gwen was also growing impatient with Orpheon's attitude. "We'd be happy to show you again. We left the arrangement in place."

"Hmm, I fear that would put too much stress on the star

aja," Rubicas said. "Let the crystals cool and recharge. Leave your apparatus where it is. We have no need of the tower tonight, and tomorrow Orpheon and I will make a point of seeing this miracle." He stroked his beard, as if reconsidering. "A window, you say? Not an actual crystal door for transport, but something that showed you images of a man —"

"Not just a man. It was my dad!" Vic cried.

"Hmm, perhaps a window would not violate the strictures of the Great Closure. I must think on this further."

"*Later,* Master Rubicas," Orpheon said sternly. "We have work to do."

Vic was clearly disappointed that they would have to wait. Because of Uncle Cap's warning about Azric, they knew they couldn't go home, but Gwen and Vic both very much wanted to bring his father here. If they couldn't be together on Earth, then at least they should all be safe in Elantya.

Sunset had already started to color the sky orange and pink, and Orpheon lit one of the crystals to illuminate the workroom. "All right, then — tomorrow it is," Gwen said. "And our friends can be there, too."

THE NEXT DAY, WHEN they all returned to the sage's tower, Lyssandra and Sharif admired the ingenuity and resourcefulness the cousins had shown, not only in discovering the scroll variations and the medallion symbol in the Cogitary, but in asking Vir Questas to let them borrow his star aja crystals.

"The power of persistence," Gwen said, anxiously studying

the arrangement of the crystals, prisms, lenses, and basin that had remained in place all night. She had measured everything so carefully yesterday, and today she had made sure that the basin was full to the very brim with water. But for some reason, the array didn't look quite right, though each crystal was on its mark. Gwen stopped herself from measuring everything again. Vic would complain that she was being obsessive compulsive.

Vic stood very close to Lyssandra while she studied the new door-opening spell. He had already read her the spell aloud while she copied it down in Elantyan. She said, "I refined these phrases. I only know a few words of Ylijan, but I sprinkled them in with the Elantyan. I believe that will help." The telepathic girl smiled. "If everything is correct, the spell should work better than it did yesterday."

Gwen hoped that using the proper languages would be enough to open a door for Uncle Cap, rather than just letting them see each other.

Rubicas and his assistant glanced over the scroll in Lyssandra's hand, at the clear crystalline ink that graced the paper like fine trails laid down by flitting moths above each line of Vic's messy writing.

Orpheon did not seem impressed. "Very well, let us try it so the sage and I can get back to work. The defense of Elantya is far more important."

Sharif sat down and crossed his arms on his chest, as if all this activity were highly entertaining. He balanced the crystal ball containing his djinni companion on his shoulder like a pirate's parrot. The sphere gave off a faint aqua glow, and Piri gazed through her curved walls, watching with curiosity and interest as the experiment progressed.

Rubicas indicated the arrangement of crystals. "You have measured the angles, the lengths for the whole array based on the crystal size?"

"Several times." Gwen lifted her chin with pride.

"More than several," Vic muttered. "Try about a thousand."

Lyssandra held up the scrap of parchment. "I am ready." Without further delay, the petite girl spoke the spell.

As her lyrical words emerged, the crystals in the array began to shimmer. Beautiful colors gleamed brighter, shifting in tone and hue. Lyssandra kept reading. She glanced up, seeing the crystals flash between the mirrors, ricocheting off prisms, as the water bubbled. She continued in a louder voice and finished the spell. The crystals grew more and more luminous.

Piri's sphere shone brighter, as if in response.

Gwen's throat was dry with anticipation. Next to her, Vic didn't blink; he didn't even seem to be breathing.

A shimmer appeared in the air at the center of the array, as before. But it looked larger, more than just a window to see Earth, much more . . . Before the doorway could sharpen entirely, the glow from the points of the crystal pattern grew incandescent. Water geysered from the basin, refogging the clear area and blotting out the image.

"Uh, what's happening?" Vic cried. "That shouldn't be —"

Still the crystals burned brighter. And *brighter.* The nymph djinni covered her eyes and tried to shield herself with her own white light.

The center of the array faded to the disappointing clarity of mere air again. Three of the aja crystals went dim like a flashlight shut off, but two glowed even more intensely. The blazing colors hurt Gwen's eyes as they sparkled from the prisms, intensified by the lenses, growing and growing.

"This isn't like what happened yesterday," Gwen said.

Like lights suddenly burning out, the crystals sparked, flashed, and then cracked, turning into blackened lumps. The last reflections spangled in the air like flash-melted snowflakes. The now-empty water basin shattered.

Lyssandra stared down at the spell in her hands, as if to reassure herself that she had read every word correctly.

Gwen sank to the platform. "So close."

Rubicas looked at the burned-out lumps and sighed. "Those were quite valuable crystals. I suspect Vir Questas will be upset that they are lost."

Orpheon shook his head. "The explanation is obvious — the array was not set up properly. At least one of the angles was wrong. Or one of the radial distances, possibly both. Such a waste of star aja." He frowned at Gwen, and she felt as if she had somehow failed. "It is a very meticulous process, and these two have never attended a single teaching at the Citadel."

The sage stroked his beard. "Hmm. We are fortunate no one was hurt."

Gwen climbed to her feet, indignant. "But that's not it at all. I measured and remeasured!" Orpheon gave her a patronizing look.

Rubicas sighed again. "No use arguing about it now. Orpheon and I have to get back to our spell. We are very close to a breakthrough. Now, can you all help clean this up?" He didn't seem to be casting blame. Gesturing to the ruined array, the sage looked once more at Gwen. "I expect you have some apologies to make to Vir Questas, too." Then the old man and his assistant descended the spiral staircase back to his laboratory.

Gwen was dismayed and confused. Vic said, "It's not your fault, Doc. I watched you — in fact, I watched you until I was sick of it. You didn't make any mistakes."

"Yet something obviously went wrong with the array," Sharif said.

"I can't understand it," Gwen repeated. "I was so careful. I used chalk to mark the positions." She paced over to the two blackened crystals, then to the other intact ones. She lifted an undamaged crystal. "See? There's my chalk mark." She went to the others, proving that she wasn't imagining things.

The intact crystal had a distinct chalk mark. When she went to the blackened ones, she found marks there too. But then something caught her eye. Several inches to the side, she saw another faint mark. "Wait a second!" She bent closer. There was definitely another chalk mark, but someone had rubbed it away. "This crystal was moved!"

Vic peeked under the second blackened crystal and searched until he spotted another faint shadow of a chalk dot. "Yup, here it is again. Somebody shifted this crystal for sure."

"I knew I should have remeasured everything!" Gwen clenched her fists.

"My people have a saying: A small amount of suspicion at the right time often prevents disaster," Sharif said.

Angry now, her violet eyes flashing, Gwen looked at her friends. "If I made a mistake, I'd admit it. But this wasn't my fault. Somebody sabotaged the experiment. Somebody knew we were going to test this crystal array — and they didn't want it to work."

"Why would anyone do a crazy thing like that?" Vic said.

Gwen narrowed her eyes. "To stop us."

20

ALL NIGHT IN THE Citadel dormitory, Vic watched his
cousin stew over the sabotage of their experiment. He felt just
as incensed, but also mystified. At Ocean Kingdoms, when his
dad had mentioned going away to lie low, Vic had never expected it would be to a place like Elantya. His father's warnings through the magical window had convinced him that he
and Gwen would have to stay here in the island realm.

So, they had to fit in somehow and take advantage of the
unexpected new realities here. But if someone had wrecked
the crystal array to prevent them from making contact with
his dad again or opening a door to Earth, maybe Elantya
wasn't quite as safe for them as his father had hoped.

"We have a lot to learn," Gwen said.

"No kidding." Vic could barely keep himself from rolling
his eyes.

"So it's time to start."

The next morning, when the cousins followed Lyssandra and Sharif to the Citadel for their first official day of courses, Vic tried to keep an open mind. Unfortunately, he'd had more than his share of bad luck at Stephen Hawking High with a couple of prison-warden staff members who looked at school rules as unshakeable laws, and teachers who did not understand his quirks or reward his unorthodox (though often effective) ways of learning.

If a subject interested him, Vic could sit still for hours and concentrate until his legs cramped. At such times, Gwen joked that she could come in with a brass band and he wouldn't even look up. But for most subjects, his attention span was not very compatible with all the distractions in a standardized classroom.

Vic let out a soft groan. "Just what I needed: a whole new batch of instructors telling me how stupid I am."

"That is not how our sages teach," Lyssandra reassured him. "During a discovery session, for example, a sage guides discussions and asks thought-provoking questions so that all in attendance may come away with a richer understanding."

Well, that did sound more interesting than chalkboards and essay questions. "So it's kind of like a classroom lecture, Jeopardy-style."

Lyssandra touched a hand to his arm and drew the context from his mind. "Ah, I see. The participants are not told what conclusions to draw. Many perspectives are offered, and spirited discussion often continues in small groups long after the discovery forum has ended."

"No homework. No worksheets. No essays. And no wrong answers — sounds like my kind of class after all," Vic admitted. "I wonder what the final exam looks like."

Lyssandra smiled. "Life is the 'final exam.' Our discovery today, however, leads into a praktik, where we will put our learning to use."

The Citadel buildings were linked by covered walkways and interspersed with arches, gardens, fountains, and water clocks. Even the sculptures moved with crystalline engines powered by sunlight.

Sharif expertly began to roll Piri's glowing ball up and down his arms and balance it on his hands. As he continued contact juggling, flickers of pink light showed how much the nymph djinni enjoyed the ride.

Lyssandra led them into a brightly lit, well-ventilated chamber. When the four companions took their seats on a stone bench, apprentices and other novice students — novs — arranged themselves around the hall. Six long tables were covered with bowls of powder, beakers of colored liquids, and rough-cut gems that sent out tendrils of smoke whenever light hit them.

"Oh!" Gwen looked around at a loss. "We didn't bring any school supplies. I have no way of taking notes."

"Did you bring your mind?" Sharif tucked Piri back into her mesh sack. "That is all you need."

With conscious effort, Vic decided not to tease his cousin.

To his surprise, the anemonite Sage Polup was their instructor. The many-eyed jellyfish genius in a mechanical body was utterly unlike any teacher Vic had ever had — a good sign. "I hope he doesn't give homework."

"Our purpose today," Sage Polup began, "is to examine a variety of crystals and their compounds to learn how each refracts, absorbs, and emits magical properties." His voice bubbled in stereo from the speakers in his artificial body.

"In other words, it's a chemistry class," Gwen whispered to Vic.

"What is the primary engine of our magical power?" Polup asked.

As the novs and apprentices began to answer the sage's questions, Vic discovered that his mind wasn't even tempted to wander. He learned that Elantyan magic is powered by seven distinct forms of aja crystals, and each one was passed around and discussed. Fire aja is always red, sun is orange, dust is yellow, sea is green, wind is blue, sooth aja — for telling lies from truth — is white, and star aja, the rarest form, is violet.

"I will not explain their properties to you. You will witness them for yourself. That is the best way to learn."

At the end of the discovery portion, the anemonite sage called the students to the experimental tables. Vic stood with his cousin, fascinated by the liquids and powdered crystals set out for the students to sample.

The different forms of crystals ranged in consistency from powdered sugar to pea gravel, and all had odd properties. Some flared with dazzling light; some released colorful fumes. Other powders, when mixed together, melted into a flowing liquid that balled up and rolled, as if it were alive, but quickly dried and collapsed back into fine crystal grains when it fell into shadow.

As Sage Polup moved his mechanical body among the groups of students, the floating anemonite watched them all with his ring of eyes. "When I lived under the waters, I had no opportunity to study dry aja crystals. But the merlons forced us to perform all manner of tests and make elemental discoveries."

"I suppose you couldn't use fire, either," Gwen said. "When I took Chem Lab, we heated substances with a Bunsen burner."

Polup stopped next to her station. "Certain flames do burn under water, and there are undersea vents where lava flows. The merlons direct great armored turtles to carry experiments to these volcanic cracks for them so they can study the effects of the elements. I was taken to the flaming cracks only once, shortly before I escaped the merlons."

"So how'd you ever get away?" Vic asked. "I bet it was quite an adventure."

"That is not a tale for this class," Polup answered. "The waters in which the merlons live are dim and cool. In their cities, kelp gardens and coral shelves filter the light from above. Suffice it to say that the merlons do not like intense heat or bright lights."

The strange sage moved off, talking to other students. Vic continued his experiments — or messing around, as he thought of it — until he and his companions thought they had exhausted the possibilities.

Polup clanked back to the center of the hall and called for

them to stop. "When dissolved and suspended, crystal powders can be made into aja ink, with which we write our spell scrolls. Crystal powders in specific patterns can also draw magic from the world or the elements and bind it into a form that we can use."

Two journeysages set up pictures of simple geometric shapes — circles, triangles, trapezoids — and a few complex designs that Sage Polup showed only briefly. "By drawing such patterns in crystal powder, we can unlock useful energies. These complicated designs" — he indicated the special drawings — "should not be used by novices and apprentices. But you may begin with the simple patterns."

Picking up fistfuls of powder and letting the grains dribble out as if he were making a sand painting, Vic tried to draw a triangle. When he was finished, the outline shuddered and then snapped into a perfect shape, as if linear magnets were drawing iron filings into a grid. "That's cool!"

Gwen made a ragged circle that also snapped into a perfect round outline. Lyssandra touched the rectangle she had drawn. "Mine is very warm."

Gwen tentatively touched her own circle. "This is cold."

Vic felt an unexpected breeze rise from the tabletop above his triangle. Enjoying himself, he began to toy with combinations of shapes, drawing a circle around his first triangle, and was amazed when the outlines shifted position, one inside the other and then reversing. Vic didn't know exactly what purpose that might serve, but at least it was fun.

They tried combinations of designs, and each shape rewarded them with an unexpected result, from ripples in the air to a humming sound to a sweet honeysuckle smell. Nothing terribly useful, as far as Vic could see. He considered trying one of the advanced patterns, just to show off, but Sage Polup had put the pictures away and he couldn't remember what they looked like.

Suddenly, he had an idea. He pulled out his keychain with the five-sided medallion his mother had given him.

Drawn by his movement, Lyssandra's gaze turned toward Vic. "That charm with the symbol on it. I saw it — or one just like it — in a dream." She spoke in a hushed voice. "At first it spun and danced above sparkling waters, then it splashed like a porpoise in the waves. It was a very happy dream, but at the end, something pulled it, and it sank to the bottom of the ocean."

Vic grimaced. "I hope that doesn't mean I'm going to lose this. I'd be awfully upset if I did."

When Lyssandra went back to her work, he looked at the medallion again. Rubicas had been excited to see it, so maybe the design would have some interesting properties. Holding the disk in one hand, he tried to duplicate the loops, angles, and swirls in crystal dust on the table and hoped the magic itself would know to make the lines straight and the curves smooth.

In the last two years, missing his mother, Vic had spent a lot of time in his room, just staring at the medallion, trying to interpret its meaning. He had always wondered what the unusual markings represented. When he completed the last loop, he called to his cousin, "Look, Doc. I made the symbol on our —"

Suddenly the new pattern shimmered and brightened. At

first, it began to glow, then to blaze. "Whoa!" He stepped back, blinded by the glare.

The other students gasped and pointed. Sage Polup swiveled in his mechanical body, and the teaching assistants came running forward.

Gwen groaned. "*Now* what did you do, Taz?"

The pattern blazed alarmingly hotter. Without stopping to think — Gwen always complained about his impulsiveness — Vic swept his arm sideways and scattered the crystal powder, ruining the pattern. Suddenly the light and heat vanished, snuffed out.

He looked at the medallion's symbol that was now scorched into the stone surface of their experimental table. Next to him Sharif brushed powder off of Piri's eggsphere and his colorful silken clothes.

Sage Polup tilted his head tank down, and after a long, tense moment of silence, said, "That is a pattern of great power."

"Sheesh, no kidding." Feeling sheepish, Vic lowered his head. "I . . . I don't think I'll try it again, at least not until I've had some more training."

"A wise decision," Polup said.

"That's enough chemistry for me." Vic looked over at Gwen. "Maybe we should consider taking a different sort of class next."

Lyssandra wore her mysterious smile. "Good. Tomorrow we can start another praktik — several days on a training voyage. The *Golden Walrus* sets sail at dawn. You will enjoy being at sea."

21

DESPITE HER INTEREST IN oceanography, Gwen had never been aboard a true sailing ship before. One time, Uncle Cap had taken them to eat dinner on a replica clipper ship at a touristy harbor in Southern California, but it was just a restaurant and had never actually sailed the seas. The *Golden Walrus* had a solid wooden hull, a swaying deck, and a spiderweb of rigging. And it was really going to sail out of the sheltered harbor onto Elantya's open seas.

When Lyssandra described the navigation field trip, Gwen had jumped at the chance, and Vic had agreed as fast as the words could come out of his mouth. This would be even better than Ocean Kingdoms amusement park!

Just before dawn the following day, Sharif and Lyssandra accompanied the cousins to the harbor. Each carried a small bundle of clothing wrapped in oil cloth to protect it from the elements. Although Sage Rubicas had seen to it that they were given a change of functional, if not stylish, work clothes, Gwen and Vic still wore their jeans and rumpled Ocean Kingdoms shirts.

The *Golden Walrus* was a wide, sturdy vessel with a broad deck, a tall main mast, and a small foremast that stuck out at an angle above the water at the beaked prow of the ship. The mainsail, topsail, and foresail had Elantyan symbols sewn in bright patterns across the field of orange fabric. Toward the stern, a long, heavy steering oar extended into the water.

Vic pointed to the reinforced hull planks and weathered deck rails. "Sheesh! That thing is old."

Lyssandra pursed her lips. "The *Golden Walrus* served for over a century as a slow cargo transport between the crystal doors. Now the ship is most often used as a floating classroom for the Citadel."

"I hope it doesn't leak."

As usual, Sharif carried his carpet under one arm, with Piri hanging like a pendant in the net around his neck. He kept a hand firmly on one end of the rolled carpet — a reminder that they had emergency transportation, if necessary.

Excited to be aboard, Gwen edged past her cousin and trotted up the gangplank, which rose a good four meters above the water. The moment her foot hit the ship's gently rolling deck, Gwen knew this was the real thing. The *Walrus* was a work of nautical art, a demonstration of superior craftsmanship. If she ever got into oceanography as a career, she would serve on high-tech modern craft, but this vessel had a mythic and adventurous charm. A sailing ship!

Gwen looked back down at her companions on the dock. "Hurry up, Vic. You've got to see this!"

Accustomed to keeping his balance even on a thin flying carpet, Sharif strode smoothly up the creaking ramp and joined Gwen on the deck. Lyssandra wobbled just enough that Vic, who had hung back to walk with her, gallantly offered his arm.

"Strange," mused Sharif, leaning an elbow on the rail. "I have never seen Lyssandra waver before. It is most fortunate Viccus was there to help her."

Gwen smiled at the petite girl's convenient unsteadiness. "Right. Most fortunate." It was becoming painfully obvious that Vic was attracted to their interpreter; Lyssandra shouldn't need telepathy to pick up on that!

Though the ship was docked in a calm harbor, it seemed to shift moment by moment, never exactly where Gwen's feet expected it to be. Ignoring her sense of queasiness, she called to her cousin, "Glad you could join us, Dr. Distracto. What was the problem? Did the big bad ship worry you?"

Flushing slightly, Vic glanced away. "I was just waiting for Lyssandra . . . uh, and studying the ship. It's very interesting."

Lyssandra let go of his arm as they stepped aboard. "Then you will be even more interested when you see everything up close."

Moving so fast she could have been a jaguar, Tiaret emerged from the hold below. The girl from Afirik looked entirely recovered now, and restless. "My friends! I heard from Sage Abakas that you would be aboard."

Vic stared at her in astonishment. "Tiaret! I didn't expect you to set foot aboard a ship again anytime soon!"

The girl scowled. "The surest way to overcome fear is to squash it before it can grow. I sail again to prove to myself there is no need for apprehension."

"I understand," Sharif said. "As my people say, 'Fear is a weed that thrives in shadow.'"

Vic nodded his approval. "Pretty gutsy, especially considering you don't know how to swim yet." Tiaret reacted uneasily to the words, as if she had managed to avoid thinking of drowning as a possibility until now.

A knowing smirk curved Sharif's full lips. "And if merlons attack? Will I need to rescue you again?"

"No, that will not be necessary." Tiaret thumped the sharp end of her teaching staff on the wooden boards. "If they attack us, then we will kill them."

Lyssandra gestured to the group of friends. "Come, I will give you all a tour."

"How do you know so much about the *Golden Walrus*?" Gwen took a step to follow her, suddenly feeling unsteady. She heard the ropes creak, and water sloshed against the side of the boat. When she looked up, the masts seemed to be weaving back and forth.

"My mother teaches the galley skills portion of this training voyage."

Gwen flinched as memories of cooking with her own mother flooded her mind: her mother teaching her to make savory soups, the two of them baking meringues that her mom called "cloud cookies," she and her dad cutting up vegetables, fruits, or meats for her mother while Fyera created exotic meals, her mother packing up food for a picnic that they would all eat together on the beach. . . .

Vic grinned. "We get to learn how to cook on a ship? That's great!"

Gwen's stomach churned at the very thought of food, and suddenly she was very dizzy. The deck was barely moving, but it felt like a slow rising and falling roller coaster, rising . . . falling . . . rising. "Yeah, great," she said faintly as she tried to follow her companions. Her stomach clenched and heaved.

Unable to fight off the nausea, she grabbed at the ship's railing and leaned over the side while the light breakfast she had eaten cascaded into the water below.

TO GWEN'S CHAGRIN AND great annoyance, Vic showed no sign of seasickness. None at all. And she was the one who wanted to be a marine biologist!

Throughout the tour of the *Golden Walrus*, while her stomach continued to roil and jitter, Vic displayed every bit of the inquisitive enthusiasm that she wished she had the energy to show. Full of energy, he was more excited about the training voyage than he had ever been in school on Earth.

After exploring the captain's cabin, the foredeck, the cargo holds, and the crew quarters, Lyssandra took them to the galley, which was rich with spicy and sweet aromas. She introduced her mother, Kaisa, a small but robust-looking woman with a cloud of red curls.

Kaisa gave a comforting smile upon hearing of Gwen's seasickness. "Oh, that is easy enough to fix." She rummaged among her spices and dried herbs. "A bit of shinqroot. Always helps settle a stormy stomach."

Gwen accepted the remedy, nibbling on the dried root. She felt her insides calm quickly.

With feline grace, Tiaret slipped further into the galley. Although she looked fully ready to wrestle lions, she asked for a bit of the shinqroot too. "If it helps me keep my strength and my balance, I should be prepared as well."

Kaisa flashed an infectious smile. She touched head and heart, then offered her hand to Tiaret, who responded in kind. "Ah, so you are the new student from Afirik? You must show me your recipes from the savannahs."

The dark-skinned girl cocked her head to one side, then nodded. "And you must show me your best fighting techniques. Sometimes kitchen implements make superior weapons."

Lyssandra's mother chuckled. "I would love to. But first, Lyssandra, please show everyone to the sleeping quarters so they can store their possessions. The first lesson will begin soon, and we set sail in an hour."

AFTER ROPES WERE CAST off from the docks, the *Golden Walrus* sailed out of the harbor onto the stippled, open seas. Vic had never imagined there could be so many back-breaking chores on a ship.

The students ranged in age from seven to thirty. The novices — including Vic, Gwen, and Tiaret — spent the first three hours of the morning learning about anchors and rigging, tie-downs and how to raise and lower the sails. Afterward, a prim and flighty sage named Snigmythya taught them the basic rules of etiquette for sailing aboard a crowded vessel. Intermediate novs like Sharif started the voyage with storm-preparation drills. Next, the more knowledgeable apprentices like Lyssandra were paired with novices and assigned basic ship maintenance duties.

Even though it wasn't kind, Vic nevertheless couldn't help but be gleeful when he saw Gwen — still a bit pale and seasick — paired with the "more advanced student," a small slip of a lad who couldn't have been more than seven years old. Vic's own partner, Lyssandra, surprised him by working harder than even the brawny sailors.

Because the *Golden Walrus* had only three sets of navigation instruments, students had to take turns learning their skills with the mirrors and sun-angle measuring devices, while the rest attended to their assigned list of chores.

They hauled buckets of salt water up on a block and tackle, then dumped them across the deck. Trainees used brushes to scrub the deck, coiled ropes, scrambled up and down the rigging to check sails, and oiled anchor chains. Some hung over the side in harnesses to chip away barnacles and scrape algae. They also took watches by twos on the lookout platforms, keeping an eye out for sudden storms, approaching sea monsters, or anything unusual.

By the time the cook's chime rang for lunch, Vic's stomach was growling loudly enough to scare away grizzly bears — if any of them had happened to be swimming toward the ship. They ate a plain but filling meal of thick brown bread, cold smoked fish, slabs of pungent cheese, and a crunchy yellow fruit called sussu that looked like an apple but tasted more like watermelon. The choice of beverages was limited to water, hot "blackstepe," or pale green "mos ale" that had a refreshing bite.

Lyssandra sat on the bench next to Vic and set a mug of cool mos ale on the table for each of them. "This is good for you, with plenty of nourishment. At the end of the meal, drink at least one cup of blackstepe. It revives tired muscles and will also help keep you alert."

Thanking the petite girl, Vic dutifully gulped the gingery mos ale between bites of bread and cheese. Then he drank a full mug of steaming blackstepe and soon felt energy flowing back into his aching limbs. "I feel like I could work all day now."

"Good," Lyssandra said with a knowing smile. "We will need to."

During the hottest and sunniest part of the day, the seas were calm. Colorful oiled fabrics were stretched across the deck to provide shade and shelter against a brief tropical rain that swept through. The Elantyan students concentrated on the mathematical lessons that Sage Abakas assigned them. Next, since her own Master Kundu had not survived the journey to Elantya, Tiaret demonstrated simple fighting techniques, which were very different from the quick-reflex *zy'oah* skills their mother had taught them. Vic wondered if the *zy'oah* movements were also Elantyan or if they had come from another of the crystal door worlds. Afterward,

Lyssandra's mother taught them some of the basics of cooking at sea.

For several hours after dark, the students worked with sextants and astrolabes, learning how to tell direction by the stars. For Gwen and Vic, this included learning Elantya's unfamiliar constellations: the Sage Springs, the Seahorse, the First Door, the Aquit Sisters, the Master Key, the Fallen Sussu, Therya's Bow.

When all was quiet and their work was finished, the students, crew, and sages gathered on the main deck. While everyone found a place to sit, Lyssandra played a lyre and sang a lively song about the stories behind the constellations. Vic watched Lyssandra's fingerwork with interest. Piri's globe twinkled in pink and gold while Sharif contact-juggled to the music.

Captain Dimas, a leathery-faced man with kindly eyes, walked to the center of the circle and illuminated a pile of sun aja crystals in a small brazier atop a barrel. "And now comes a time loved by all who sail the seas. This is a time of tales. Who would like to begin?"

Without hesitation Sharif volunteered. He seemed to enjoy telling his story as much as he enjoyed having a large audience. "Not long ago, in the flying city of Irrakesh, there lived a great Sultan who had many beautiful daughters and two fine sons. The Sultan ruled his kingdom with wisdom, justice, and compassion, and his people loved him. He had many trusted advisors, but one grew dominant to the point where the Sultan would listen to no one else.

"The wily and charismatic vizier advised the Sultan with caution at first, but when he was completely trusted, the vizier began to change his advice. He urged the Sultan to dismiss unnecessary courtiers, to suspect former allies of being traitors and assassins, and to impose heavy taxes on his loyal subjects. Only the Sultan's older son Hashim dared speak out against the scheming advisor. The Sultan did not listen."

Sharif looked around, and his voice faltered. "No . . . the Sultan did not listen, until it was too late. Only when, through darkest magic, the vizier murdered poor Hashim, did the Sultan come to his senses. But nothing could bring his older son back. Grieving and broken, the Sultan commanded that the evil vizier be thrown from the flying city."

Vic saw a glint of real tears in Sharif's olive eyes, which reflected the light of the sun aja crystals. "When the guards brought him to the high balcony for his execution, the defiant vizier was unafraid. He did not plead for his life, did not recant his crime. He seemed happy that Hashim was dead.

"Before the guards could throw the vizier from high Irrakesh, he began to laugh. His features shifted into a familiar face of evil that every child in the flying city learns to fear." Sharif narrowed his eyes. "He was *Azric,* in disguise and walking among us!"

Tiaret held her training staff, her dark face etched with a frown. The other students and crewmembers muttered, both intrigued and disturbed by the story.

"Then Azric astonished everyone by leaping from the city. Even as he fell, his body transformed. Sprouting great batlike wings, he took flight, laughing and screeching as he soared away."

Before he sat down again, Sharif said, "That Sultan is my father, and Hashim was my brother." His jaw tightened. "Believe me when I tell you this. Even if he is the most powerful dark sage in the universe, Azric will regret the day I find him."

22

THE FIRST NIGHT OF the training voyage would have been more enjoyable if Gwen hadn't known the merlons were prowling out there. Sharif's story about Azric — who had, apparently, made the killer whale attack her at Ocean Kingdoms — didn't help, either.

Captain Dimas and the four sage instructors had interior cabins, while the novs slept in hammocks belowdecks. With the hatch covers open, the students could sway in the fresh ocean breezes that stole down into the hold, and hear the lapping of the water against the hull. Gwen stared up through the hatch at the stars. Each time she found herself searching for familiar star figures like Orion or Cassiopeia, she was reminded that Elantya was an entirely different world.

When she needed to, Gwen nibbled at the shinqroot Kaisa had given her to settle her stomach. It took effect quickly and she wondered for the fiftieth time why her cousin had not been afflicted with seasickness. It wasn't fair . . . but then again it wasn't fair that her parents had been killed in that car accident. It wasn't fair that she and Vic had been thrown into this strange world far from Uncle Cap. It wasn't fair that the Elantyans and merlons were at odds with each other, and that Gwen and Vic could not go home.

But there it was, one of the fundamentals of human existence: Life was not fair. You just had to learn to deal with what you had. Maybe that's why somebody put "for richer, for poorer, in sickness and in health" in the marriage vows: good luck or bad, you never knew what life would throw at you.

"Suck it up," she muttered to herself as she put her hands behind her head and stared upward. "Let's see what you've got."

Beside her, Vic was awake as well. From his own hammock, he said, "I'd feel safer if one of those guardian galleys had followed us. I mean, we're just a training ship out here on the open sea."

"Sage Abakas and Sage Snigmythya have read spells to make the bottom of our ship invisible from below," Lyssandra said. "Swimming merlons will not be able to see us from underneath."

"Tiaret is worried enough for all of us, though she tries not to show it," Sharif said. The girl from Afirik had insisted on taking the first watch, pacing the deck in the starlight. Meanwhile, he rested comfortably with his rolled flying carpet stashed beneath his hammock beside Piri's glowing cloth-wrapped sphere. "I doubt she will sleep."

"It's gonna be hard to sleep," Vic agreed. "At least *I* don't get seasick." Gwen had a sudden urge to go over and start his hammock swinging wildly, but she was too tired to make the effort.

As she finally started drifting off, Gwen heard a faint buzzing in the air that grew louder, like a swarm of angry wasps. She blinked and sat up.

Lyssandra was also awake, looking up into the starlit night. "Something is coming." Other students had heard the noise and were stirring, slipping out of their hammocks. Gwen, Lyssandra, Vic, and Sharif rushed up to the main deck with the other students following. Kaisa emerged from her quarters near the galley, rubbed her eyes, checked to see that her daughter was safe, and went back inside.

One of Captain Dimas's crewmen stood at the bow sniffing the air, his head tilted into the night. Water lapped up against the side of the ship. Tiaret was clearly agitated, pacing over to her friends without taking her eyes from the darkness. "Be alert! There may be danger."

Cabin doors opened, and the teaching sages came out. Captain Dimas called for his crew, and they scrambled up from belowdecks, ready for a fight.

The buzzing sound in the impenetrable darkness grew louder, more ominous. The vibration grated on Gwen's ears. The humming grew impossibly loud and was joined by strange high-pitched chirpings and splashes.

Vic stood next to her, anxious. "That doesn't sound good, whatever it is."

"It's all around us!" Gwen ran to the deck rail and peered into the endless darkness. "But I still can't see what's making that noise." The captain marched up and down the deck, checking ropes and rigging.

Sharif squinted, staring out into the empty night. Finally he pointed. "There! A whole swarm."

"And they will be hungry!" Captain Dimas said.

The crewmen took up the cry. "They will devour anything in their path!"

"Locusts of the sea!"

As if they had been drilled many times but never faced the actual danger, the rugged crew scurried around on deck. Some grim-faced sailors carried long boat hooks, holding the stout handles in two-fisted grips. Others snatched up spare oars from the lifeboats tied to the side of the hull.

Lyssandra and Sharif stood side by side, tense and alert. Tiaret held up her teaching staff, ready to strike. Gwen looked at her cousin, then waited for somebody to give her an answer. She still couldn't identify the threat, but she was smart enough to be frightened.

The hum grew louder until her teeth vibrated, as if she were standing in the path of an oncoming tornado. Suddenly, instinct told her to duck and something flashed past her, a flying thing the size of a dove but with silver skin and bright red . . . wings? Fins? Gwen flinched and another shot in front of her face. Now dozens of scaled creatures filled the air. Flapping spiny fin-wings, they slammed into the ship's sails, the hull, the thick masts, reminding Gwen of a swarm of giant bugs hitting a windshield.

"Has a flock of birds gone insane?" Vic asked.

When Gwen got a better look, she noticed their *jaws.*

"Flying piranhas!" Lyssandra said. "They can gnaw a ship to splinters!"

"Oh dear! Oh dear! They will strip our flesh from our bones." Sage Snigmythya flapped her thin hands as if to shoo away the attacking swarm.

Sage Abakas was cooler in the crisis. "Not if I can read our spell scrolls fast enough." The mathematics instructor dashed into his quarters and returned juggling three baskets of scrolls. Lyssandra took the baskets from him, and he began pulling scrolls open and discarding them as he searched for useful in-cantations. Snigmythya pitched in, grabbing spell scrolls and skimming the complex loops and whorls of silvery aja crystal ink. Lyssandra knelt by the baskets and salvaged scrolls as the sages discarded them.

Tiaret did not wait for spells. She waded in, twirling her teaching staff and using the blunt end like a heavy baseball bat to smack the creatures out of the air.

Gwen and Sharif picked up a pair of wooden buckets and swung them to deflect fish from the sages. Vic threw a small fishing net over a cluster of the predators, but it took them only seconds to chew their way through it.

More and more flying piranhas surged in, squeaking and humming, their long fins flapping. With spiny appendages, they fastened onto anything they struck. Diamond-sharp teeth slashed. The fish gnawed through rigging ropes and sail lines as if the thick braided cables were no more than fine spider silk.

A flying piranha slammed into Gwen's shoulder, and she

slapped it away, again reacting with an instinct born of her *zy'oah* training. The fish felt hard and slimy, and after knocking it to the deck boards, she stomped hard with the heel of her right foot. She heard scales and fish bones snap, and she kicked the wounded creature away. The piranha continued to writhe on the deck and scratch the planks with its sharp teeth.

Gwen got a good look as the thing lay twitching. The undersea creature seemed to have been built out of a dozen different bad dreams. Its spiny wings were tipped with thorns like the lionfish she had seen at Ocean Kingdoms; its head was crusted with misshapen mossy growths. The serrated needles of teeth lining its jaws were able to slice through rope, cloth, wood, and no doubt, skin. The fish's face was studded with two main eyes and a row of milky sensors above a set of whiplike whiskers, like those on a catfish. The creature showed no sign of intelligence, only a hunger to chew on anything in its way.

The injured fish died after a moment. And a thousand more took its place.

Flying piranhas kept soaring by, chewing and splintering the deck rails, boring holes through the hull. The students and crew worked together to knock away the fish as soon as they alighted on skin and clothes, protecting their lives above everything else.

Finally, Sage Abakas found a useful scroll. Unrolling it, he uttered incomprehensible syllables while touching his chest, then said one last word. The silvery ink glowed slightly. Since Lyssandra was closest to Sage Abakas, he touched her shoulder and repeated the incantation. The mathematics instructor moved to Gwen, Sharif, and then Vic. "Now you are all protected."

Gwen felt no different after Abakas had shielded her with his spell, but suddenly the flying piranhas didn't notice her. She seemed to have turned invisible; when one of the voracious fish struck her, it seemed to be entirely by accident. Unfortunately, as the mathematical sage erased the piranhas' potential victims one at a time, the creatures concentrated on the unshielded people, who became all the more prominent targets.

Abakas tossed the scroll aside after he had read from it several times and used up all the stored magic. By then, though, Snigmythya had found another scroll imprinted with the same spell, and she began to read protection onto the students and crew, while Abakas found a third protective scroll to shield frantic fighters.

When the second and third spell scroll weakened, the protected people gathered around the last few to defend them. Gwen's bucket broke and she seized a wooden awning pole and flailed at the invading piranhas to chase them away.

Next to her, Vic yelled over the buzzing roar. "That's too small! We need something wide and flat!" Tiaret, thrashing with her teaching staff, was having the same problem. "I've got an idea!" Vic dashed into Kaisa's galley.

Abakas used the dregs of energy in his spell scroll to protect Snigmythya. Lyssandra found one more in the baskets of stored scrolls, and the sages rushed to protect Captain Dimas and finally Tiaret, who did not want to be bothered in the middle of a fight. She barely stood still as the spell was cast on her.

While the warrior girl kept battling, the two sages huddled by Lyssandra over the baskets, sifting through scrolls, searching for anything else that might help in the crisis. Muttering and fumbling, Snigmythya read a spell that summoned up a brief wind storm. The ship rocked, and the attacking fish swirled around in the violent gusts, disoriented, then fell back upon the boat. In the meantime, the blustery air currents snatched the scroll right out of Snigmythya's hand, and she watched it flutter off into the water. The wind soon died down by itself.

Flushed, Vic returned, holding four of Kaisa's widest iron pans by the handles. The metal clanged as he ran. "Mom always told me I could make a weapon out of just about anything. Think of this as a big flyswatter!"

He shoved one of the heavy pans at Gwen, who took it with a quick smile. "Good idea, Taz!"

Vic handed a pan each to Sharif and Lyssandra. Sharif nodded his approval. "These are weapons the fish cannot eat."

Alerted by Vic, Kaisa now appeared on deck wielding a pair of wicked-looking chef's knives and began slashing at the aquatic attackers.

Vic dove into the fray with his metal pan, smacking at the voracious fish. Gwen could see that her cousin's childhood *zy'oah* training had also taken over. Like the star player on a Little League team, he swung right and left, sending fish pinwheeling out into the dark sea. Each time he struck an incoming piranha, it made a thunk and a clang. "Home run! It's out of the ballpark!"

Gwen, Sharif, and Lyssandra went after the winged

predators with their new weapons. Soon stunned fish flopped and twitched on the deck. Kaisa dispatched any that showed signs of reviving.

By now the broad orange sails of the *Golden Walrus* were shredded. Ribbons of cloth dangled from the yardarms. At the water line, the fish had settled onto the treated hull planking, grasping the few remaining barnacles with sharp fin-spines so they could gnaw on the hull.

Captain Dimas bellowed, stomping fish with his boots, sweeping his leather-sleeved arm sideways to knock them off the deck rails and the masts.

To Sage Snigmythya's dismay, the piranhas dove into the scroll baskets and tore the spell scrolls to shreds, making the magic useless. "Oh, they did that on purpose!" she moaned. "On purpose!"

Abakas raised his voice with a warning to be heard above the clamor. "Everyone, listen! Your protective spells will not last long!"

Captain Dimas said, "I have never known a swarm of flying piranhas to stay in one place for this long. They usually sweep in, rip everything to shreds, and then continue."

Tiaret skewered two more fish with the point of her teaching staff. "Then these are not normal flying piranhas."

"No," Lyssandra said. "Not normal at all. They are being . . . guided."

Sharif growled, "It must be merlon magic!"

"Thanks to our camouflage spell, the merlons could not see our ship from beneath the water," said Abakas. "But if the flying piranhas are indeed their spies, the merlons will soon know where we are."

"Oh, my! Now we are doomed!" moaned Snigmythya. "Doomed."

"In danger, perhaps," Tiaret said, setting her jaw. "But not doomed yet."

From out of the darkness, the flying piranhas kept coming, thousands of them swarming over the ship. They stripped the sailcloth down to shreds, and left teeth marks on the thick yardarms and masts.

One nipped Vic between the shoulder blades. He yelled, slapping with his hands, and Gwen knocked the creature away. "The spell must be wearing off. We're not protected anymore."

"Quick — everyone inside the cabins or get belowdecks!" The captain looked sickened, but still determined. "If we do not protect ourselves, we — along with this vessel — will become skeletons." His face creased in a grim frown. "My beautiful vessel . . ."

While students jumped through the hatch covers into the hold and pulled the grates into place, Gwen, Vic, and their friends ran to the captain's cabin. All of them crammed inside and Tiaret slammed the wooden door shut behind them. Captain Dimas threw the stout iron bolt, and they all crowded together, listening to the constant battering and chirping as the predators continued their relentless assault.

Gwen heard cracking and splintering sounds, and endless buzzing as the piranhas smashed against the walls, the deck.

One of the deadly fish crashed into the cabin's small crystal window. Stunned, the creature fell aside, leaving a slimy smear on the glass. Then a second fish hit even harder, as if drawn to a new target. A crack split the crystal pane.

A third flying piranha hurtled headfirst into the window, finally shattering the glass. Its spiny fins caught on the jagged pane. Stuck halfway through the hole, it snapped its needle-like teeth, squirmed its scaly body, and pushed with its fins to propel itself toward the people huddled inside.

Vic went forward and pounded the fish's thick body with his pan, driving it onto a sharp crystal splinter from the broken window. The skewered piranha squirmed, its mouth agape, its big-finned body filling most of the window.

As they all held their breath and listened, the sounds of skittering, flapping, and chirping seemed to be dying down. The deadly swarm was finally moving on. Two straggling fish fell upon the dead piranha carcass pinned in the broken window frame, chewing out mouthfuls of stringy meat. Leaving the half-eaten body behind and their dead strewn on what remained of the deck, the last piranhas flew away, flapping into the night.

When the humans heard nothing for a few moments, Captain Dimas creaked open the door of the mangled cabin so they could look at what remained of the *Golden Walrus*.

Portions of the deck were splintered, the rails nicked, gouged, and chewed. The sails were completely gone. Only a few strands of gnawed rope lay curled about. In the distance, the colors of dawn began to tinge the horizon, but the ship was far from sight of land.

"We survived the flying piranhas," Sharif said, "but we cannot last long out here. We are stranded."

"This ship can no longer sail." Captain Dimas was grim. "If the merlons come now . . ." But he did not complete his thought.

23

WITHOUT THE HUNDREDS OF dead, slimy fish that stank up the deck, Vic would have considered it a beautiful daybreak. But the *Golden Walrus* had no sails, the masts were splintered, and even the steering oar was damaged. Their ship was adrift far from land out in a merlon-infested sea.

All of that spoiled the mood, regardless of the clear sky and colorful dawn.

Sharif's expression was somber, as if he knew exactly what he had to do. The boy from Irrakesh stood out on the deck and faced the sages and the forlorn-looking Captain Dimas. "With my carpet, I can race back to Elantya for help."

Captain Dimas said, "We will not last long in such a condition."

"Then I will urge them to bring their swiftest rescue ships." Sharif's olive eyes were serious and intense.

Saga Abakas scowled. "Go, then, young man! No telling how soon the merlons will come."

"Merlons? We barely survived the flying piranhas." Sage Snigmythya wrung her hands. "Oh, my! Most of our spell scrolls were damaged or used up. And there may be much worse in store for us. Much worse."

"Take someone with you," the captain said, looking at the bedraggled survivors. "You may need an extra set of eyes and hands. You never know what trouble you might run into, even in the air."

Though Sharif preferred to fly alone, he agreed. "I cannot concentrate on flying and solving problems at the same time."

Tiaret rubbed a cut on her arm as if it were no more than a mosquito bite. "That way at least a second person will be rescued, if something goes wrong here." Then, as if to make clear that she wasn't volunteering to go, the girl from Afirik added, "*I* will stay behind to defend the ship."

"Take Gwen," Vic suggested. "She doesn't weigh much, so she won't slow you down, and she's got pretty good reflexes." Kaisa's big pans lay where the fighters had dropped them, but Vic ruled them out as too heavy for Gwen to wield while seated. He grabbed one of the oars from the splintered deck. "Here, use this to whack anything that comes too close — you know, in case you get dive-bombed by pterodactyls or something. The handle will give you a bit of reach." He smiled at his cousin's surprised expression. "You *know* you want to go, Doc. Besides, you get seasick — no point in staying here and barfing on the merlons."

"Eww." Gwen wrinkled her nose. "Maybe I'll just get airsick."

Sharif retrieved his flying rug and his djinni sphere from the hold. Back on the debris-strewn deck, he unrolled his carpet and settled Piri's glowing ball in her mesh sack around his neck. The nymph glowed green with anxiety and uncertainty to see all the damage. Sharif's face was grim as he gestured brusquely to Gwen. "Make yourself comfortable behind me, but please do not fall off. That would cause complications."

Vic wasn't sure whether or not the boy from Irrakesh was joking. Gwen obviously didn't think it was very funny. "Then I'll do my best to keep things simple." She crossed her long legs and tried to sit securely on the thin rug with the oar on her lap. "Ready to go," she said. Clutching the gold tassels around the fringe, she fixed her gaze on Vic's face, and her expression told her cousin that she was not at all ready to leave him behind. Were those actual tears brimming in her eyes?

Sharif traced the embroidered patterns with his fingertips, as if he were gunning a fast car's engine, and the carpet lifted off the deck. Vic and the stranded students, crewmen, and sages waved up.

Gwen stared down at them, looking seasick again. "We'll be back with help as soon as we can! Just stay safe until then."

As the carpet streaked away, Tiaret stood solemnly next to Vic and Lyssandra, her teaching staff even more battered and stained than before. "I hope I have not used up all of my luck — I have already been rescued once."

"Luck had nothing to do with that," Vic answered. "It was our *skill* in finding you."

The young woman turned her amber eyes toward him. "Then I hope Sharifas has not used up all of his . . . skill."

Hundreds of dead flying piranhas lay in the sun as the day grew warmer. Wearing an expression of distaste, Vic and the other novs kicked them off the decks into the sea. The ocean around them was quiet . . . maybe too quiet.

Though he didn't know the exact distance to Elantya, Vic tried to calculate how long it might take for Sharif and Gwen to fly back to the island and for rescue ships to be sent out. "It'll be at least half a day before the flying carpet gets to Elantya, right?"

Lyssandra stared out at the sun-dappled water, as if she were listening to quiet thoughts from deep in the ocean. "Yes, and after that the Pentumvirate will tell the captains of any fast ships in the harbor to prepare for departure — at least a few more hours." She sighed. "Even with magical guidance and propulsion, and even if the rescue ships launch immediately, we cannot hope for any vessels to arrive sooner than two days from now."

Vic swallowed hard. That sounded like an impossibly long time. "What about the gliders we saw over the city? Does Elantya have any big aircraft? Any extra flying carpets stowed away somewhere?"

"No carpets, and no aircraft that could come so far out to sea." Her brow furrowed. "Maybe Sharifas will return with more spell scrolls — or he could carry a powerful sage to protect us."

Kaisa brewed a strong batch of medicinal greenstepe and served the restorative to the injured. Snigmythya and Abakas sat together in the open sun, scratched and bruised from their fight against the predator fish. Their once-fine robes were now stained and torn. The two sages bent over the few spells that had survived the piranha attack, salvaging tatters of paper and assessing how they could use the remaining magic for defense if — *when* — the merlons discovered the damaged ship. Lyssandra had also collected several simple spell scrolls that novs or apprentices had brought along.

Abakas held up a long scroll with dense and ornate writing. "Here's a complicated one, called a 'bubble of death.'" He pursed his lips.

"That sounds promising," Tiaret said.

"And ominous," Vic added. "What does it do?"

"Apparently, it steals all the air within a certain circumference, suffocating every living thing — including the spellcaster, I presume."

"Oh my," Snigmythya said. "We probably don't want to use that. Not that."

"Besides," Captain Dimas added, "it wouldn't help against undersea creatures that can breathe water."

Several of the written incantations were mere fire-lighting spells, the sort that any child or unskilled worker could read repeatedly before the imprinted magic was used up. Merlons would not like fire, but a flickering spark offered little protection against them.

In the meantime, Tiaret worked with Vic, Lyssandra, and other bedraggled students to scrounge makeshift spears and clubs from the wreckage. They stashed these and other weapons around the deck where they could be grabbed instantly, as soon as an attack began.

Captain Dimas ordered his men to patch as many holes as possible on the hull to keep the *Golden Walrus* afloat for as long as might be necessary. Shadowy forms in the water — sharks, or merlons? — made them loath to dive over the side and work below the waterline. From inside the hold, however, the sailors managed to patch the leaks well enough to keep the merlons from breaking through weak spots.

By mid-afternoon, clouds had begun to gather, turning the sky gray and blocking out the sunlight. A lookout on the skeletal mast shouted a warning, and Tiaret directed her tawny gaze out to where shark fins cut the water, circling closer. She gripped her teaching staff, her mouth set in a determined line.

Standing near the stern, Vic looked down at the waves and saw murky forms deep below, shaped more like sleek humans than fish. "Forget the sharks! Come and look at this!"

The merlons had arrived.

As if responding to his voice, one of the figures poked its head above the waves. Fine green and gold scales covered its body. The creature's face was flat, the nose little more than a nub to cover slits. Huge eyes flashed oily dark. Long flowing seaweed strands sprouted from the head where hair should have been. Gill slits like raw cuts ran down the side of the head, and a pair of circular membranes pulsed at the center of the forehead like a pair of flat, blind eyes.

"Ugly!" Vic said.

"Merlons," Lyssandra corrected him.

More scaly humanoids swirled around the stranded ship,

blinking in the cloud-filtered sunlight. Nictitating membranes folded over to keep the eyes wet. Sharp teeth flashed when the merlons opened their wide mouths.

Captain Dimas rushed the youngest students belowdecks with three sailors to serve as guards. Then, as he and his crew crowded to the edge of the deck with their makeshift weapons, the merlons closed in around the helpless ship.

At first Vic was more curious than afraid. He spotted both male and female merlons — slippery, lithe, moving in the water with a grace that reminded him of otters. All the merlons wore thick mother-of-pearl and coral necklaces, and heavy armor made from jagged shells. One of the creatures even had a pair of long, thick tentacles sprouting from its head like demonic horns.

Ignoring the captain's shouted threats, the merlons flexed their webbed hands and sank their claws into the hull planks. Now Vic saw the exotic weapons they carried: clubs with spiny sea urchins on the ends, perforated swords made of sharpened shells, spiral knives fashioned from what looked like narwhal horns.

Tiaret thrust one of Kaisa's wide frying pans into Vic's hands. "Viccus, prepare yourself to fight." Turning to the others, the girl shouted quickly, "The tympanic membranes on their foreheads are their ears. Sage Polup told me those are sensitive spots. Those, and the eyes! Hit them there if you can — but by any means possible, *hit them.*"

The scaly creatures began their attack.

24

NO MATTER HOW FAST the flying carpet went, Gwen feared it would be too long before emergency ships could reach the stranded *Walrus*. Her heart sank.

"I hate to leave them behind," she said. "We should be there to help them fight." She grasped the battered oar Vic had given her for defense, and hoped she wouldn't need it.

Sharif stroked Piri's glowing sphere and glanced back at her. "Out here alone in the open on a small carpet, we are far more unprotected than they are, Gwenya."

"If that's your idea of a comforting speech," Gwen said wryly, "you may want to take a few classes."

He flew onward as fast as the carpet could go. Inside her glowing sphere, the female djinni bent forward, extending tiny hands as if her magic could help the carpet go faster. Maybe it could. . . .

They cruised low over the ocean, flying for hours. Though the sea offered no landmarks, Sharif seemed confident of their route, reminding Gwen of Uncle Cap, who never stopped to ask directions. Gwen's blond hair whipped around in the moist, salty breeze. At any other time she might have enjoyed the freedom of this reckless flight.

The hypnotic, sun-dappled waves made her feel sleepy, but she didn't dare doze and risk falling off the carpet. Sharif concentrated, sometimes letting his olive-green eyes fall closed as his fingertips touched the carpet's golden maze of embroidery. Gwen envied his self-assurance. "Are you ever afraid?" she asked.

Sharif sat up straighter. "My people have a saying: a mind that knows no fear is the mind of a fool."

"So . . . is that a yes, or a no?"

Instead of answering directly, he said, "I cannot swim, yet we are flying less than a camel's height above the deepest water I have ever known. Can you guess my answer?"

The boy from Irrakesh went up a notch in Gwen's estimation. "I guess you're not as foolish as I thought."

He gave her a sardonic smirk. "You are most perceptive."

Unexpectedly, a choppy section of white froth appeared in the water ahead of them, as if a pot had begun to boil. "Sharif, what's that? Over there."

The young man glanced down before returning his concentration to the embroidered patterns. "A school of fish feeding."

"Must be an awfully large one."

Like popcorn popping, scaled bodies leaped out of the water, jumping from the roiling froth and flapping sharp wingfins. Within seconds, more than a hundred of the deadly fish took to the air and homed in on the soaring carpet.

Gwen felt a knot at the pit of her stomach. "It's the flying piranhas again!"

"The merlons must be controlling them. They have tracked us."

"How can they possibly be hungry after last night? They ate half the ship!"

"They are always hungry." Sharif hunched over and tried to go faster, but the flying carpet had already been racing along at top speed. He took the carpet higher, as well.

Gwen gripped her oar with both hands, ready to make a desperate stand. Her palms were sweaty, but the wooden implement was her only way of defending them. She would not let go of it.

Her skin crawled as the flying piranhas made their familiar buzzing sound. The ravenous fish streaked toward them like a pack of flying wolves, jaws snapping. They beat their wings and sprayed droplets of water, driving up to intercept the flying carpet.

Sharif tried to lift them higher as the creatures swarmed around them. Gwen fought off a flurry of flapping fins and snapping jaws. With her back to Sharif so that she had more room to move, she swung the oar to bat fish out of the air. Each time she felt a solid impact, a little victory sparked inside her, but she didn't take the time to keep score.

Gasping with the effort, Gwen struck down another piranha and another. The mindless fish displayed no sense of self-preservation, focused only on bringing the flying carpet down. Sharif flew upward at a steep angle, and the deadly fish kept up.

Five piranhas snapped at the dangling golden tassels, then began chewing the embroidered fabric, fraying the intricate threads. She whacked them with the flat of the oar, dislodging two fish, but others held on like shredding machines.

"They are damaging my carpet!" Sharif growled. "My father had it made for my brother Hashim, and then gave it to me after . . . Azric." He took one hand from the embroidery to claw at a chewing fish and ripped the creature away. As soon as he was distracted, though, the carpet dipped and wobbled. Sharif zigzagged to throw the fish off, urging the carpet to greater speed.

Piri's crystal globe strobed bright red as she angrily shook her tiny hands at the fish. The glowing djinni danced about in helpless fury, as if wishing her magic were more mature so she could help in the fight.

As it rushed through the air, the magical rug began to unravel. Gwen didn't know the magic or science that drove the carpet, but she guessed that if the material were too damaged, Sharif wouldn't be able to keep them aloft.

"Let go, stupid fish!" By the time she dislodged two clinging piranhas, seven more had darted in to strike. She saw one creature bite at the white fabric of Sharif's flowing sleeve. Before she could do anything, another flew into Gwen's shoulder-length hair, tangling in the strands like a panicked bat. She thrashed and shook it away.

Behind her, Gwen heard two of the sharp-toothed fish slam into Sharif's unprotected back. Somehow maintaining control, Sharif lifted his hand again from the embroidery patterns to knock them away. The flying carpet began to lose altitude. "Gwenya, you must fight them so that I can concentrate on the carpet, or we will crash."

She wanted to argue that she was doing her best, but he was right. She would have to do better or they might not survive, and her cousin, the crew, and the students on the *Walrus* would never be rescued. She turned at an angle so she could better cover herself and him. "Can you get higher, Sharif? They're flying fish — I doubt they can climb very far."

"I shall try. But there is a limit . . ."

The carpet tilted upward again so that Gwen had trouble holding on. She swung the oar, knocking a piranha away from Sharif's head. A fish snapped at the mesh bag that held Piri's eggsphere, but the djinni flared bright orange, disorienting the creature enough that Sharif managed to swat it away as they continued their mad flight.

Sharif pulled the carpet up at an even steeper angle. Some of the piranhas had fallen behind now and gave up the pursuit. But others, sensing that Gwen was poorly armed and vulnerable, converged on her. They snapped and tore at her hair. One nipped her cheek, drawing blood.

Gwen was astonished when six of the mindless fish acted in concert, cooperating as they clamped onto the flat blade of her oar. Together, they chewed and split the wood while at the same time they weighed it down with their heavy bodies.

She jerked the oar from side to side to fling them off, but the oar was overbalanced in her hands and her palms were slick with sweat and fish slime. The long handle slipped out of her fingers. Gwen lunged for it just as another flying piranha bit her left forearm. She yelped in sudden, helpless pain, and the oar went over the side of the flying carpet. Lost.

"No!" she shouted, making a last desperate grab — and lost her balance on the tilted rug. With a sickening lurch in her stomach, Gwen realized she was falling. Frantic, she reached up to grab for the tassels. Her fingers caught a few of the loose threads, but they snapped under her weight, and she dropped away from the flying carpet. Gwen tumbled toward the water far below.

Piranhas swirled all around her, intending to strip the flesh from her bones before she could hit the waves far below. But she was falling too fast. She couldn't even scream.

Falling.

Terror clamped its icy hand around her heart. Blond hair whipped around her face, and she knew she was going to crash into the water. After a fall from this height, the waves would feel as hard as cement. Gwen saw the water rushing toward her and knew what it must feel like to be a skydiver without a parachute.

Her logical mind suggested in desperation that in this strange world where magic sometimes worked, perhaps she could take flight and soar away. In a place where carpets and piranhas could fly, why not her? Gwen held out her arms, instinctively flapping and struggling. Air whistled through the rips in her Ocean Kingdoms sweatshirt.

High above, Sharif swooped the flying carpet around and lunged downward with a force superior to gravity's. He zoomed past her.

When Gwen saw him, she drew her legs up against her chest like a cannonball, hoping she could land softly. Sharif flew beneath, did his best to match her speed, and then rose just enough to scoop her up, like a collector catching a butterfly with a net. Gwen flopped with barely a bounce on the embroidered fabric.

"I never let a friend down," he said.

As soon as she was back aboard, he flew forward at a steep ascent, but the damaged carpet couldn't gain enough altitude to escape all of the fish. There wasn't enough power left. Gwen flattened herself out on the mangled purple rug, clutching the ragged edges and breathing heavily. Her heart was pounding too hard for her to say more than two words. "Thank you."

The flying piranhas chomped and buzzed. They continued to tear at the fabric, ripping more strands loose, so that a fringe of ragged threads dangled like a lion's mane in all directions.

The carpet wobbled, its flight path uncertain. Sharif hunched over in concentration, but so many of the stitched spell lines were unraveling, he could barely control his erratic course. The relentless predatory fish kept after them.

Though she could barely move her trembling body, Gwen forced herself to sit up again. With scratched and bloodied hands she slapped at more fish, protecting Sharif at all costs. They raced onward, too close to the choppy waves for Gwen, who could think only a few seconds ahead, just trying to survive.

She was not at all certain they would ever reach Elantya.

25

WITH THE SOUND OF a rattlesnake being pressed with a steam iron, merlons swarmed up the side of the *Golden Walrus*'s hull, raking the already-scarred wood with their long claws.

Before the first ones came over the rails, Tiaret was there to meet them. Her lioness eyes blazing, her face drawn in an expression of fiery determination, she looked fearsome enough to make a bull elephoar run in terror. "I see you need to learn my lesson again. Do some of you still carry battle wounds from when Master Kundu and I fought you?" She bared her teeth. "Perhaps I need to emphasize my point more."

Showing no hesitation after her previous ordeal, Tiaret attacked the enemy vanguard. As a merlon's head appeared over the deck rail, she swung her teaching staff. The polished stone cracked the first intruder in the center of its forehead. The merlon warrior let out a wet-sounding wail that thrummed from a bladder in its throat, and slipped over the side to splash back into the sea.

Vic tightened his grip on the cast-iron frying pan and swung it menacingly from side to side. "Time to kick some fish butt." He picked up a second pan from where it lay on the deck, holding one in each hand. He knew, though, that merlons were going to be a lot harder to knock down than a few flying piranhas.

The aquatic attackers edged forward, gurgling incomprehensible words. Using a defiant voice, Lyssandra shouted back at them in the same language. The merlons spun, surprised that she could speak to them. Instead of heeding the telepathic girl's threat, two of them charged her.

Seeing his friend in danger, Vic came at the merlon warriors with his iron pans, pounding one of the creatures on the back of its scaly head and hitting the other in the throat. His mother would have been proud of his swift, flowing reflexes. The first merlon reeled, grunted, and lurched toward him, brandishing a sea-urchin club. Before he could lose his nerve, Vic squeezed his eyes shut and swung again with all his might.

He surprised himself this time by striking the sensitive tympanic membranes in the middle of the merlon's forehead. The creature grabbed its head as if Vic had deafened it. With a hollow yowling sound, the creature stumbled on the slippery deck and fell through the broken guard rail and into the waves.

He grinned as he had a sudden idea. In order to hear vibrations underwater, the merlons' ear membranes had to be quite sensitive . . . and noises were a lot louder here above the surface.

As two more creatures approached, Vic held the two flat pans in opposite hands and brought them together like crashing cymbals. The metal clanged like a gong, sending vibrations all the way up to Vic's shoulders.

The echoing noise was deafening, and the merlons staggered backward as if Vic had hit them with a fire hose. He banged the frying pans together again, and the merlons reeled from the hideous din. Cringing and hissing, they finally dove overboard.

"Thank you, Viccus," Lyssandra said. "They did not seem interested in talking."

He stood beside her, sweating. "Sure thing. Unfortunately, you might have a chance to return the favor in just a few seconds." He held his pans in aching hands, ready to swing again in any direction. He was glad now for all of his *zy'oah* training. He wondered if his mother had ever been here in this world, and if she had even fought merlons herself. . . .

Six more hissing aquatic warriors climbed onto the deck. Tiaret spun like a whirlwind. The blows from her teaching staff sounded like a hammer striking wet meat. Yelling in anger, Captain Dimas and his crew also fought right and left, but the merlons kept coming.

After conferring, Kaisa and Snigmythya worked together. Snigmythya grabbed small pieces of splintered wood and hurled the kindling in the face of the nearest merlon, while Lyssandra's mother read a brief household spell from a tattered scroll. Though the pieces of broken wood were too small to cause direct harm, Kaisa's fire-lighting spell took hold with a vengeance. The timing was perfect. All the splinters burst into flames, and the flash of fire caused the merlon warrior to flail wildly. The long strands of seaweed hair smoldered and curled. Grinning at the surprisingly simple victory, the two women tried their trick again. Snigmythya threw more kindling at two oncoming merlons, and the ensuing flash drove the pair back.

Captain Dimas used his physical strength, throwing himself at one attacker. Ducking under a scalloped scimitar, he grabbed the enemy's arm. They wrestled, and Dimas tried to strangle the warrior, which proved ineffective on a creature with gills. With his free hand, the merlon raked claws down the captain's chest, ripping his shirt and his skin. Dimas gasped, lost his grip on the slimy scales, and reeled off-balance.

Too late, Vic shouted a warning, as a second merlon seized the captain's tunic, drove him to the rail, and threw Dimas overboard into the dangerous waters, where merlons quickly fell on him. Though the captain fought to the last, the enemy creatures dragged him under the water.

Horrified, Vic let his attention waver, and before he could react, a merlon wrenched one of his frying pans out of his grip. Vic yelped, twisted with a sudden fluid movement, and swung his other pan, landing a glancing blow on the merlon's head crest. The creature tossed the first frying pan over the side rail. Vic backed closer to Lyssandra, holding up the last pan like a club.

Seeing their captain fall, the rest of the *Walrus*'s crew snarled for vengeance. They already understood this was a fight to the death. The sailors did not give up, even though merlons continued to emerge from the water. The muscular men threw themselves into the fray, using clubs, lengths of metal chain, broken pieces of deck rail, the tip of a boat hook.

Kaisa and Snigmythya used their brief fire spell again, but they were running out of fuel and the flashes in the air were too small, designed primarily for lighting candles and torches, without enough heat to burn the merlons.

Vic saw a snapped yardarm rolling on the deck. Since he could no longer clang his pans together, he stopped the heavy pole with a foot, then shouted to Lyssandra. "Pick up the other end! The two of us can carry it!"

After looking at him in confusion, the petite girl touched his arm and understood what he intended. Holding the long beam between them, Vic and Lyssandra rushed at two aquatic warriors. The horizontal pole bowled over the attackers, knocking them back into the ocean.

"Another two down," Vic ranted. "About a million more to go. Right now, I sure would be happy to see the Elantyan cavalry."

"Elantya has no cavalry. We are a small island, without any horses —"

He gave her a wry smile. "You're supposed to be telepathic. How come you can't figure out what I mean?"

"Your head is full of strange cultural references. Right now I am too busy to sift through them all."

"I'll explain it later — once we survive," Vic said.

Sage Abakas rushed forward with a long, thin scroll. "The only remaining option is the bubble-of-death! But we cannot use it, since the merlons do not breathe air. It will suffocate us instead."

"Wait! That spell steals all the oxygen, right?"

"It takes away the breathable air, yes. It will have no effect on —"

Vic let out a heavy sigh. "Doesn't Elantya's great Citadel have a basic biology class! Fish live underwater, but they still need oxygen. Their gills filter it out of the water, just like our lungs filter it out of the air. I bet if you cast that bubble-of-death *into the water,* the merlons won't be able to breathe either!"

"Air? In water?" The sage did not seem to understand.

Tiaret swung the heavy end of her staff to crack a merlon's skull, then followed through to drive the sharp point into the ribs of another attacker. "Whatever you do, Sages, I suggest you do it soon. I . . . I would trust Viccus."

Abakas saw even more merlons swimming around the hull, and clearly realized that they would overrun the *Golden Walrus* soon. "I have always taught that one learns best by experimentation. . . ." He read the incantation in its incomprehensible magical language. As he finished the last phrasing, Abakas pointed at the sea around the ship and yelled "S'ibah!"

Suddenly the blue-green color changed, becoming black and still. A pool of swift death spread outward like a stain, sucking all the breathable oxygen from the sea. As the dark boundary swept past the swimming merlons, they struggled and choked. Rows of gill flaps on the sides of their heads opened and closed like gasping red mouths.

In a panic, merlon warriors tried to swim beyond the zone of death, but the black suffocation continued to spread. Unable to get out of range in time, one of the scaled warriors floated belly-up, then slowly sank again, dragged down by the weight of his shell armor and weapons. A pair of motionless sharks drifted up to take its place.

With no new attackers climbing up from the water, the battered and bleeding crew redoubled their efforts against the enemies on the stained deck. They killed two of the scaled warriors, and drove three more overboard into the deadly water.

Stillness descended like a sudden rain shower. In a moment of quiet, the survivors stood panting, ready for another attack that did not come. The merlons had been driven off for now, and the wrecked vessel was protected by the black zone of suffocating water.

Groups of silvery fish also floated to the surface, dead — innocent bystanders in this conflict. Vic felt sorry for the fish, since they had done nothing to warrant being slaughtered, other than swimming in the wrong place at the wrong time. But then, he thought grimly, Captain Dimas had also perished, murdered by the merlons — and *he* had done nothing to provoke this attack. None of the people on the *Golden Walrus* had done anything to earn this. Apparently the merlons wanted to kill all land-dwellers for no particular reason. The undersea people intended to destroy ships and keep the Elantyans away from the oceans.

"Uh, how long does that bubble of death last?" Vic asked Sage Abakas.

The mathematician looked befuddled, as if surprised that his spell had worked at all. "I am not certain. According to all the records I have read, such a spell is used only as a last resort. In the old wars, such sages always died. Only a few distant onlookers have ever lived to report on the spell's effectiveness."

"A dangerous spell to bring aboard a training ship," Lyssandra said.

Tiaret nodded. "We must use dangerous weapons now that we are at war."

"Actually, you see, I included the spell scroll by accident," Snigmythya admitted. "I thought it said Bubble of Flowers. I packed in a bit of a rush." She looked embarrassed. "A bit of a rush."

The sages stood together on the splintered and splattered deck, counting their injuries and their dead. In addition to Captain Dimas, two sailors had been killed. With Kaisa directing them, Vic, Lyssandra, and Tiaret tended the wounded as best they could.

"Now that it is over with, I must say that all of you did quite well," said Snigmythya as if grading a homework lesson. "Quite well. Students, teachers, and sailors. You proved your mettle. Very good, very good."

"A satisfactory trial run." Tiaret thumped her teaching staff on a patch of intact deck.

"*Trial* run?" Vic asked, surprised.

The dark-skinned girl stared at him. "Think of it as practice, Viccus. The merlons will be back. They know we are here and helpless."

Night was about to fall. "So . . . how soon do you suppose Sharif and Gwen can get to Elantya?" Vic asked.

"Not soon enough," Lyssandra said quietly.

26

WITH THE MERLONS DRIVEN away, the rest of that day and the long night were nerve-racking but uneventful. Tiaret prowled the deck, never allowing her concentration to waver. The students, sages, and sailors did not go more than a few minutes without looking over the side of the ship at the water, wondering when the attackers would return.

By morning, there was still no word from Sharif and Gwen. Vic's stomach twisted itself into knots of worry for his cousin. Logically, stranded out here with the merlons planning new ways to sink the damaged ship, he was in a lot more danger than Gwen. But he had already lost his mother, Uncle Rip, and Aunt Fyera. He wasn't sure when — or if — he would ever see his father again, not to mention Earth. He was in a strange world in the middle of a bizarre, unpredictable war. Gwen was all he had left, and she had been gone so long. . . .

By the next afternoon, a lookout on the tall mast pointed toward a storm brewing on the horizon. The wind picked up, blowing directly toward them. Vic smelled a metallic odor in the breeze. The storm did not seem natural.

Without Captain Dimas, the crew seemed disorganized, but Kaisa, who had been on more voyages than even the first mate, proved ready to make decisions. Her first decision was to put Tiaret in charge of security. Though the girl from Afirik was no older than most of the students, she had more experience in battle than anyone else onboard. Putting to use what she had learned in the Grassland Wars, Tiaret began planning immediately and collecting weapons. Kaisa assigned half of the crew to Tiaret and set the other half to work preparing the ship for bad weather.

Vic and Lyssandra worked together to lash down any remaining loose equipment and supplies. Tiaret came up behind them, moving as silently as a savannah cat. "We cannot avoid the storm, but we can prepare to fight. I have already posted guards belowdecks, in case the merlons try to break through the hull." She strode off to continue her work.

When they finished their preparations, the telepathic girl pointed out at the sea. Under the lowering gray skies, enormous writhing creatures rose and sank, their massive coils slithering over and around one another. Vic was fascinated in spite of himself. "Tell me those aren't —"

"Sea serpents? Yes. The merlons herd them and train them." She indicated the waters directly below them. "I am more concerned with what is swimming beneath the ship."

The bubble of death spell had dissipated, and the sea had

returned to its normal green-blue — which meant the *Golden Walrus* was once again vulnerable. Vic saw human-shaped shadows gliding deep, as if afraid to approach too closely. They made no threatening moves. Yet.

Uneasy, Vic said, "You've been on a lot of voyages. I guess you're used to stuff like this."

The telepathic girl shivered. "Not at all. This is hardly a . . . typical training voyage. I have never experienced such danger, except in dreams."

Vic let out a long breath. "Well, you look as cool as a snow cone to me."

She put a hand on his arm, read the meaning of his thought, then gave her head a rueful shake. "I am not cool right now. I know that you, and the others, consider me to be a . . . distant person. I have friends, but I keep myself apart."

"But why? You don't need to keep yourself apart from me."

She shook her head. "It is because of my telepathy. I see things in my dreams and in visions when I am awake, things I do not wish to see. It is easier not to become attached, to put up barriers, keep everyone at a distance. I am afraid, but I do not bother to show it anymore."

She crossed her legs on the deck, put her elbows on her knees, and held her head in her hands. Her dark copper curls fell forward, hiding her face from Vic. "Sometimes I cannot escape the images that come into my mind. But for now my thoughts are filled with what my eyes have recently seen — flying piranhas, sailors dying, storms, sea serpents, and attacking merlons."

Vic cast about for something comforting to say; in the end,

he settled for patting her awkwardly on the back. "Maybe you need to replace those images with something nicer." He kicked himself mentally. How stupid was *that*? They were in the middle of a crisis, didn't even know if they were going to live until the next day, and he was telling her to think pretty thoughts? Great way to make her feel better!

Vic was pleasantly surprised when she moved closer to him without turning her head. "Tell me about the place you come from, Viccus. It must be full of wonders, since you and Gwenya wish so much to return there."

"Not that your island is so bad, but it's not home. And my dad's there. I know I can't go back right now, but if he could be with us, like he wanted, maybe I wouldn't miss home so much."

Vic leaned toward her until their shoulders were touching, and he thought of the things he missed about Earth. "I guess we do have our share of wonders, now that you mention it. Nothing like the nifty magic system here in Elantya, mind you, but we've got some pretty neat stuff." He tried to think of his favorite kitchen appliances. "Like microwaves that can cook meals really fast, and they can make popcorn in three minutes. Everybody in the house can smell it!"

"Popcorn?"

He chuckled. Of course she didn't know what popcorn was. "Just try to pick up as much as you can while I talk." He described cars and jets and the amazing speeds at which they could travel.

She glanced at him. "Truly?"

"No kidding. And we have this power called electricity that

doesn't come from crystals or magic or mirrormills. We use it all sorts of ways, like to make our microwaves run, light our houses, play music, talk to each other from far away, send email, refrigerate foods so they don't spoil, even open and close doors. And we have lights you can turn on or off just by clapping your hands."

Lyssandra's shoulder was still touching his, and Vic could tell she was drawing the pictures from his mind as he spoke. The telepathic girl gradually began to relax. "And this eeleg-eeleg —"

"Electricity."

"Yes. Could it power a ship such as the *Golden Walrus?*"

"If the battery was big enough." Then he thought of something else she would enjoy hearing about. "Another cool thing we can do is tell stories with pictures made out of light. We watch the stories in movie theaters, or we can watch them at home on something called television."

"And these are also powered by eeleg-tricity?" Lyssandra asked.

"You catch on fast. We have lots of oceans, and I love to swim in them, especially during the summer. And we have mountains that are so high that they're covered with snow in the winter. You know snow — ice, frozen water?"

Lyssandra smiled. "My mother came from a world that has snow and ice for many months of the year. She has told me, and I have seen images, but I have never gone through a crystal door to visit it."

"In these mountains I like to go skiing or snowboarding."

He remembered family vacations he had gone on years ago — Uncle Rip and Aunt Fyera sitting by the fire in the ski lodge, his dad holding his mother's hand while they rode the ski lift to the top of the slope, his mother breezing down the mountainside without using any ski poles, Gwen struggling with her first skiing lesson, falling in the snow and trying to get up but only wallowing in deeper, his own early attempts at snowboarding.

Catching an echo of the images, Lyssandra seemed fascinated. "But how —"

"We strap smooth boards to our feet and slide down snow-covered hills."

"And these are powered by eeleg-tricity —"

"Nope. Skis don't need electricity to run. Just gravity. But sometimes we use electricity — well, engines, really — to get to the top of a slope. We sit in special chairs that are tied to a rope and a pulley, like the ones that raise a ship's sail. Once we get to the top, we can start the run back down."

Lyssandra looked strangely at him. "But if you wish to be at the bottom of the hill, why do you go to the top of it? Simply to slide down?"

"You're missing the basic concept here." Vic laughed, lost in this reverie about Earth and family. "Because it's *fun*."

Lyssandra's face grew troubled again. "Does your world have wars? Or are you safe from enemies like the merlons?"

"Oh, I think every place has wars, sooner or later." Vic decided the telepathic girl needed some serious cheering up. She had too many visions of terror swirling around in her head.

He would just have to provide some better images for her, so he hurried to add, "What if I tell you a story about a war you'll be very interested in?"

The quiet girl's eyes regarded him dubiously. "If you say so, Viccus."

Closing his mind to storms and sea serpents, merlons and flying piranhas, Vic slid his arm around Lyssandra's shoulders and concentrated. He hoped she would be able to see some of his favorite vivid pictures.

"This war starts a long time ago in a galaxy far, far away. . . ."

IN THE STORY, the hero had just entered a deep, dangerous trench and was attempting to destroy the villain's fortress. Evil henchmen chased the hero, intent on killing him. All seemed lost when —

Something hit the side of the ship with a *thump*.

Instantly alert, Vic and Lyssandra scrambled to their feet and looked over the rail. Tiaret came running. They were relieved to see that the noise had been caused by a broken yardarm that the churning waves washed against the ship.

Then Lyssandra gasped, and Vic's breath left him in a rush. Immediately below them, a merlon climbed onto the broken yardarm and floated there.

Tiaret sounded the alarm with a loud, piercing whistle. "Merlons!"

The unnatural storm was almost upon them. Cold droplets spattered from above. The ocean had turned a dark gray, and in it Vic could see the shadows of swimming merlons. The sea serpents were closer now, much closer, yet they hovered at a distance, waiting.

Shouts carried the word around the ship. All remaining students, sages, and crew took up whatever weapons they had and stood ready to fight. Just before the wallowing ship slid into the trough of a wave, Vic caught a glimpse of something large in the distance coming toward them. A sea serpent? Another school of flying piranhas? He couldn't be sure. A distinct chill was in the air. Rain began to fall.

At a signal from the merlon on the floating yardarm, scores of aquatic warriors surfaced and swam toward the ship. It looked like a final assault.

As the ship crested the next wave, several merlons began to scramble up the hull. With dread, Vic glanced out toward the additional looming threat of the sea serpents, but the rain fell harder, and he couldn't see the enormous creatures clearly. The raindrops were fat and cold and heavy, like a barrage of small water balloons. In less than a minute his hair and tattered clothes were drenched.

With a sound like two cars colliding, something large and heavy crashed against the side of the ship. The scaly, sharp-jawed head of a sea serpent rose up. In a flash of lightning he saw that armored plates were strapped to its head. The serpent had rammed the training vessel.

Another impact struck from the opposite side. Vic could see three more greenish sinuous serpents streaking in, guided by merlons. A sailor called from belowdecks, "That last one cracked our hull! We are taking on water."

"Get everyone out of the hold!"

"We are sinking fast!"

The *Golden Walrus* dropped into another trough in the waves, and the first merlon set foot on deck. As before, Tiaret welcomed it with her teaching staff. Reeling from the blow, the creature stumbled backward and grabbed a handful of Lyssandra's long wet hair, yanking her off her feet on the rain-washed deck. Vic's reflexes took over. Without thinking, he sprang forward and kicked the attacker soundly in the center of its forehead. With a high-pitched squeal, it let go of Lyssandra's hair. Tiaret smashed the merlon again with her teaching staff.

Another merlon appeared over the side of the ship, and Lyssandra snatched up a chunk of broken wood and clubbed the creature, while Vic pushed it backward. The merlon toppled into the ocean just as the *Walrus* floated to the top of another wave.

"Sheesh, why don't they just wait an hour?" Vic panted. "We'll all be down under the water soon enough." The sinking ship already tilted at an alarming angle.

"Look there!" Lyssandra pointed off into the storm.

Vic squinted through the punishing rain. A great *boom* echoed across the water, followed by another and another. Water ran into his eyes and mouth and streamed down his back. But what he saw made him laugh with relief.

"Look — they're here! They made it." Vic gave a joyful shout. In the distance, but getting closer by the minute, a group of Elantyan guardian galleys sliced like swift knives through the rough water. They were firing bright flashes, like magical cannons, at the sea serpents that drove toward the disabled ship.

At the prow of the lead galley stood Sharif and Gwen, waving to them. As the boom of cannon fire came closer, the merlons gave up the battle and dove back into the ocean. The survivors aboard the *Walrus* cheered.

"Well, I asked for the Elantyan cavalry." Vic grinned. "Looks like they've arrived."

27

AFTER WHAT THEY HAD ALL been through, Gwen was sure the voyage back to Elantya would seem like a vacation.

The Elantyan navy swiftly drove away the merlons lurking around the damaged *Golden Walrus*. Loud cannons scared away the sea serpents. When the weather sorcery no longer held, the rain and wind suddenly died down, and the storm clouds dissipated.

Weary novs, apprentices, sages, and crew were taken aboard Elantya's lead guardian galley, the *Bright Warrior* — and not a moment too soon. The damaged training ship wallowed and tilted from all the seawater rushing in through its broken hull. Splintered masts dipped toward the water. Shortly after the refugees and a few valuable possessions were taken aboard the galley, the *Golden Walrus* sank quietly beneath the waves, leaving only a spreading wake of debris on the water. Captain Dimas's crew watched with dismay as the vessel disappeared into the realm of the merlons. . . .

But at least the survivors were safe.

The rescue ship was roomy and well-lit, and their host Admiral Bradsinoreus saw to it that the bedraggled survivors received clean, dry garments. On deck, Elantyan sailors bustled about, turning the fleet around. Lyssandra's mother had already taken over the military kitchen, handing out mugs of mos ale and blackstepe and bowls of thick, hearty stew.

Gwen and Sharif sat at a wooden table and exchanged stories with their exhausted but exhilarated companions. The friends compared scratches, bruises, and cuts as if they were badges of honor. With a heavy sigh, Sharif spread out his now-ragged flying carpet, unwrapped a bundle of purple fiber and gold sun crystal thread from his pack, and began the painstaking process of repairing the damage the flying piranhas had done.

"Sheesh," Vic said, "I'm glad those munching fish didn't take a big bite out of you or Gwen."

Gwen shuddered. "Not that they didn't *try*." She watched Sharif's laborious needlework. "Are you sure you can fix that?"

"Fortunately, yes. I have no great skill at weaving, but all I need to do is sew any holes closed, and the magic in the carpet should finish the repairs — or so I am told. I have never tested its healing properties before. It has never been so terribly damaged before."

"I wish I could repair our clothes that easily," Gwen said. The cousins had finally had to give up their tattered Ocean Kingdoms clothes and dress like Elantyans. Gwen wore a drapey robe of soft white material that was gathered at the waist and came with a loose drawstring capri to wear underneath. A lavender cloak hung over her shoulders. Vic wore similar garments in cream and turquoise, though they were not gathered at the waist.

Gwen pointed to his toga. "I've got a pair of earrings that would be really cute with your dress."

Vic punched her lightly on the arm. "Okay, but I refuse to wear high heels."

In spite of the joking, Gwen missed their tee shirts. She felt as if she were leaving a part of herself behind. With each day, each amazing or frightening experience here, her life was changing. The Elantyans welcomed the two, and their new friends had — literally — put their lives on the line for them. But she feared her life would never be normal again.

GREAT CROWDS GREETED THE ships' arrival back in the Elantyan harbor. Families and friends of those who had been on the teaching voyage gathered on the docks. The five members of the Pentumvirate stood at the forefront of the crowd, wearing their bright robes.

"We rejoice that so many of you are still alive," said Etherya, the Vir of the Arts and leader of the council. The white-robed woman had dark hair caught up in ringlets high at the top of her head. "And we grieve for those who have died."

"They were murdered by our enemies!" said Helassa, the

stern Protective Vir. Anger colored her cheeks as red as her robe. "First Captain Argo's ship, and only a few days later, the *Golden Walrus*. The merlons have declared outright war."

Sage Polup clanked toward the end of the docks in his steam-powered walker. "The merlons have come to hate all land-dwellers and resent the very existence of this island in their oceans. It grieves me to know that I am the only anemonite ever to escape their bondage." Gwen watched the floating jellyfish creature inside the head tank. She could understand Polup's distress, knowing his people were held captive while he remained free. "Even now, my enslaved people are being forced to create new weapons for the merlons."

"We must never let down our guard," Helassa warned. "We must build up Elantya's defenses." Sages Abakas, Snigmythya, and Admiral Bradsinoreus left with the Pentumvirate.

Lyssandra walked down the ramp with an arm around her mother. Gwen felt her throat tighten when a burly bearded man shouldered his way through the crowd accompanied by a young boy with shoulder-length coppery hair — presumably the telepathic girl's father and little brother. They ran forward to meet each other with massive bear hugs. Lyssandra only had time to glance back at Gwen and Vic before her family swept her into the crowd.

Reaching the crowded docks, the cousins stepped to one side and watched as novs, crew, and apprentices were welcomed back with open arms. Although they were glad to be safe in Elantya, this joyful homecoming was a sharp reminder to Gwen that *they* were not home.

As the docks began to empty and the celebration died down, Gwen had an acute sense of homesickness. She and Vic could always return to their quarters in the Citadel. Sharif and Tiaret would be there, but they were friends . . . not *family*. She wished at least Uncle Cap could be with them.

Dr. Pierce had wanted to send them here, to keep them safe. Now that Gwen had seen the deadly merlons attack a helpless training ship, she wasn't sure she or her cousin were going to be any safer in Elantya.

Unless they could find Vic's mother, somehow. Or unless they found a way to bring Uncle Cap through the crystal door to Elantya.

But they had no idea where to start.

28

THE NEXT DAY, WELL-RESTED, the group of friends bounded up the path to the laboratory and its tower, which was now overgrown with thick grapevines from the spell Rubicas had read.

Inside, the lab was abustle with activity. The old sage and his assistant seemed to be everywhere at once. From time to time, one of them would call out a number or a name. The other would agree, and Rubicas would hurry over to a high lectern carved out of marble. Without bothering to perch on the stool behind the writing table, the sage picked up a stylus, dipped it into an inkpot, and scribbled a line or two on a parchment scroll. Apparently, they had not stopped working on their ideas in all the time since the companions had set off on their training voyage.

While Vic and his friends waited for Rubicas to notice

them, Orpheon gave a warning shake of his head. The bearded sage held up one finger in their direction, as if to press it against their lips for silence, then dashed back to his writing desk and skritched furiously at the scroll.

After what seemed like an eternity, the sage finally lowered his finger. He stared at the scroll a minute longer, then smiled up at the visitors. "Welcome back. I'm glad to see you survived. All of you."

"It was a close call," Tiaret said.

Vic walked to the wall aquarium and stared at the four aquits swimming about. Remembering everything the *Walrus* had been through, he said, "Now I can see why these little guys think the open sea is too dangerous."

Orpheon glanced sidelong at the tank, and a brief grimace flashed across his face. He stayed pointedly on the other side of the room.

The sage tugged at his white beard, and his gray eyes lit with enthusiasm. "Hmm, while you were gone, we had a breakthrough — a new sort of spell that could well protect Elantya. Would you like to see? It is only a small spell so far, you understand. It may take months, even years, to expand it sufficiently, but it has the potential to shield Elantya from all attackers."

"Congratulations!" Vic said.

"That is a bit premature," Orpheon muttered. "We have not tested it yet."

"Hmm, testing. Would you like to assist us? It should prove quite enlightening," Rubicas said. The companions quickly agreed. He picked up the scroll, with its silvery ink still wet, and strode to the center of the chamber.

Sharif and Vic moved forward, jostling each other in their eagerness to see, but Orpheon said, "Stand back. I will let you know when you can participate."

They were even more confused when the handsome apprentice handed Gwen a curved scimitar, then gave a javelin to Vic, throwing stones to Lyssandra, and a sling and several sharp-edged crystals to Sharif. Tiaret already had her dragon's eye teaching staff. Orpheon showed them where to stand so that the five of them were spaced evenly apart facing the master sage.

Looking at his sharp javelin, Vic asked, "So, uh, this is the first time you've ever used this spell?"

"Yes. Let us see if we succeed." Facing his armed helpers, Rubicas began reading from the scroll. It took almost a full minute for the sage to finish reciting what he had scribbled down. He blinked. "Well? Did it work?"

"I don't see anything," Gwen said, "so I would deduce that the spell was a flop."

Rubicas raised a bushy white eyebrow. "Hmm. The eyes see only what may be seen."

Vic muttered to Lyssandra beside him, "I hope that's not one of Elantya's best proverbs — I'm pretty sure we all knew that."

The sage's lips curled in amusement. "Very well, then you and your companions may join me on this side of the room now."

Curious and confused, they all walked toward Rubicas. Vic

had taken no more than three steps when he smacked into something solid and unyielding. He yelped, then reached out to feel an invisible barrier. "Cool! It's a forcefield, like in *Star Trek*."

"A shield, yes," Rubicas said.

"Oh, now I can see it," Gwen said, sounding embarrassed for having missed something so obvious. "It's clear but all shimmery." Intrigued, Tiaret tapped the barrier with the dragon's-eye stone at the end of her teaching staff.

Vic rubbed his bruised nose. "Yup. It's like dad always says about problems — you just have to look at the situation from the right angle."

"Try your weapons. See if you can touch me."

Gwen poked at the shield with the point of the scimitar while Vic prodded it with his javelin. Tiaret showed a great deal more enthusiasm as she swung her teaching staff, clearly confident she could halt the blow in an instant if something went wrong. The dragon's-eye stone bounced off the shield.

"Excellent," Rubicas said, standing behind his protection with his arms crossed. "Marvelous."

Lyssandra's throwing rocks had no more effect. After placing a crystal in his sling, Sharif swung vigorously and let the projectile fly directly at the sage. It ricocheted off the shield and hit the nearest wall before falling to the floor, just missing the bank of aquariums. The languid glow eels shone brighter in alarm. The aquits swam away, miming scolding gestures.

Looking smug and satisfied, Orpheon hurled a heavy crystal against the invisible wall with all his might. The assistant genuinely looked like an enemy trying to hurt the master sage, but the spell field rebuffed his attack.

Now convinced he would cause no real damage, Vic stepped back to throw his javelin, which struck and clattered harmlessly to the floor. Gwen took a firm two-handed grip on her scimitar and swung it harder, again to no effect. The blow sent a jolt up her arms, and she dropped the thrumming blade.

"Splendid. I believe this spell will be more than capable of defending us from merlons!" Rubicas raised his hands and said, "A'o'ah, S'ibah." The shield dissolved. He walked toward them, and nothing stood in his way.

While the sage seemed exceedingly pleased with what he'd accomplished, Orpheon was more of a wet blanket, as usual. "This small test scroll was extremely complex. Expanding the shield into a dome with an effective radius will be a much more difficult task."

The old sage scratched his left eyebrow. "Hmm, there must be a way. If we make use of large resonating lenses . . . or amplification rods. Or both! Yes, that is indeed the necessary next step."

Lyssandra's cobalt-blue eyes lit up. "Master Rubicas, several of those are kept in the storage tunnels beneath the city. My father was in charge of the Elantyan anniversary celebration two years ago. I remember where he put them and could get them for you right away."

"Children should not be going down to the —" Orpheon began.

"Excellent, Lyssandra." Ignoring the sour warning, Rubicas set the spell scroll aside on his work table. "We have no time to lose. You will need all your friends to help you carry the

resonating lenses and amplification rods — and be careful."
He grabbed his assistant's sleeve. "Come, Orpheon. We must
speak to the Pentumvirate immediately. This could be our
best chance to save Elantya."

Leaving the draft spells on the table, they all rushed out of
the laboratory.

29

GWEN FOUND THE CAVERNS that riddled the foundation of Elantya fascinating. The entrance to the island's underground passages was not far from Rubicas's tower, and Lyssandra led the way down a long, chilly tunnel.

"Cool secret passages." Noting hundreds of storage alcoves carved into the rock wall, Vic joked, "Not enough cupboard space up above?"

The telepathic girl explained, "We store food and supplies here, as well as seeds and roots for our garden plots. The temperature in these caves keeps perishables from spoiling as quickly and keeps our wines and ales cool."

"Like an old root cellar," Gwen said.

"Two years ago we had a grand Elantyan celebration. My father was in charge of the light show, and afterward he stored the equipment out of the way in the deepest tunnels. He doubted the components would ever be used again, but it would have been wasteful to discard them. He will be very pleased that his foresight can help Sage Rubicas now."

As they continued, the tunnels became narrow, cramped, and dark. Tiaret prowled along, wary of what might come out of the shadows. Lyssandra felt along the wall and exclaimed in annoyance, "Tunnel workers are supposed to leave suntips here to light the way. Every suntip is gone!" To forestall Gwen's question, she added, "A suntip is a slender wand with a chip of embedded sun aja. We use them for portable light." In vain, she felt in another of the alcoves. "Who would take them all?"

Sharif stepped forward. "Piri, it is your time to shine." A warm buttery glow instantly filled the tunnel from the djinni's globe.

Vic got out his keychain and turned on the LED flashlight. "It's not as bright as Piri, but this should help. Sharif can lead, and I'll bring up the rear."

"These passages have been here since the rising of Elantya," Lyssandra explained. "Many smaller tunnels connect to each other, forming an extensive maze that almost no one knows completely. Some are used by maintenance workers to move quickly from one part of the island to another. A few branches simply terminate in dead ends."

Tiaret stopped suddenly. "This side tunnel looks freshly excavated." Vic shone his flashlight. The unexpected passage abruptly continued downward at a steep angle, its walls and floors strangely smooth and slippery.

Lyssandra's forehead wrinkled. "We are deep in the seldom-used passages, near where my father's equipment was stored. There should have been no new digging."

Sharif raised the glowing globe to cast a warm, scintillating light all around them. "Then we had better investigate." As they descended into the sloping tunnels, the rock provided barely enough traction to keep from sliding. The passage quickly widened to a low-ceilinged cavern twice the size of Uncle Cap's solarium.

"We must be at sea level by now," Gwen determined, looking around.

Lyssandra shook her head in confusion. "This passage was not on any map or diagram. I did not know Elantyans were digging additional tunnels."

"Could this be part of Vir Helassa's new defense plan?" Sharif suggested. "Tunnels to get to the merlons, perhaps?"

The close, thick air smelled of fish and rotting kelp. At the far end of the chamber they were shocked to find a pool of water that rippled and lapped, as if from ocean currents. Sharif submerged Piri's globe in the mysterious pool, and her glow gradually changed to the orange of agitation. Through the water, the friends could clearly see an undersea passage leading away from the bedrock of the island and out toward the deep sea.

Vic cleared his throat. "At the risk of stating the obvious, it seems like this passageway would make it easy for merlons to get *in*."

"I agree with Dr. Einstein here," Gwen said.

In alarm, Lyssandra pointed to some large objects stacked near the tunnel entrance: thick transparent cylinders and mirrored parabolic crystals like satellite dishes. "Those are the amplification rods and resonating lenses Sage Rubicas needs. Someone has moved them here!"

Sharif shone Piri's light around the grotto. Numerous sacks of grain, crates of preserved food, and heavy bags of crystal dust had been dragged down to the rocky chamber. "The merlons appear to be stealing our supplies."

"Now that's a low blow," Vic said.

With narrowed eyes, Tiaret scanned the chamber, assessing defense strategies. "The Pentumvirate did not consider that the enemy might approach from beneath the island." She studied the watery passageway. "Observe how smoothly the rock was dissolved. It appears that the merlons used powerful sorcery."

Lyssandra knelt at the edge of the pool. "If the merlons did this, they must have sent diggers ahead to prepare the way. Their magic is most effective where the water touches the rock." She shook her head. "We always assumed they would come at us from the sea. We did not worry about the ground beneath our feet."

The girl from Afirik growled, "A merlon invasion force is probably even now ready to slip into our city. They mean to overwhelm us."

Gwen drew a deep breath. "Then it's up to us to warn the city. Let's get some guards down here, and construction workers to seal up that pool." She jumped back from the edge, startled. "Wait, I saw something down there! Shadows shaped like —"

"Merlons!" Vic finished for her.

In a gush of bubbles from below, aquatic warriors streaked upward like scaly otters. A pair of amphibious men burst out of the pool passage with a heavy splash, surging up like monstrous jack-in-the-boxes.

Gwen was closest to the sacks of powdered crystal dust. In a defensive reflex, she yanked a bulky bag from the moist floor and threw the heavy weight at the nearest merlon, which bowled the creature into its companion. The sack burst, spraying the glittering powder over both scaled warriors.

Two more merlons came up behind them, pushing the first pair out of the way. From the pool many more amphibious attackers slithered up.

"We've got to get out of here!" Vic shouted. "Call for help!"

"We must stop them from getting into the city." Tiaret stepped forward and began to make a good accounting of herself with the teaching staff.

Beside her, Lyssandra kicked open one of the wooden crates, splintering the sides. Crowded inside were sealed jars of food, which she began to throw at the merlons. One hard container smacked a creature on its sensitive tympanic membranes. Other jars bounced off greenish scales and shell-plate armor. Gwen joined her, and both of them began pummeling the invaders. Jars shattered, and syrupy preserves splattered the hissing merlons.

"Hey, Doc — I've got an idea!" Vic shouted. He turned and

bolted as fast as he could up the passageway from which they had come, shining his LED flashlight ahead of him. Just like that, he was gone.

"Taz! Where do you think you're going?" Her cousin raced out of sight up the slippery, narrow passage toward the surface. "If we don't stay and hold them off, who will?"

Sharif tucked Piri's glowing ball into the mesh pouch to free his hands. The merlons cringed from the bright light. The boy from Irrakesh picked up another sack of crystal dust and used all his strength to swing it forward at another dripping creature that emerged from the watery passage. The merlon slashed with a scalloped sword, and the sack split open, spraying dust across its scales and into its face. The hard crust clung to the merlon, covering its eyes with grit. The blinded creature dropped into the pool to wash itself off.

But more merlons emerged, far more than the small group of defenders could hope to stop.

After dragging Tiaret from the fray, Gwen, Lyssandra, and Sharif pulled the crates together to form a barricade in front of them, blocking the narrow passage up which Vic had just fled. Gwen looked over her shoulder, irritated with her cousin, but soon the merlons' clawing against the crude barrier demanded all of her attention. Sea-urchin clubs and shell-tipped spears jabbed at them through the stacked crates. They would tear through the blockade before long.

A merlon warrior slashed with a narwhal-horn dagger, and Gwen deflected it with a crate lid she had torn free to use as a shield. "I wish we'd brought some spell scrolls with us — even a crystal-lighting spell."

Switching languages, Lyssandra echoed the bubbly sounds of the merlons. The creatures paused as if taken aback, glared at her, and then advanced with renewed vigor.

"What did you say to them?" Tiaret asked.

Lyssandra gave a faint smile. "I told them that if they did not leave, we would make them into a fish stew."

"I don't think they found your threat convincing," Gwen said. A merlon knocked a crate aside and dove toward her, but she ducked with her *zy'oah* training made her duck and hit it in the forehead with the crate lid. She desperately wanted to know where Vic had gone. Had he just run away? She didn't think her cousin was a coward. She had seen him battle flying piranhas, and he'd put up a good fight on the *Golden Walrus*. What other explanation could there be?

Removing the eggsphere, Sharif faced the encroaching merlons. "Piri, I need you to do something for me." He glanced down at the nymph djinni. "It is difficult and dangerous, but I know you can do it."

Flickering orange, the tiny female nodded, understanding what he wanted her to do. With pride, Sharif held the sphere toward the hissing merlons, who worked to shove aside the crate barricade.

Then, inside the crystal ball, the djinni's tiny feminine form crossed her arms and legs, and her hair rippled, crackling with red electricity. Sharif shouted, hoping their aquatic attackers couldn't understand Elantyan. "Everyone, close your eyes!"

Gwen instinctively did as her friend told her. Lyssandra and Tiaret both put a forearm over their faces.

A powerful burst of white light shot through the chamber, so intense it burned even through Gwen's tightly closed eyelids. Startled, the merlons hissed and roared. When Gwen opened her eyes again, she saw bright spots as if she had looked directly into a camera flash. The blinded merlons were reeling. Their scaled, moist bodies smoked from the intensity of the flash.

Exhausted and drawn, Sharif folded his shaking legs and sat on the rocky floor. Inside her eggsphere, emitting a barely visible yellow glow, Piri appeared to be unconscious, as if she had used all of her power in the single blast of light.

The chamber was now dim, but Gwen and her companions were not dazzled as the merlons had been. "Come on, we've got to use the advantage!" She climbed over the barricade, snatched one of the sea-urchin clubs from a stunned merlon, and swung it like a baseball bat. The impact against the attacker's armor knocked them both in opposite directions.

The blinded creatures were beginning to grope their way back to their feet. Lyssandra played tug-of-war with one of the creatures, trying to yank its spear free. Tiaret jabbed with the pointed end of her staff. Sharif, still too weak to fight, stayed behind the barricade.

Gwen knocked one of the off-balance warriors into the pool, from which even more merlons were emerging. Scrambling back over the barricade with Tiaret and Lyssandra, Gwen knew they couldn't last long against such an army. They should have called for help from the first moment they saw the merlons. Maybe that was what Vic had done! He could be returning any second now with the full Elantyan guard.

From behind, she heard skittering, sliding footsteps as someone ran down the passage. "Here I come!" Vic slipped, caught his balance against the wall, and then continued to run headlong, shining his LED flashlight in front of him. Her cousin barely slowed as he bounded into the chamber. Gwen caught his arm and spun him to a halt.

Ahead of them, the hissing merlons angrily tore at the weak barricade.

"Lyssandra! I need you." Vic clutched a rolled piece of parchment in his hand. The telepathic girl staggered away from a merlon's thrusting scimitar, and Vic caught her before she could fall. "Here, you've got to use this! You're the only one who can!"

Lyssandra took the scrap of paper. "What is this?"

Vic held up his miniature flashlight, so she could see the scroll. "It's the shield spell Sage Rubicas was working on. He left it on his lab table when he and Orpheon went to see the Pentumvirate, so I grabbed it." He panted. "I just didn't think it was so far away!"

Gwen looked at her cousin, surprised and pleased. "You stole that spell from Rubicas? It was just a rough draft."

"Sure, but we saw that it works, right? Oh, and I think help is on the way. I sounded an alarm, sort of."

"How could you sound an alarm?"

"Well, I snatched the spell and ran. Somebody yelled after me, but I couldn't stop. I yelled, 'Sound the alarm and follow me.' Guards were chasing after me when I came down here." He grinned. "They should be here any minute."

Gwen shook her head. "I suppose that's one way of doing it."

Lyssandra held up the draft scroll and said in dismay, "I cannot read this! Only some of it is in Elantyan. Parts of it are in the ancient language. I am not sure if —" Then, steeling herself, she began to read the words aloud, stumbling with her pronunciation.

Gwen helped Sharif move behind the copper-haired girl. Tiaret waited, ready to fight if the spell didn't work. Several merlons extended their clawed, webbed hands and tore at the weakening barricade. Other aquatic warriors smashed it with their shell-edged swords and sea-urchin clubs.

As soon as the girl's strengthening voice finished the incantation with a firm "S'ibah!", a shimmering wall like solidified water stretched in front of the tunnel opening, forming a translucent skin just as the warriors broke through the barricade.

The magical shield blocked the surprised merlons. The enemy warriors threw themselves against the invisible wall, jabbing with their undersea weapons. But the spell barrier held.

"You did it, Lyssandra! I knew you could!" Vic looked at Gwen and gave her a cocky grin. "Pretty good idea, huh? Figured that out myself."

Gwen punched him in the shoulder. "I didn't think you would just run away."

"Viccus has proved his bravery before," Tiaret said.

"Sheesh, I couldn't stand around and explain. Somebody would have argued, and then we would have had a whole long discussion, and then you would have listed at least five reasons why you should go instead of me. That's just for starters." He gave a huff. "I don't think I've ever run so fast!"

In a surprising surge of emotion she hugged Vic. "One way or another, Taz, we're going to help the Elantyans win this war. Then they'll have tons of time to help us bring your dad here."

Vic grinned. "And find my mother."

Helpless behind the barrier, the merlon intruders snarled. Gwen looked to Lyssandra for a translation, but with a wry smile, the telepathic young woman shook her head. "You would not want to know what they are saying."

"Of course I would," Gwen said. "I want to know *everything*."

"They said that our entrails will become necklaces for their children, and —"

At last a loud clamor came from the tunnels behind them, and a breathless Rubicas, Vir Helassa, and numerous Elantyan guards appeared carrying suntips and weapons.

"I was hoping you'd all get here soon," Vic said.

At the sight of the merlons, Vir Helassa looked simultaneously shocked and filled with righteous fury. "They now dare to attack us from within our own city?" She scowled. "What is holding them at bay?"

"A force shield," Gwen said. Sharif, mostly recovered now, held up Piri's brightening eggsphere to illuminate the frustrated creatures behind the barrier.

"Ah! Not bad for a work in progress." Rubicas saw the scroll in Lyssandra's hand. "May I have my spell back, young lady?"

She gladly gave him the parchment. "I think the shield is fading already."

"I will reinforce it. Precise pronunciation is critical." Rubicas read the spell again, thereby doubling the barrier. With the shield holding, he walked slowly forward, extending the parchment, which pushed the impenetrable barrier in front of him like a slow battering ram, forcing the merlons back.

Helassa crossed her arms over her chest and watched with a look of resolve on her face. She put a guard on either side of the master sage and sent others to fetch engineers and materials to seal the off the breach in Elantya's defenses.

While Helassa continued snapping orders, Rubicas and the two guards took several more steps into the chamber, and the shield drove the invaders backward. Merlon snarls and frustrated shouts grew louder, until finally they were all crowded back to the watery trapdoor. Seeing no alternative, the thwarted invaders plunged into the sinister passage and swam away one by one.

The last merlon stood with his clawed feet planted on the rocky floor. He bowed backward, fighting the spell barrier, resisting to the last moment. Finally, still brandishing his shell scimitar, he dropped with barely a ripple into the watery passage.

30

WITH THE MERLON INCURSION foiled, the Elantyans pulled together. The once-passive undersea dwellers had become a very real threat — to all Elantyans, not just the sailors and fishermen. The entire city was now on high alert, and everyone made emergency preparations.

The Pentumvirate held two more war councils to determine how the island republic could best fight against the undersea enemy. All sages were told to prepare spells, while Vir Helassa commanded the home guard to distribute conventional weaponry that anyone could use.

All night, patrols marched along the shore and up and down the steep streets, watching for merlon spies slithering through the shadows. All citizens were ready to raise an alarm if they saw any sign of sea serpents, brewing storms, or flying piranhas. The Elantyans would not underestimate the danger again.

Surrounded by stinking fumes and hot furnaces, the anemonite Sage Polup clanked about in his chemistry labs, working to re-create an explosive chemical mixture that he and his people had discovered near the bases of submerged volcanoes.

In the well-lit Cogitary, historians studied ancient scrolls to glean all that was known of merlons from previous encounters. For millennia, Elantyans had assumed that the uneasy peace would hold between the two races. Obviously, though, something had driven them to increased violence, and the merlons had been making plans for quite a while.

Gwen offered to assist Sage Rubicas and Orpheon through the long night as they worked without rest on expanding and improving the defensive shield spell. Her cousin and their friends would be getting up early to keep watch as the fishing boats set sail at dawn. No one doubted the merlons would return soon, and in full force.

Inside the laboratory chamber, Gwen fed the fish, glow eels, and aquits, then lit three extra sun crystals to keep the cluttered room bright throughout the darkest hours. The warm, cheery illumination reflected off the pale stone walls, the aquarium tanks, the skylight, and the half-finished inventions stored on shelves. All other projects had been put on hold for now.

Orpheon was not pleased to have Gwen there "interfering." He reminded her — and Rubicas — of her "carelessness" with the aja crystal array in opening a window to Earth. When she defended herself, the assistant only scoffed at the suggestion that someone had sabotaged her carefully measured array. "You have a very high opinion of your own importance, Gwenya, if you think merlon spies would go out of their way to trouble you or your cousin!" He laughed out loud. "I do not need to look for a dire conspiracy when simple sloppiness is a more likely answer."

"Hmm, I could use some assistance," Rubicas said, "if you two are quite finished annoying each other? As Orpheon is so fond of reminding me, this spell work has repercussions for the defense of all Elantya. We should not allow ourselves to be distracted by other things."

"Perhaps we should approach this tomorrow in daylight, when we are all fresh," Orpheon suggested, not looking at all contrite. Oddly, he had been dragging his feet during much of the work.

Gwen hurried to the sage's table. "I'm ready to work as long as you need me, Master Rubicas." She used a special silky rag to polish the smooth crystal surface of a resonance lens. The concave mirror-crystals and the shining rods certainly looked impressive. They had to be flawless if they were to channel the spell across such a broad area. After driving the merlon infiltrators from the tunnels, she and her friends had carried the lenses and amplification rods up to the sage's laboratory. If they had gone searching for the stored equipment even one day later, the merlons would have dragged the components under the sea. Had they known somehow that Rubicas would need them?

Since the draft of the shield spell had worked so well against the merlons, the bearded sage was even more enthusiastic about his ideas. The principle had been proved. Gwen couldn't imagine any logical reason why the protective barrier could not be expanded to cover a wider region.

Rubicas stared at the scraps of parchment and incomplete spell scrolls. He hummed to himself, deep in concentration. "Hmm, I have had another thought. If we cannot expand the shield enough to protect the whole island, maybe we can overlap numerous smaller shields, like the links in chain mail."

Orpheon glanced up in alarm. "That would require barrels of aja crystal ink to create scroll after scroll! And an army of talented sages to copy the spells, then read them in the complex old language —"

"It seems you are being frugal in the wrong places. No one will complain about the expense or difficulty if it works."

Rubicas scribbled one segment after another, modifying lines and punctuation, rolling the sounds of the arcane words in his mouth before daring to utter them aloud. Gwen figured he was just practicing. She finished polishing the new components, then helped arrange the numerous versions of his spell, keeping a log of each effort. Rubicas himself had never been so organized.

After he recited each incantation, Gwen, Orpheon, and the sage checked to see the results. When a casting flickered and failed, he crumpled the parchment, then picked up a new sheet, trying out variations on his original spell. Gwen retrieved the discarded spells and kept them in a separate stack, never knowing when Rubicas might need them again.

Letting out a long, discouraged breath, Rubicas scribbled

out a set of symbols. "Hmm, good thing I caught that one —
such a choice of words could have led to disaster."

Outside, Gwen could hear the crashing surf and the tower's
grapevines rustling in the breezes. Night birds flew around,
gobbling moths that were attracted by the bright light spilling
through the open windows, snatching a last snack before
sunrise. In narrow alleys and wide thoroughfares below, the
Elantyan streetcrystals remained lit. Uniformed guards pa-
trolled the cobblestoned byways.

Orpheon occupied himself, but he seemed unusually tense.
Gwen decided he must be very tired. The small water clock
in the corner trickled with a gentle, soothing sound that
apparently helped Rubicas concentrate; at the moment, it
was making Gwen sleepy. By now it was only an hour or so before dawn. Even the sage started yawning and rubbing his eyes.

Scowling, the apprentice pushed himself away from his
table and crossed his arms over his chest. "Look at you, Master Rubicas! Barely able to keep your eyes open. Why not stop
for now? At least take a nap until sunrise."

"Hmm, not yet," Rubicas insisted. "I am not finished."

"If you overtax your abilities, Elantya may lose you entirely. And without sleep, you risk making mistakes in your
spell. Why not rest? A few hours will make no difference."

"Relax and rest, eh? A fine meal and a nap?" Rubicas looked
down at his unfinished spell and all the near-misses he had
crumpled and tossed aside. "I am certain the merlons would
appreciate that!" He cracked his big knuckles. "No, Orpheon,
this is too important. We can put up with bleary eyes and
headaches until I am finished and Elantya is safe."

Gwen couldn't understand why the dark-haired apprentice constantly raised problems. Every step of the way he found some objection. A time of crisis was a time to take necessary risks and to push yourself to your limits.

The apprentice stood next to the tank that held the aquits, and the doll-sized undersea creatures swam away from him, as usual. Their forms shifted, as if they had difficulty maintaining their shapes around Orpheon. Gwen had always found the aquits' behavior strange, and she couldn't imagine why the handsome apprentice didn't like the innocuous little creatures. *Some people just don't understand animals,* she thought. Shoru the killer whale probably would have munched him in a single gulp.

When Rubicas suddenly drew a quick breath as an idea occurred to him, Gwen stepped closer. "What is it? Have you solved the spell?"

"A strong verbal nuance, a new bridge to connect the parts." Using aja ink from his jar, he scribbled another line, and then, pleased with himself, recited the spell.

A shimmering curve took shape in the air and extended through the ceiling. She hoped the sweeping invisible barrier hadn't knocked anyone flat out in the streets.

"Ah, a step in the right direction! Now if the entire Pentumvirate casts the same spell, we can extend the boundary. Perhaps even a protective dome over the whole island!"

"That will never happen, Rubicas." Orpheon's voice carried a dark edge.

Gwen finally lost her patience with him. "Why are you always such a pessimist?"

Rubicas was puzzled. "Do you doubt my abilities, Orpheon?"

"Not that. I am simply stating a fact." He took a step closer. "You will never have the chance."

Whirling, Orpheon extended his hand in a clawlike grasp. He held a tiny lightning storm cupped in his palm. Green electricity arced from his finger to his wrist. The assistant's long face drew back in a sneer, and for a brief moment his lips grew wider, thicker, his teeth sharper.

Rubicas gasped. "What are you doing? What is this?"

"Look out!" Gwen cried.

As if throwing a heavy stone, Orpheon hurled the crackling ball of green fire at the confused sage. Gwen tried to block it, but the wave of light struck both of them, engulfing them. She couldn't breathe, couldn't move. The flood of light was so intensely brilliant, it saturated her mind with bright unconsciousness.

31

IN THE UTTERLY STILL hour before dawn, a bleary-eyed Vic accompanied Tiaret, Sharif, and Lyssandra down to the harbor. He hated to get up so early. Maybe Gwen had it easier just staying up all night assisting Sage Rubicas in his laboratory tower.

But he couldn't complain. Everyone in Elantya, especially the novs, apprentices, and sages at the Citadel, had their new assignments to help defend the island. By the light of lanterns and glowing streetcrystals, Vic and his friends watched the morning preparations of the fishing boats and cargo ships, as well as the guardian galleys that would accompany each trading vessel, on high alert.

The incredible spray of diamond stars overhead only made the surrounding night seem blacker. On his keychain, Vic fingered the five-sided medallion his mother had given him. What if she was really here in Elantya? But if she were here wouldn't she have heard about Vic and Gwen and tried to contact them by now? Still, she could be in some other world connected through the crystal doors.

In the crisp pre-dawn darkness, uneasy crewmen loaded weapons along with their fishnets and cargo crates. While Tiaret and Sharif walked along the docks where large and small boats were tied up, Vic and Lyssandra boarded a sharp-prowed Elantyan war galley, which would patrol the coastline. With glowing crystals on their prows, scouts in small boats helped guide merchant ships in and out of the harbor.

Stern Vir Helassa herself stood at the front of the galley, looking out at the water as the oars moved in unison and drove the warship with little more than a whisper and a splash. Elantya's Protective Vir was young to hold such a powerful position, and her hair was a striking mixture of raven streaked with gold that cascaded down her back from a clasp at the base of her neck. Her face was hard and determined, with no soft edges at all.

Having no duties while the sailors went about their well-practiced work, Vic and Lyssandra reported to the Protective Vir. "Now that we're ready for them, the merlons wouldn't dare mess with Elantya." The young man forced good cheer into his voice.

Helassa narrowed her indigo eyes, turning from her vigilant search. "Soon, Elantyans will feel the secondary consequences of these merlon attacks." A fish jumped at the surface, and the splash startled them all. Helassa sniffed with impatience.

"What consequences do you mean?" Lyssandra asked.

"By pouncing on a few ships, our enemies have thrown

Elantya's economy into turmoil. Yes, we have our own vegetable gardens, and our fishermen bring in a good haul, but this island has never been self-sufficient. We depend on regular trade through the crystal doors. If we are cut off, we cannot support ourselves for long. These days, even the fishermen are afraid to venture out of sight of land, and trading ships are more reluctant to come here with their cargoes." Helassa nodded toward the docks to where Sharif and Tiaret were still helping to load hooked harpoons onto more patrol galleys. "The merlons have already sunk our much-needed shipment of star aja crystals from Afirik."

Vic realized that he'd taken a lot for granted about this marvelous island. Elantya was clean and bright, full of magical and technological marvels. Everyone seemed so wealthy with knowledge, happiness, and personal goods that he hadn't bothered to think about where everything came from. He had seen the terraced olive groves and vineyards, and household gardens crowded with tomatoes, eggplants, and squashes. He had watched fishermen return with loaded nets; sellers in their dockside stalls hawked mussels and squirming crustaceans in wooden buckets filled with seawater.

Considering the sheer number of students, teachers, government leaders, sages, and scientists, Vic realized how many mouths Elantya had to feed. Without trade ships, wouldn't the people begin to starve?

But Elantyans would not give up without a fight. Helassa, standing on the prow of the war galley, symbolized that. She looked like a statue, beautiful, solid, and immovable.

As dawn spread a fingerpaint smear of bronze light across the east, the fishing boats prepared to set off. Twelve well-balanced fishing boats were ready to cast their nets at the edge of the harbor. With colorful sails stretched tight, the first three ships moved away from the docks using the morning breeze and a nudge of nautical magic to guide them across the smooth water.

Just ahead of the outbound ships, strange ripples began to form. Vic shaded his eyes, though the dawn still wasn't very bright. "That's weird. Lyssandra — can you tell what's going on out there?"

The girl also sensed something amiss. "I do not know."

Helassa, though, didn't hesitate. She whistled an alarm. The galley captain ordered his rowers to strike out toward the mysterious turmoil. Belowdecks, the men heaved their oars.

Aboard the first fishing boat, several men ran to the bow, pointing at something large that moved below the surface. The captain turned the steering oar, changing course to avoid the disturbance.

Though the guardian galley raced across the water, Vic could see they would not get to the fishing boat in time. Beside him, Lyssandra jerked as if she had just sensed something large and ominous and startling. "It is rising!"

Like a scene from an old giant-monster movie Vic and Gwen had watched with his dad, a fat tentacle broke the surface and curled into the air, dripping water and glistening white slime. The tentacle's inside edge was studded with suckers the size of dinner plates, each one ringed with thorny spikes. The thick back of the snakelike appendage was covered with flat, strapped-on metal plates, like a soccer player's knee-pads or a knight's greaves, but these plates were adorned with curved metal scythes.

The huge body rose, like some kind of plump sea spider, accompanied by more and more tentacles. In addition to the sharp weapons covering the monster's tentacles, heavy plates protected parts of the bulbous head. Vic did not want to imagine who might have the job of strapping battle armor on a giant squid. He yelled, "What is that thing?"

"It is a weapon of the merlons," Vir Helassa said. "We do not need to name it in order to fight it."

"You've got a point."

Helassa shouted, "All soldiers, arm yourselves!" A neosage, also dressed in red robes, rushed forward with an armful of scrolls. Elantyan guards grabbed wicked-looking spears.

The other two fishing boats tacked sideways to stay beyond the reach of the tentacled creature. The trapped fishermen on the first ship ran around the deck. They seized harpoons designed for spearing giant fish and cast them into the roiling water toward the body of the submerged beast.

One harpoon clattered off the armor plate, then disappeared into the sea; another pierced the thick appendage like a sewing needle stabbing a worm. The pain triggered a frenzy in the monster. The thrashing creature lifted three more tentacles, each as thick and menacing as the first.

Helassa's xyridium-reinforced galley raced into the deep harbor. Sailors dipped long oars into the water, pulling in well-practiced unison, making the craft cut through the water like an axe blade. Two more guardian galleys converged toward the sea monster.

Tentacles whipped around the first fishing boat. One slashed sideways, using the metal hooks of its armor plate to rip through the main sail as easily as a chef might gut a fish. Another tentacle wrapped in a stranglehold around the middle mast, clenching until the thick pillar snapped.

Water cascaded from the monster's long bulbous back, which was ridged with rough spines and lumps, as if a coral reef had grown on its body. Its two front tentacles were much longer than the others, giant grasping limbs that ended in broad, flat sucker pads. Between the two longer tentacles, a mass of smaller, equally deadly limbs writhed. In the middle, a clacking beak chomped the water into a froth. On each side of the tentacle cluster, two dead-yellow eyes showed no intelligence whatsoever.

Most frightening of all, though, was an artificial pavilion mounted on top of its conical body core. Two merlon generals stood under a curved shell awning wearing undersea armor and carrying shell-tipped spears and spiny clubs. They rode the giant squid as if it were an elephant.

Using sharp staffs and aquatic magic, the merlon generals tapped hard against the fleshy head of the monster, goading it. The thing responded with renewed frenzy, ripping the first fishing boat out of the water. Crewmen fell into the water like fleas shaken from the fur of a mangy dog. With incredible strength, the beast raised the vessel high. Water poured in wide streams from its entire length. The sturdy hull groaned, creaked, and finally shattered.

Lyssandra clutched Vic's hand. "Never in my worst nightmares did I think I would see a battle kraken. Never did I believe the merlons would unleash such a thing against Elantya!"

Helassa unrolled her defensive spell scrolls. "I underestimated the evil of the merlons." She was clearly frustrated that the galley was still too far away from the kraken to mount an effective attack. Even at top speed, they seemed to move in slow motion.

After destroying the first fishing boat, the kraken jetted forward like an armored submarine. The second boat couldn't get out of the way in time. The merlon generals prodded the kraken's sensitive head, driving the beast faster.

Raising its two longer tentacles, the monster squid slapped the second fishing boat. The kraken's heavy wake tipped the vessel halfway over in the water. The merlon generals clutched their control pavilion and bellowed orders in their strange language. Vic didn't ask Lyssandra what they were saying.

By now, Helassa's galley was close, the soldiers rowing furiously, building momentum to the point of ramming speed. "Hang on!" Vic yelled. Sleek and fast, the knifepoint prow of the patrol craft rammed into the squid's soft body with a great crash.

The impact knocked Vic and most of the Elantyan soldiers to the deck. Lyssandra was thrown to the side, almost over the railing, but Vic caught her ankle and dragged the girl back.

Some men were cast overboard, and they swam desperately back to the armor-plated galley.

Vic scrambled to his knees and threw a rope over the side. "Come on, we have to help them!" He reached down to grab a soldier's outstretched hands. He and Lyssandra hauled two of the gasping Elantyans back aboard.

Other disoriented soldiers scrambled to their feet and threw a barrage of jagged spears into the monster's hide. Many of the weapons bounced off the studded armor plates, but the Elantyan defenders were well muscled, and some spearheads sank deep into the meat.

Somehow, Vir Helassa had kept her balance at the prow, which was dripping with slime and ichor from the monster. Impatiently, she yanked her neosage to his feet, and both of them unfurled spell scrolls, chanting in the ancient language. As her red robe flapped around her from a rising magical wind, three white-hot fireballs burst against the kraken's soft, cool flesh. The third explosion struck one of its huge yellow eyes, blinding it. The neosage finished his spell as well, and a fiery blast crisped one of the sucker-studded tentacles. Without pausing, Helassa opened another scroll.

A second patrol galley came in at full speed from behind the battle kraken, and its jagged, reinforced hull ground against the barnacled back. Elantyan archers shot fiery volleys of suntip arrows at the two merlon generals guiding the beast, but the shell walls of the pavilion protected them.

Squirming in reflex, even as the merlon generals pounded its sensitive flesh, the kraken writhed out of the way, then ripped a tentacle sideways. One spike-armored blow split the second galley through the deck and snapped its keel. The wreckage sank so swiftly that the Elantyans barely had time to jump clear.

In pain from its numerous injuries, the battle kraken went into a full destructive rage. The merlon generals could no longer control the monster. It surged toward all the boats still tied up to the docks.

32

WITH VIC AND LYSSANDRA gripping the rails, the guardian galley streaked after the battle kraken. Though the merlon generals could not control their beast, they seemed pleased with the destruction the kraken was causing. With a flurry of spiked tentacles, the sea creature sank smaller boats trying to race away.

"Row!" Helassa shouted. "Faster!"

Though the war galley had been damaged from ramming the monster, the impact had also torn an angry-looking gouge in the creature's hide, knocking off one of the wide armor plates. Slime and blood oozed into the water. In pain, the kraken thrashed at anything that moved.

Finally, it reached the wharf. As people fled the docks, the armor-plated tentacles smashed down. Hooked metal scythes splintered the wood. Thick appendages crushed unmanned boats and knocked pilings aside like toothpicks.

Heavily loaded cargo ships wallowed helplessly and sank to the muck on the bottom of the harbor. Their masts stuck out above the surface like the tips of dead trees in a drowned forest.

From behind, the galley rammed the kraken's fleshy body again, and tentacles whipped backward, slamming into the deck and prow. The red-robed neosage was hurled like a pebble into the roiling water. Vir Helassa tumbled down the slanted deck, dropping her spell scrolls.

A tentacle seized a soldier who rushed forward with a long harpoon. "Look out!" Vic shouted, too late, as the crushing appendage lifted the soldier into the air. The soldier lost his grip on his weapon before the kraken tossed him aside like a gnawed chicken bone.

Lyssandra rescued one of the rolled spell scrolls that Helassa had dropped. Vic saw a tentacle coming toward the petite girl, and moved faster than he could think. With a flash of his surprisingly fast reflexes, he grabbed the hooked harpoon dropped by the doomed soldier, twirled it around, and speared the descending tentacle with all his strength.

The kraken reacted as if it had touched a hot match, jerking back from Lyssandra. Smelly ichor splashed all over Vic, and he smeared it away from his face. "Eww!"

Picking herself up, Lyssandra flashed him a grateful smile for just an instant, then unrolled her scroll and read aloud as fast as she could. Stumbling a bit on the ancient language, she created a fireball, weaker than the ones Helassa had made.

Even so, the blazing sphere sizzled outward and struck the pavilion protecting the two merlon generals. In a flash, one of the supports and side walls disintegrated, leaving the enemy commanders exposed.

The bright light stunned the nearest merlon general. His scales smoking from the heat, he flailed his goad and grabbed for support, but tumbled off the head of the battle kraken. Down in the frothing water, the tentacles thrashed, and the fallen merlon was himself drawn into the creature's sharp clacking mouth.

Furious, the surviving enemy general prodded the kraken. In a reflexive twitch the huge sea beast shoved Helassa's galley aside, driving it up against the docks. Pilings splintered, the armored hull cracked, and the galley came to ground halfway out of the water.

"We're stuck!" Vic grabbed Lyssandra's hand. "Time to abandon ship."

They stumbled and ran down the slick deck, jumped over the rail, and landed on what was left of the dock. As soon as they caught their balance and got back to their feet, Vic and Lyssandra ran at full speed up the dock to the rocky shore. Vir Helassa and the soldiers evacuated from the galley right behind them.

A hammering tentacle crushed the abandoned galley, and another one shattered the dock. Then the battle kraken turned to the other vessels tied up to the wharf.

Rushing to relative safety, Vic scanned the milling defenders on the shore for any sign of Sharif and Tiaret, shouting their names. By now the dawn had brightened, and he could see. Finally he spotted the bobbing light of Piri in Sharif's hand as he and the warrior girl ran toward them. They were all glad to find each other still alive.

"Sharif, you've got to go fetch Master Rubicas. He's up at the laboratory working with Gwen and Orpheon. We need his help! Maybe he has a kraken-withering spell, or something."

"The master sage will certainly have some magical weapons," Lyssandra said, "though I have never heard of a kraken-withering spell."

"He will know which spells can help us." The boy from Irrakesh unrolled his carpet onto the paving stones. "I am on my way!"

"And bring my cousin, too!" Vic called as the embroidered carpet rose into the air. "If it's not too much trouble. She'd hate to miss this."

Sharif waved back at them as the flying carpet streaked off toward the high, vine-covered tower above the sage's laboratory. "You three stay here and save the harbor."

"Oh, sure, *we* get the easy part." Vic wiped slime from his hands and face. Then he saw scaly hordes of merlons emerge from the water — a whole invading army. Undersea foot soldiers climbed onto the remains of the docks and engaged the fighters on dry land. "As if we didn't have enough problems!"

"I see work to do here," Tiaret said.

Before Vic could stop her, Tiaret charged in among the aquatic attackers, swinging her teaching staff to bash heads with the dragon's-eye stone.

Vic grabbed a harpoon that had been thrown from the shipwrecked war galley. "Here we go again."

33

GWEN WASN'T SURE HOW long she remained unconscious. She found herself sprawled on the stone floor, her arm twisted awkwardly under her. When she stirred, scattered scrolls rustled around her, and her sleeve brushed against tinkling shards of broken crystal.

Then, as her eyes focused, she saw Orpheon across the room gathering scrolls and scrap parchments. Satisfied, he turned to stand over Master Rubicas with what looked like a small scimitar made of glass. Apparently he didn't think his stunning spell would be sufficient against them.

"You leave him alone!" She tried to shout, but her voice came out as a faint gurgle. The aftereffects of the strange stun spell made her queasy, and when she lurched herself into a sitting position, Gwen fought back waves of nausea.

The apprentice looked up, his dark eyes flashing, and she

saw that they were now slits, not round *human* pupils at all. "I intend to kill you both. It does not matter in which order you die." He stalked toward her with the long dagger while Rubicas groaned, still far from consciousness.

Gwen struggled to stand up, but sickening dizziness crippled her. Orpheon looked as if he might laugh. He came closer with his curved knife.

Behind him, a strong voice called out. "I see I have arrived just in time!" Orpheon whirled, and a sudden flash of light dazzled him. While the apprentice was blinded, Sharif ran forward and slammed into him. The unexpected impact knocked his curved glass dagger to the floor, where it shattered. Inside her still-glowing eggsphere, Piri twirled, waving her hands in a little victory dance.

Orpheon hissed, writhed like a sea serpent, and ducked away. The illumination from Piri's globe finally caused Rubicas to stir. The bearded sage made a miserable sound and lifted his head as if it had become a heavy weight. He blinked, propped himself up on his elbows, and looked around. "What? What is happening?"

Seeing himself outnumbered, the treacherous apprentice held tightly to his stolen scrolls and parchments and bolted toward the arched laboratory doorway. Gwen cried a warning, but seeing that they were hurt, Sharif stopped to check on Rubicas and then on her. "Are you all right?"

"Don't let Orpheon get away —" Gwen began. Moving with inhuman speed, the apprentice was already out the door and running down the corridor.

Sharif didn't go after him, though. He had an emergency of his own to report. "The city is under attack, Master Rubicas! A great battle kraken is smashing the harbor."

The old sage shook his shaggy head and hauled himself to his feet, groaning as if he had a terrible migraine. "I have never experienced such a stun spell." He sat up, remembering what had happened. "Orpheon! This is not a magic that I have seen before — but I have heard of it. Merlon magic."

"Orpheon is working with the *merlons*?" Sharif asked in disbelief, helping Gwen to her feet. "My people say, 'Misplaced trust may blind an honest soul to the truth.'"

Gwen remembered seeing the other man's features shift at the last moment. Could Rubicas's own apprentice — who had worked with the sage in the laboratory for more than a year — be some kind of a spy for the sinister ocean kingdom? More thoughts tumbled into place. Had *Orpheon* been the one who sabotaged the aja array, preventing Gwen and Vic from opening a crystal door for Dr. Pierce? And if so, why?

She and Sharif looked around the laboratory chamber. She saw to her dismay that one of the large curved resonance lenses had been shattered, the jagged shards strewn across the floor. The transparent crystal rods were broken.

"I have to think!" The sage rubbed his throbbing head. "What could Orpheon have been after? Why did he do this? What did he have to gain? Why is it so dark in here?"

Piri's light shone brightly enough for Gwen to see that the glow eels lay dead on the floor. The aquarium had been smashed. It was pure malice. Why would anyone want to do that? Gwen frowned at the dead glow eels, the ruined aquarium, the puddles of water spilled on the floor, ruining many of the old scrolls. The four aquits lay drying out at the bottom of one tank, huddling together for survival in shallow puddles. The small sea creatures lifted their tiny arms, begging for water in which to immerse themselves.

Alarmed, Gwen hurriedly looked around. To her relief, she spotted the trickling water clock in the corner of the room. She and Sharif gently lifted the aquits two at a time from the damp floor of their broken tank and dropped them into the water clock's reservoir. The bowl was crowded once they got all four aquits inside, but the creatures stood gratefully under the trickling flow as if it were a miniature waterfall. They splashed each other, gasping with relief as the moisture revived them. Although they preferred salt water, this would have to do for now. Too many emergencies were happening at once.

Looking anxious, the boy from Irrakesh said, "Master Rubicas — the battle kraken! We need your help."

"Mmm. I must find my spell scrolls." The sage looked down at his worktable and groaned. "Oh, no!"

All of the draft spell parchments had been taken, even the crumpled discards that Gwen had rescued.

"My prototypes of the shield barrier spell are gone. Everything!" He hung his head. "The scraps, the drafts, the iterations."

Gwen was ready to strangle Orpheon if ever she laid eyes on him again. No doubt, Rubicas could remember the basics, but it would take him a long time to re-create all the work —

certainly not in time to use any of it against the monster currently attacking the harbor.

She realized the second terrible thing. "Not only did he steal your spells from us, but now he can give the secret of the shield barrier to the merlons! We have to find him!" She ran to the window, pushed aside the newly grown grapevine leaves, and looked at the brightening dawn. "He can't have gone far!"

Sharif held up his embroidered carpet. "Fortunately, we can go faster." Piri's eggsphere rippled through a spectrum of colors, in empathy.

The old sage stood on wobbly legs. "Orpheon knows everything I was working on! He knows our defenses, my methods, and so much about Elantya." Rubicas grabbed Sharif by the shoulder. "You and Gwenya must find him. If Orpheon escapes, then the merlons will know everything! Go!"

He didn't have to tell them twice.

34

THE AIR SMELLED SO STRONGLY of the merlons' rank body odor that Vic could barely draw a breath without gagging. Even cafeteria fish sticks smelled better than this.

In the harbor, another guardian galley circled around to pummel the kraken. From the damaged pavilion on the monster's head, the remaining merlon general shouted commands trying to direct the massacre. The squidlike beast smashed together two small fishing dinghies. Merlon invaders splashed toward shore carrying their scallop-edged scimitars and sea-urchin clubs. The Elantyan guard forces and citizens armed with makeshift weapons rushed down to the harbor to defend the island.

With a groan, Vic slapped his forehead. "Why couldn't I have thought of this *before* Sharif flew away? It would work, I know it!"

Lyssandra looked at him. "What is it, Viccus? Do you have an idea?"

"Yup. A way to use those mirrormills you showed us. But we need to get into the air. I don't suppose Elantya has an air force — balloons or something?"

"No." The girl raised her eyebrows. "But we do have pedal-gliders."

"That's right!" Vic wanted to give her a hug. "Can you fly one? Do they seat two people?"

"Of course, and of course."

Tiaret ran up, panting, her clothes and hair in disarray from fighting the merlons that climbed up onto the docks. Oddly, she was grinning. "Fifteen so far! The merlons have learned to stay away from me — which means I must now run after them."

"Viccus and I are going to attack from the sky."

Tiaret accepted the comment without question. "And I will continue the fight on the ground." The wiry girl from Afirik swung her teaching staff with a swish, and droplets of merlon blood and slime flew off.

BY NOW MORNING'S WATERY light lit the island. From the air above the harbor, the carnage looked even worse than Vic had imagined.

Lyssandra easily piloted the small, lightweight craft. The fluttering glider did not feel stable or safe, but riding it was certainly exciting. Breezes through the open framework rustled the fabric sides and flaps. Apparently, even Elantyan children played with the little vehicles.

"You see, we already know the merlons don't like bright light," he explained. "And I remembered you telling Gwen how your mirrormills magically store the power of sunshine in special battery jars. So why not —"

Still pedaling the glider over the mayhem in the harbor, Lyssandra kept her attention on flying. "Now I understand." She nodded. "I thought it strange when you asked for the luminous jars from the mirrormills."

He reached down to untie the first of several cloth-wrapped pouches dangling from a strut in the flying contraption's framework. "Take us over target number one!"

Lyssandra navigated them above a group of twenty merlons that had moved in their soft-jointed gait onto the gravelly shore. Seeing them flying high overhead, the merlons raised their clawed hands and angrily swung scallop-edged scimitars at the unreachable opponent.

"Ready? Bombs away!" Vic undid the cord and, careful not to touch the hot glassy surface of the storage jar, released a silvery-white cylinder over the merlon soldiers. "These guys don't know what's coming."

The undersea invaders looked up at the tumbling luminous jar. When the mirrorglass cylinder struck the rocks, it burst in a blaze of light and hot crackling fire. Sparks and sunshine flowed out in a wave that left the merlons smoking, blistered and senseless. Blinded, the aquatic attackers ran into each other searching for relief and finally crashed into the seawater, producing bubbles and hot steam.

Lyssandra laughed in delight. "The magic of sunshine!"

Vic blinked the bright spots from his eyes. "You're not kidding."

Lyssandra pumped the glider's pedals. From far below, they could hear the cheers of Elantyan fighters who had seen the dazzling blast. "Hurry, Viccus. We have five more jars."

He unleashed three more sunshine bombs in quick succession upon merlons who emerged onto the shore. The scaly army had no defense against the blasts of light and sunshine, and many of them staggered back into the cool water, burned and defeated.

Next, Lyssandra guided the small aircraft out over the battle kraken itself. "I'm going to use the last two at once," Vic shouted above the noise from below. Then, switching to a fake Jamaican accent, he said, "Time to fry some calamari, mon!" He let go of the remaining pair of luminous jars, dropping them onto the barnacled back of the sea monster.

The bright flashes sent the creature into a thrashing fury. Enraged, its back smoking from large burns, the kraken collided with another entire dock, then sank a newly painted yacht. Elantyans fled from the deadly tentacles.

"That's all folks!" Vic wished he had more of the sunshine bombs. There hadn't been enough to finish the job. Lyssandra turned the glider about and headed back toward the city.

The battle kraken remained unstoppable.

35

SHARIF WASTED NO TIME. As soon as Gwen grabbed the fringe tassels, the flying carpet soared away faster than any athlete could run.

Peering down into the frantic streets, Gwen said, "Orpheon's taller than most people, and he's probably still wearing the short apprentice's tunic he used when helping Sage Rubicas. Even so, how are we supposed to spot one person in all that chaos down there? Everyone is rushing toward the harbor."

"It should be easy, Gwenya," Sharif said with a quirky smile. "He will be the only one running the opposite direction."

With the city alarms blaring, people scrambled out of their houses, cinched their robes tight, and gathered homemade weapons. At intersections, streetcrystal lamps blazed with golden or sapphire light, crackling with magic energy.

Sharif banked the carpet sharply. "If Orpheon is working with the merlons, he will want to get to the sea as fast as possible. Perhaps he has arranged for another merlon spy to meet him at the water."

As far as Gwen could tell, none of the running Elantyans below looked like Orpheon. "Why would any person shift his allegiance to the undersea people? What could a human hope to gain from the merlons?" The apprentice had always rubbed her the wrong way, sneering at her, blaming her for the accident with the aja crystals when he must have sabotaged the array himself.

Sharif clenched his jaws, clearly upset. "We can ask those questions when we catch him. Irrakesh reserves its most unpleasant prison cells for traitors. I hope Elantya has similar accommodations."

Gwen leaned forward, trying to ignore a brief flash of dizziness from being so high up — and saw a tall man duck furtively into the shadows. The man was working his way along a sheltered street, moving from doorway to doorway, away from the harbor.

"Sharif! Circle around." Gwen pointed to the alley. "I think I saw him!"

As the flying carpet banked, the sneaking stranger looked up in surprise. As soon as he saw the carpet and its riders, Orpheon bolted. He raced with long-legged strides away from the buildings toward the hillside vineyards on the island's outer highlands.

"Follow him with your eyes, Gwenya," Sharif said as he concentrated on guiding the carpet.

Holding on, she shouted, "Orpheon! We know what you've done. Stop, or you *will* face the consequences!"

Sharif gave her a strange frown. "What consequences can you and I impose?"

Gwen shrugged. "I was hoping to intimidate him."

The traitor wasn't intimidated, though. He put on a burst of speed and ran under an ornate arch topped with baskets of hanging flowers.

The flying carpet sped onward, cruising low, but the apprentice sprinted inhumanly fast. Seeing the pursuit close in, he left the whitewashed dwellings behind and headed toward the sea.

From the carpet, Gwen could hear the crashing surf. "Hurry! We don't want him to get to the water."

"There is no shore up here, Gwenya. Only cliffs. *High* cliffs. He will be trapped."

Orpheon raced up a steep rocky path bounded by grapevines tied up on posts. The assistant moved so swiftly that his pumping arms tore away dark-green leaves. Gwen wondered if the merlons had provided the apprentice with some kind of stimulant or enhancement to give him such a boost of speed. "That would be just great," she muttered. "Spies on steroids."

As the carpet got even closer, she saw that Orpheon had strapped five or six scrolls to his belt and carried three others rolled in his hand — the stolen shield spell scrolls!

Kicking up dust with each step, Orpheon ran through the vineyards, but Sharif did not relent, chasing him toward the high cliffs. After two years on the island, Rubicas's apprentice must know there could be no escape in this direction. According to Sharif, the gravel path would hit a dead-end up ahead.

"Trust my carpet, Gwenya. We will catch him. He has no place to go."

As they closed in, Orpheon halted as the narrow path turned a corner. The traitorous apprentice found himself faced with an abrupt end to his path. The sheer black rock dropped away to deep water. Seabirds, a few clumps of moss, and succulent flowers found places in the lumpy stone wall, but no human could ever climb down the spray-slick cliff. Foamy waves curled against the jagged rocks far below.

Orpheon stared longingly down the cliff toward the deep water, then faced his two young pursuers as Sharif landed the carpet. Blocking off the spy's escape, they stood together, but Gwen did not forget that Orpheon had already stunned a powerful sage like Rubicas. "Be careful, Sharif."

The young man from Irrakesh showed no concern. "You have nowhere to run, Orpheon." Piri's shimmering ball hung in its pouch around his neck.

"Give us those scrolls back and nobody needs to get hurt," Gwen added, recalling a hundred tough-guy movies she had seen. She tensed her muscles, remembering the *zy'oah* self-defense moves her mother had taught her. Special Elantyan training? So many things to wonder about. . . .

"You know nothing of what you speak." Orpheon sneered at them as if they were no more than insects. "Elantya is doomed. The merlons will destroy you all. They will sink this island beneath the waves and return the ocean to its purity, as it was before filthy land-dwellers came through the crystal doors."

"Get over yourself!" Gwen said. "Elantyans have done a lot of good here."

Sharif added, "They unified the whole network of civilizations and stopped the dark sages' armies with the Great Closure."

"Great Closure?" A flash of fiery hatred ignited behind Orpheon's eyes, an incomprehensible fanatical gleam. "Azric has made his promises. The merlons will kill all land-dwellers, destroy Elantya. Then the sealed crystal doors will once again be opened."

"Azric!" Gwen cried. "With the merlons? *He's* the one who's been riling them up?"

"The merlons will help him reverse the Great Closure. Azric's immortal armies have had centuries to grow more powerful, and once they are unleashed, all worlds will fall!"

Sharif let out a low growl. "Azric has been trapped outside ever since the Great Closure. In disguise, he walked among us on Irrakesh — and killed my brother." Sensing Sharif's outrage, Piri flashed blood red in her crystal ball, startling Orpheon. He raised a hand to shield his eyes.

Without thinking, Gwen seized the chance and yanked the scrolls out of the traitor's other hand. Orpheon jerked backward, but Gwen wouldn't let go. The two strained and tugged — until the parchments ripped.

Gwen stumbled off balance, but Sharif caught her. Triumphant, she held fragments of the precious scrolls, while the spy held the other torn scraps. "At least the merlons won't get them now. Sage Rubicas can piece the rest together."

Orpheon flung away the tatters in his hand, letting them blow over the cliff. But he still had several intact scrolls in a pouch at his waist. "You are fools, both of you! Naïve dreamers."

Gwen balled her fists. "I still don't get it. Why would any human willingly serve the merlons?"

Orpheon sneered at this. "You assume I am merely human? That was your first mistake." His body shimmered, his skin grew rough, lumpy, then scaly. His eyes enlarged, as did his mouth. His hands became webbed, and claws hooked out of his fingertips. "I was one of the original generals in Ulkar's army, countless centuries ago. We sacrificed a Key after he opened a crystal door and the blood magic gave us the power to control the cells of our bodies. Now I can take any shape I choose." His amphibious lips curved in a cruel imitation of a smile. "Azric is not alone in his fight."

Shocked, Gwen and Sharif rushed Orpheon, hoping to seize the last scrolls, but the transformed apprentice easily dove backward off the cliff. His sleek aquatic body dropped downward in a clean arc.

The two looked over the cliff edge just in time to see the shape-shifter plunge smoothly into the waves and disappear with barely a ripple.

"Now that's something you don't see every day," Gwen said.

36

WITH HIS FEET ON solid ground again after the pedal-glider flight, Vic turned back toward the harbor, where Tiaret and the Elantyan soldiers were still fighting the remaining merlons. Lyssandra surprised him by slipping her arms around him. "That was an excellent idea, Viccus. Your sunshine bombs saved many lives, and possibly turned the tide of the battle."

"Sure." He flushed in embarrassment but hoped she wouldn't let go of him anytime soon. He had no idea how even the greatest sages and warriors could defeat the gigantic armored squid. "I don't suppose Elantya has any, uh, super weapons stored in a warehouse somewhere?"

The telepathic girl cocked her head as if listening to something inside her mind. She pulled away and turned to the steep harbor road. "Maybe. Here comes Sage Polup."

Several struggling novs — students he had met in the anemonite sage's "chemistry" class — worked together to carry a hollow tube the size of a telephone pole. Leading them was Polup's clanking, hissing walker.

Vic took Lyssandra's hand and ran with her. "Come on, let's help! I can't wait to see what crazy things Sage Polup came up with."

As the anemonite genius guided his apprentices forward with their heavy metal tube, Vic took a handhold next to the sweating novs. "I'm guessing this is like a big cannon?"

The jellyfish brain drifted inside the aquarium container. "I did not wish to create weapons, but Elantya must be defended."

Lyssandra touched the robot to pick up images from the anemonite brain. Her cobalt eyes sparkled. "Ah, I see. I hope it will be effective."

"What is it?" Vic asked. "Some of us aren't telepaths, you know."

Lyssandra slipped in next to him to help carry the weapon just as Polup answered. "I have created a dangerous mixture of chemicals and magic. Crystal dust and spells, all ready to be activated with a powerful symbol." In one of his thick artificial hands, Polup held a disk inscribed with a design in aja ink. Vic wasn't sure, but he thought it was one of the dangerous symbols the anemonite had warned them never to use.

"I had the spell and the recipe for a long time, but never have I risked concocting it. Now the threat is great enough. This cannon will launch a ball of Grogyptian Fire, which burns hot. Water does not extinguish it. The monster cannot seek safety under the waves, for the chemical will continue to burn."

"Sounds like Greek fire," Vic said, remembering a chemistry experiment he'd always wanted to try, but his father wouldn't let him have the materials. "Phosphorus or magnesium, a metal that burns hot under water and —"

"It is Grogyptian Fire," Lyssandra repeated. "Think of what you know, Viccus, then multiply it by a thousand through the addition of magic."

"Cool."

She gave him a curious sidelong glance. "No, it is extremely *hot*."

With the exhausted and frightened novs, Vic and Lyssandra carried the heavy metal cylinder toward the end of the dock. The battle kraken advanced, smashing everything in its reach. Seeing them, especially incensed to notice the anemonite escapee, the last merlon general, once more in control, used his goad to drive the monster closer to the main wharf.

Though Sage Polup was afraid of being recaptured and enslaved with his people, his heavy walking body stood its ground. Behind the cannon, Polup fumbled with his symbol disk. "When I ignite the crystal dust, the cannon will launch our projectile," he said through his speakers. "We have only one opportunity."

The apprentices struggled to hold the heavy cannon steady. The battle kraken raised its tentacles. By now the suckers were covered with splintered chunks of wood.

Polup extended his symbol disk to the crystal-dust fuse, but before the anemonite genius could touch the powerful design to the fuse and fire the weapon, a tentacle slammed into the wharf pilings. The whole dock reverberated; two of the struggling novs stumbled. Vic planted his feet, straining to keep his grip on the heavy cannon.

Jarred loose, the symbol disk slipped out of Polup's artificial hand. He clumsily tried to grab it, but the ignition key tumbled to the dock boards, struck the splintered wood, bounced, and fell through a wide crack into the water.

The anemonite let out a wordless, bubbling cry. The students gasped in astonishment. "Now how will we fire the cannon?"

The kraken came closer. Another tentacle slammed the wharf. When two merlon soldiers clambered onto the dock and lurched toward the cannon, one of the novs let go and ran. The others were stranded. Polup stood stock still, as if he had forgotten how to make his artificial body function.

"Wait!" Vic yelled. "I've got an idea!"

The merlons swung their spiked clubs. One more nov fled, and the others could barely hold the heavy cannon. The hissing undersea invaders came within striking distance, ready to cut down the students and Sage Polup.

Vic let go with one hand, eliciting moans of dismay from the trembling helpers. "I need to try something."

Suddenly Tiaret rushed in among them, slashing from side to side with her battered teaching staff. The startled merlons turned toward this one-girl whirlwind. One blow from her staff cracked an attacker's ribs even through its seashell armor; another swing shattered a sea-urchin mace. She called in a hoarse voice. "Viccus, whatever you intend to do — do it now!" She grabbed one of the cannon handles, planted her bare feet, and struggled to hold the weight.

He dug in his pocket and drew out his keychain, the five-sided pendant his mother had given him — the powerful design that had caused such a surprising reaction in the chemistry class. He knew it was just instinct guiding him, but somehow the instinct seemed *right*. "I sure hope this works."

Lyssandra rallied the terrified apprentices. "Hold the cannon steady! We have one more chance."

Sage Polup looked at the medallion. "Be cautious, Viccus. A symbol of such great power may be quite unpredictable in unskilled hands."

"Do you have anything else to fight that mega-squid?"

The sage swiveled his aquarium head. "No."

The kraken reared up, and the last merlon general stood tall, like an overconfident conqueror. Spike-armored tentacles waved about, and the sharp beak of the monster's mouth clacked, hungry for the taste of more flesh.

Vic slammed his mother's medallion against the crystal dust fuse. The pattern glowed intensely hot, burning his fingers, but he did not let go. The crystal dust ignited. With a deafening roar, an enormous molten projectile of Grogyptian Fire shot like a comet from the cannon.

"Ha! Take that!"

The recoil and shockwave knocked all of the students to

their knees, and the massive cylinder clanged to the dock. Even Sage Polup reeled for balance in his heavy body.

The blazing torpedo streaked toward the battle kraken and exploded in a direct impact. Beneath the monster's remaining unblinded eye, the flame burned like a torch, digging deep into the soft flesh — driving the monster squid wild. Its tentacles thrashing, the creature churned the water, but the sun-hot flames just burned whiter and more fiercely.

The spiked greave on one of its lashing tentacles bent back and smashed the pavilion where the last merlon general stood. The bone struts snapped. The shell covering shattered, and the tentacle grasped the merlon commander. The kraken flailed the struggling general, then smashed him into the water.

Sage Polup regained his balance and his senses enough to clomp to the edge of the dock. Vic, Lyssandra, and Tiaret went with him. They watched the squid writhe until it dove beneath the surface, where it pumped jets of water through its body, retreating from the harbor at top speed. The sun of Grogyptian Fire remained embedded in its body, still burning in spite of the water. Weaving and swirling, the kraken finally disappeared from the harbor.

"An impressive weapon," Tiaret said.

"Will the fire ever burn out?" Lyssandra asked the anemonite scientist.

Sage Polup swiveled his jellylike body in the tank. "I do not know. This is all an experiment to me. I fear I have killed the creature, and that makes me sad, for it is yet another beast that the merlons have enslaved for their war effort."

"It had to be stopped," Vic said. "Do you know how many lives you saved?"

"I know," Polup said in his bubbly voice. "I feel no guilt, merely sadness."

Vic held the still-warm medallion tight in his hand, thinking of his mother, and Gwen's, and of his dad's crystal door experiments. He still had so many questions.

He and his cousin had a lot more research to do.

37

THAT EVENING AFTER THEY had both eaten and washed up, Gwen came into Vic's small chamber and sat at the end of his sleeping pallet.

She studied the floor for a few minutes in uncomfortable silence, then asked in a low voice, "Are we human?"

"Of course."

"But our moms weren't from Earth."

"Nope. That part I'm pretty sure about," Vic said. "What I want to know is why our parents never mentioned it. Seems like a pretty important piece of family history to leave out."

"Maybe they thought they could protect us from whoever killed my mom and dad." Gwen sighed. "You know, I always thought that losing them would be easier if I could make some sense out of it. But now that I know my parents were *murdered*, it's worse. Azric wanted them dead — and wants me dead, too." Her head snapped up, her violet eyes narrowed. "But not you. Or your parents . . . Why? Are you immune, or —"

"No," Vic broke in. "You were just an easier target at Ocean Kingdoms. Anyway, he wanted to kill my mom, too. When she escaped, Dad says she was trying to lead Azric away from us. All I know is she's still alive. I can't explain why, but I can feel it."

"Kind of like Lyssandra feels things?" Gwen asked.

Vic shrugged. "I'm not sure. What do you think about the dreams and prophecies she's always coming up with? Are they real? I mean, are those legends she quotes really about us?"

"No way." Gwen was emphatic. "Here's why: Number one, I've just barely gotten used to the fact that we are in another world. Two, there are lots and lots of worlds. Three, we're finding out that we don't know as much about our moms as we thought. Four, your dad wanted us here to keep us safe, but we arrived in the middle of some insane war, so —"

"Seventy-seven?" Vic suggested.

Gwen plowed ahead. "*Five,* we're not really safe at all. We are actually fighting in the war. My brain is already running over with all the impossible things I'm being asked to believe. So, when a telepathic girl with copper hair starts tossing prophecies around, maybe you can understand why I'm not ready to accept that. Six, we're some sort of chosen ones out of a prediction written thousands of years ago. It's way too bizarre."

Vic looked resigned. "According to Dad, we shouldn't even try to get home. We can bring him here, but only by creating an impossible door or opening one that — from the sounds of it — is permanently locked. So that's what we'll have to do."

A thought occurred to her. "If it's permanently locked, how did our moms get to Earth? And Azric?"

"Huh," Vic said. "Good point. They weren't there before the Closure, so there must be a way to open a door. We'll *find* a way."

"Meanwhile," Gwen said, "we take classes and fight slimy ocean warriors — eww — and sea serpents."

"Not to mention giganto-squids and magic-wielding shape-shifters," Vic added. "And we look for my mom."

"In other words, our best hope is to work with Master Sage Rubicas."

THE NEXT MORNING WHEN the five friends reached Rubicas's chambers, the old sage was deep in thought at his writing desk. The marble floor of the central chamber was strewn with equipment, crystals, and soggy spell scrolls, as if he had ransacked the whole tower for something.

"Wow," Vic commented, "somebody whose filing system is worse than my own." Rubicas did not look up.

"This looks worse than the disaster after we came through the crystal door from Earth." Gwen cleared her throat. "Can we help with anything, Sage Rubicas?"

"Hmm, possible. Very possible," the old man murmured, again without looking up.

"We will recover," announced Tiaret. "We will survive. The

merlons have been driven back, their battle kraken defeated, and Elantya remains strong and undefeated."

Sharif stood at a window, looking out to the city. "Crews are already working hard to repair the harbor. My people have a saying: 'Great efforts yield great rewards.'"

Lyssandra clicked her tongue. "Orpheon left quite a mess, did he not?"

"Orpheon did a lot more than that," Vic grumbled. Though the aquariums were too damaged to use, the rescued aquits now swam in a large basin of sea water.

Rubicas blinked at them when Gwen started to pick up some of the clutter. "Hmm, well, not quite. That is to say, my traitorous apprentice caused some of this damage, but I am responsible for my own share of the mess. I have been trying to reconstruct the shield spell, mostly from my own memory. I think it can be done. You see, I pieced together a framework from the fragments Gwenya and Sharifas brought back. Then I used bits of existing spells to fill in some of the blanks."

Vic nodded as if he understood perfectly. "Like subroutines. You just lifted them out of other spells."

"Hmm," Rubicas agreed absently. "I have made a good start, as you can see. Though I could not always find the precise materials I needed. I must have set them somewhere." He indicated the disorganized pile of spell scrolls at the foot of his marble lectern. "I did not realize how much of my work Orpheon kept in order . . ."

"*Order?* Sheesh, I wouldn't be surprised if he hid stuff on purpose," Vic said.

The sage looked forlornly around his laboratory. "I have much work to do, and I no longer have anyone to keep track of all my spells and research."

"You have us," Gwen said. In her mind she was already putting together a logical organization system for his writings. The old sage had always piled his work, arranging it by a system only he understood, and then Orpheon had probably "helped" by sorting spells to diminish the sage's effectiveness. "I've got some ideas on how to put all this into a rational and efficient order. First, I'd sort your scrolls and notes. Second, I would catalog all of the finished spells. Third —"

"Oh, great," Vic said. "Once she starts organizing, I always end up getting sucked into the job."

"Ah, yes, that is what I wished to tell you. Due to the urgent nature of my work, the Pentumvirate has agreed to grant me the use of several novs. I am convinced that each of you is vital to my success somehow. Lyssandra has had some dreams indicating that you five did not come together merely by accident, but by design. Therefore I told the esteemed virs that I wanted all of you to be my apprentices — if you are willing, that is."

"If you believe my skills will be of use to you," Tiaret said, "I am willing. We all have a part to play in the Great Epic, and this will be an important tale."

Lyssandra's eyes warmed with pleasure. "Thank you, Sage Rubicas. I accept your offer. I will transfer my apprenticeship from Translation and Diplomacy to you."

"Of course, it would be my honor to help the master sage," Sharif said.

When Gwen and Vic also agreed, Rubicas grew thoughtful. "Hmm, if you two intend to help me, first we must know the limits of your potential."

"You mean you want us to take an aptitude test?" Vic groaned. "I've taken those before. Anybody got a Number 2 pencil?"

"Everyone in Elantya has natural aptitudes," Lyssandra said. "But we may be unaware of what they are. We need to be *shown* our potential."

Gwen knew that their mothers had great secrets and some kind of power. Fyera and Kyara had pried open a crystal door to Earth, even after it had been sealed off in the Great Closure. Gwen and Vic knew that their five-sided medallions, with their intricate symbols, held some kind of power here in Elantya, but they didn't understand it yet. If this test could tell them anything about themselves, she wanted the answers.

"Yes," Gwen said, "we need to know."

"Usually they test to see if you have the potential to become a Key," Sharif explained. Piri's sphere glowed white with pride in the mesh pouch. "My brother Hashim had trained to become a Key, and I scored very high. Now that I know Azric is involved in this merlon uprising, nothing will stop me from using every power I possess to defeat him." His skin flushed darker.

"I have not been tested yet, either," Tiaret said.

"We've all been kind of busy since you were rescued from the shipwreck," Vic pointed out.

The girl from Afirik looked at the cousins with her amber eyes. "Then we should waste no more time." She rapped her teaching staff on the floor. "It may be useful to know our capabilities before the merlons attack again."

Gwen's heart had leapt at the idea of helping Rubicas. What better opportunity could there be to reach Uncle Cap than to work for the man partially responsible for bringing them here? A healthy dose of skepticism tempered her enthusiasm, though. "That's quite an honor, Sage Rubicas, but Vic and I are from Earth. I doubt we'll qualify as potential Keys."

Vic gave her his stop-being-such-a-killjoy look and started talking a mile a minute. "If I had told you a month ago that we were going to come through a crystal door to a magical island where there are real wizards called sages and real spells — not to mention nymph djinnis, and skrits that fetch and deliver things, and giant battle krakens — you would've said that was pretty unlikely, too. Why is it any more fantastic to think that you and I might be potential Keys?"

"Okay, Taz." Gwen held up her hands in surrender. "You're right. We should just let them test us and see what happens."

Lyssandra lifted her pointed chin. "I will take them to the testing center, Sage Rubicas. There is no need for you to interrupt your work."

"This testing . . . uh . . . it doesn't hurt, does it?" Vic asked. "You don't need a scraping from inside my skull, for instance?"

Lyssandra's coppery hair rippled as she shook her head. "Your potential is part of you, Viccus. We only need you to be present. The crystals will do the rest."

Gwen gave a wry smile. Of course it would be based on crystals. Everything in Elantya seemed to have something to do with crystals.

Most important, she wanted to understand the mystery of Kyara and Fyera Pierce. How much "magic" had their mothers given to their children? If the "twin cousins" actually turned out to be Keys, then maybe they could open crystal doors themselves and find where their mothers had come from.

And where Vic's mom had gone.

Gwen felt an ache in her heart as she thought of all the things she didn't know about her own mother. Had Fyera kept secrets from Gwen's father as well? Uncle Cap obviously knew more than he had ever told her or Vic. If she could uncover the answers, the information might be important not just to her, but to Elantya and other worlds as well.

38

THE CRYSTAL DOORS CENTER was larger and more elaborate than Gwen had imagined. Built and decorated with materials from every world that traded with Elantya, the open structure was supported by ornate pillars that stood like tree trunks throughout the echoing halls. Various wings were filled with offices, writing desks, and ledgers documenting trade routes. Large, intricate charts on the walls showed the locations of all the crystal doors surrounding the island.

Elantyan workers moved about in alcoves, managing stacks of scrolls and identification tablets, which they arranged in racks with numerous cubbyholes like post office boxes. After only a glance, Gwen already admired the strict organization. "This looks like a hall of records."

"Here we keep all the information about the Keys in Elantya and the crystal doors they can open," Lyssandra said.

"Any merchant or traveler who wants to go to a specific world must use an appropriate Key. They come to the Crystal Doors Center, where one of our Key assistants searches the records and finds someone capable of opening the desired door."

Sharif stepped forward. "For instance, if you wanted to go to my flying city of Irrakesh, you would have to find a Key from my own world — perhaps even myself, once I am sufficiently trained."

"So I'm guessing this is like a bus depot," said Vic. "Everybody comes here from wherever, and they have to find a ticket to get where they want to go."

"Some Keys ask a large payment for their services," said Lyssandra. "Others consider it their duty to keep trade and passage open to Elantya. Most Keys consider themselves guardians, and are very careful about whom they allow through a crystal door to their worlds."

Pecunyas, the green-robed Vir of Agriculture and Trade, met them at the arched entrance. After Lyssandra explained why Sage Rubicas had sent them, the vir narrowed his eyes. "Yes, three of you," he said in his nasal voice. "Come into the main gallery. We have the ability to test many at a time, which is useful when large numbers of students arrive in Elantya."

Under pentagonal skylights with prismatic edges, an airy open gallery had two concentric rings of egg-shaped crystals standing atop delicate pedestals. Pedestals alternated in the inner and outer rings. Gwen studied the geometrical arrangement and realized that if she connected the pedestals in the rings with straight lines, they would form pentagons, a ubiquitous symbol in Elantya. Vic looked around at the arrangement of crystals, as if imagining ways he could take the equipment apart and reassemble it into something better.

"So what exactly do we do for this test?" Gwen asked.

Lyssandra stepped forward. "It is a simple thing." She walked to one of the milky crystals and touched it. After only a second, the crystal began to glow with a pleasant orange tint. "This shows that the crystals recognize me, that I have potential."

Not to be outdone, Sharif went to the next crystal. "And I've been tested as well." He gripped the smooth surface, and the object shimmered a greenish-blue even more intense than Lyssandra's crystal. His full lips quirked in a smile. "The brightness of the glow is an indication of the person's ability." He seemed to imply that as a prince, his light should shine stronger than the others.

While Sharif and Lyssandra kept their test crystals glowing, Tiaret drew a breath, closed her eyes, and lowered her chin as if summoning memories. "My Master Kundu was convinced of my potential. I do this to honor him. I hope I can carry on the work he meant to do when coming to Elantya."

Completely engrossed in her test, Tiaret held her hand above the egg crystal for a few moments, then lowered her palm to the smooth surface. The crystal remained dark at first. Gwen thought the girl from Afirik was going to fail, until a white light like a tiny spark began to shine from inside the crystal. It grew brighter, and brighter, and finally Tiaret's crystal shone as brightly as Lyssandra's. With her other hand, she rapped her teaching staff on the floor in a gesture of triumph.

Gwen nibbled at her lower lip and said to Vic, "Now it's up

to us. I'll go first." She walked calmly to one of the crystals, but he rushed to another one.

"You've got to be kidding. Don't try to pull rank on me —"

Gwen rolled her eyes at her impulsive cousin. Ignoring him, she touched the ovoid crystal at the same time that Vic touched his. Suddenly, their testing crystals erupted with blazing, scintillating light, as if fireworks had gone off in their hands.

Vir Pecunyas stepped back, gasping. "I have never seen such a bright —"

Amazingly, the crystals held by Lyssandra, Sharif, and Tiaret also brightened tenfold. The radiance became blinding from all five beacons. Then other crystals around the gallery — those usually used for illumination and decoration — ignited as if picking up the excess energy that Gwen and Vic had unleashed.

"It is the five of you together!" Pecunyas looked at the astonished faces of Lyssandra, Sharif, and Tiaret. "You each had potential, but when added to those two, the synergy is incredible. This is unprecedented."

Travelers and merchants who had come to the Center looking for someone to open a crystal door stared and whispered in awe. Bystanders rushed down the halls of the large building, spreading the news.

The light from the five ovoid crystals intensified, and Gwen's instinct was to yank her hand away before the gem could explode. But she felt no danger, no heat, only a pleasurable tingling sensation all the way through her body.

Sages came running now, their multicolored robes flapping, and stopped in astonishment to watch the display of power.

Even after the students took their hands away, the crystals continued to glow.

In the eggsphere around Sharif's neck, Piri spun and somersaulted, shimmering pink with happiness.

Tiaret's eyes were luminous. "If we learn to make use of this power, the merlons cannot prevail against us."

"This is *so* cool," Vic said.

Lyssandra looked both shaken and filled with awe. "It is like the prophecy song we teach to little children. They sing it while they play a little game."

"The question is, *what* is the prophecy?" Gwen asked. "What does it say?"

Lyssandra swayed to the rhythm of the words as she sang in a soft voice,

"Crystals five will shine like suns,
Thus reveal the Chosen Ones.
When the learning time is done,
Chosen Ones may choose as one,
Heralding the final fight,
Sages Dark with Sages Bright."

Vic scratched his nose. "Sheesh, that sounds pretty serious — whatever it means. Uh, what are we supposed to do with that?"

Gwen gave Vic a punch in the shoulder. "At the moment, Dr. Distracto, I think we've got enough mysteries to solve without adding enigmatic prophecies to the mix. I say it's high time we searched for some answers about our mothers."

"Right. And try to bring my dad here while we're at it," Vic agreed. "Family now, prophecies later."

"And what of the rest of us?" Lyssandra asked, looking worried. "Do we not belong together?"

Vic put one arm around the telepath and the other around Gwen. "Yup. You're our friends. We have a lot to learn, and we need you. I have a strange feeling that you're stuck with us."

Gwen smiled at this unusual display from her cousin. She drew Sharif and Tiaret into the circle. "In other words, I think we just became a sort of family, too."

About the Authors

REBECCA MOESTA (pronounced MESS-tuh) is the daughter of an English teacher/author/theologian, and a nurse — from whom she learned, respectively, her love of words and her love of books. Moesta, who holds an M.S. in Business Administration from Boston University, has worked in various aspects of editing, publishing, and writing for the past 20 years and has taught every grade from kindergarten through college.

Moesta is also the author or co-author of more than 30 books, including *Buffy the Vampire Slayer: Little Things*, and the award-winning *Star Wars: Young Jedi Knights* series, which she co-wrote with husband and *New York Times* bestselling author Kevin J. Anderson. A self-described "gadgetologist" Rebecca enjoys travel, movie-going, and learning about (not to mention collecting) the latest advances in electronics.

*   *   *

KEVIN J. ANDERSON is the author of more than eighty books, including *Captain Nemo, The Martian War, Hidden Empire, A Forest of Stars,* and many popular *Star Wars* and *X–Files* novels, as well as bestselling prequels to *Dune,* cowritten with Frank Herbert's son Brian. He has also written dozens of comics and graphic novels for Marvel, DC, Wildstorm, Dark Horse, and Topps. He has over seventeen million books in print in 29 languages. His work has appeared on numerous "Best of the Year" lists and has won a variety of awards. In 1998, he set the Guinness World Record for "Largest Single-Author Book Signing."

*   *   *

For more information on
Rebecca Moesta or Kevin J. Anderson, see

www.wordfire.com
or
www.elantya.com

When the learning time is done,
Chosen Ones may choose as one,
Heralding the final fight,
Sages Dark with Sages Bright.

Gwen and Vic's adventures on Elantya
continue in *Ocean Realm,*
Book 2

Coming June 2007